STONE GARDEN

STONE GARDEN

AND OTHER STORIES

Alan Spence

◆

PHOENIX HOUSE

London

To
JANANI

First published in Great Britain in 1995 by
Phoenix House, Orion House,
5 Upper St Martin's Lane,
London WC2H 9EA

Some of these stories have appeared in the following: *Scottish Short Stories* (Harper
Collins), *Modern Scottish Short Stories* (Hamish Hamilton/Faber), *Panther Book of
Scottish Short Stories, Identities* (Heinemann), *Edinburgh Review, New Edinburgh
Review, Words, Writers in Brief* (Book Trust), *Beloit Fiction Journal* (USA), *Scotland on
Sunday, London Magazine, Best Short Stories 1994* (Heinemann), Some have also been
broadcast on BBC Radio.

A CIP record for this book is available
from the British Library

ISBN 1897580 58 4 Cased
1897580 63 0 Paperback

Typeset at The Spartan Press Ltd,
Lymington Hants

Printed by Butler & Tanner Ltd
Frome and London

CONTENTS

RUPERT BEAR
AND THE SAN IZAL

I opened the Rupert Bear book and laid it flat on my lap. Not that I could read it. There were too many words, a dense block of print under each frame. But I followed the story in pictures, made my own sense of it.

The house was quiet, filled with the strangeness of being alone. My father was at work, my mother had gone out to the shops. I was not long up out of bed, had been sick, with a fever, for a week. That was why I wasn't at school.

I sat in the kitchen, keeping warm by the fire.

The Rupert book was one of three I had been given at Christmas. The others were the Beano Annual and a book of Bible stories. I had kept all three close by me this past week, read through them and through them again. The Beano book was the easiest. The words were simple, came out in balloons, straight from the characters' mouths. The Bible stories were too difficult, solid columns of narrative and only one picture to a page. I had busied myself by colouring some of the pictures with stubs of wax crayon. But the lines were a scrawl, were never neat enough, were all the wrong colours. In one picture I had given God an orange face and green hair, a black crown and a cloak made up of all the colours I had, one on top of another. And I couldn't contain the colours within the outlines. They streaked over onto other things in the picture – clouds, a bird, the sun. Frustrated, I had scored a heavy black line across the page and scribbled over the words that I couldn't read. That was why I had put the book from me and turned instead to Rupert Bear.

The Rupert stories were very mysterious. Rupert lived with his mother and father in a snug house, a thatched cottage with its own garden. But he was forever wandering off, sometimes on his own, sometimes with his friend Algy. He would discover a secret door or a hidden passage that led through to some enchanted place. There was a beautiful little Chinese girl called Tiger Lily. Her father was a Conjurer and could make magic. He would set Rupert off on fantastic adventures. But no matter how far away he went, how strange the worlds he entered, he always found his way back. Home. Safe.

My mother had been gone a long time. I was hungry.

I climbed on a chair and ransacked the kitchen cabinet, but there was nothing. A bottle of sauce. Salt and pepper. A packet of rice. Nothing I could eat. Left in its greaseproof wrapper was the last slice of a pan loaf. The ender. Outsider. It was curled and beginning to go hard, but it didn't look too bad. There was a lump of margarine, solid from the cold and hard to cut and spread. But I managed to slice a bit off, scrape it and press it on to the bread. The whole mess was crumbly and uneven. I sprinkled sugar over it. A sugary piece. The bread was dry and tasted half-stale. I laid it down on the table after a bite or two, closed up the kitchen cabinet, put the knife I had been using into the sink.

The Rupert book was lying open, face-down where I had left it, and looking I noticed something I hadn't seen before. The front and back covers made up one long picture, carried on over the spine. Before, I had seen them as separate, now I could see it whole. It was a wide vista. Rupert was in the foreground, cresting a hill, overlooking a valley, a few of his friends coming up the slope behind him. Tiger Lily and the Conjurer were in the valley itself, walking towards a golden pagoda. The valley was a magic land, flowery and lush. Trees grew around the pagoda and along the banks of a stream. There were parrots among the trees, tiny lizards in the grass, a black dragon coiled on an outcrop of rock. And in the sky, throwing a weird light over everything, was a shining globe, a planet, bright yellow and green against the deep blue of the sky. The Conjurer's arm was outstretched, finger pointing at the globe. I felt like crying, for no reason.

I got up and went through to the room, to look out the window for my mother. From the room I could see our street and another leading off it down towards the docks. Rows of grey tenements, a factory, wasteground. There were only a few people. A huddle of men at the corner. A scatter of children on the wasteground, too young for school, or off sick like me. Women moving from close to shop and back again, but no mother. Through the thin walls I could hear a radio playing in the house next door. *Yellow bird, up high in banana tree* . . . I liked the song, but not the singer's voice. I went back through to the kitchen, feeling cold.

Mechanically, I picked up the bread I had left on the table and took another bite, chewed it to a dry pulp, sweet sugary grit between my teeth. I couldn't finish it, threw the last hard crust into the bucket.

The kitchen window looked out over the back court, the backs of the buildings, a grey square. My mother's washing, pegged on a line, hung limp. A dog snuffled in the midden, among the rubbish and the ash. Nothing else moved. There was nothing to see. In the sink lay the knife I had used, still streaked with margarine. I turned on the tap, let the rush of water splash over it, but it didn't come clean, was still smeared, the cold water clinging in globules to the blade.

Beside the sink was a dark green bottle of disinfectant. The name was in big red letters on the label. SAN IZAL. And in smaller letters, under a red cross, was the word POISON. That had been spelled out to me, with a warning to leave it

3

alone. I unscrewed the cap and sniffed at the San Izal. I loved the strong smell of it, a smell you could just about bite. I wanted to take a sip, but it was poison. If I swallowed it I would die. My father said when you died that was it. Finished. There was nothing else. My mother said you went to Heaven to live with God. I thought of the God I had coloured in the Bible storybook, with his orange face and green hair. The strange feeling of sadness, of wanting to cry, was still on me, an emptiness inside. I put the cap back on the bottle, sat down again with my books.

I didn't try to read, just opened out the Rupert book, sat staring at the picture on the cover. I looked at every inch of it, saw every detail, every blade of grass, every figure. Rupert. Tiger Lily. The Conjurer, pointing. And again and again I was drawn to that globe in the sky, that perfect radiant sphere. The feeling was centred in my stomach and had something to do with the picture. I wanted my mother.

I held the book close to me and crossed once more to the sink. I wanted to drink the San Izal. The liquid was dark brown, treacly brown, but when you poured it into the sink it turned white. I tucked the book under my arm. I lifted the bottle and opened it. The dark smell from the green bottle. The circle of light in Rupert's sky. To be dead. To be finished. To be with God. To be nothing. The empty feeling inside. The lack. If I swallowed the poison I would know. I heard my mother's key turn in the door and she was here, she was home. The tears came now. I couldn't hold them back. I had put down the bottle and dropped the book on the floor. My mother dumped her message bag on the table, and 'Hey, what's the matter?' she said, laughing and hugging me. 'What's the matter?' And I wanted to tell her but I couldn't. I had no words.

4

BLAND UMBRELLAS

It's still there after all these years, and it still makes me smile. The shop is just at Notting Hill Gate, across the road from Finches pub and a few blocks along. Presumably it sells umbrellas, and the proprietor is a Mr Bland. But there's something surreal about the sign, painted in big black letters on the gable end of the building. BLAND UMBRELLAS. It's a found poem, an urban haiku, especially when seen through a drift of grey drizzle, like this. I always meant to photograph it, print it up on a postcard with a title on the back. But I never did.

It was Ray who first pointed it out to me. From the top deck of a Number 9 bus. Jabbed the air with his long bony finger. Drew my attention to the sign as the bus swung past.

'Now there's a poem for you. One of those found efforts.'

'Could call it Rain in the City.'

'Make it a homage to Edwin Morgan. Or Ian Hamilton Finlay.'

'Next time I'll bring a camera.'

That must have been 1968. The year we left school. Our trip from darkest Glasgow was a quest, for the Golden City, the Wonderful Land, the End of the Yellow Brick Road. Our mission was to boldly go, explore strange new worlds, seek out new life. Here be dragons, and girls with kaleidoscope eyes.

★

It was early morning when we set out, the streets still quiet. Next to nothing in our rucksacks. The essentials. We had kitted ourselves out from Paddy's Market, Ray in an old army greatcoat, me in a fireman's jacket and a big widebrimmed hat. We felt good.

We caught a red bus out of town, to Hamilton, to hitch from the start of the motorway. We were buoyed up on a wave of manic energy, excitement spilling over easy into laughter at the sheer freedom of it. This was it. We were on our way. Down that road. We would be in London in no time. No time at all.

From Hamilton Roundabout to Finchley Central took twenty-five hours.

Somewhere outside Carlisle we were stranded for five hours. The wind caught my hat and blew it into a ditch. Climbing down to fetch it, I fell full length and my hand, flailing, grabbed a clump of stinging nettle.

'Very Beckett,' said Ray. 'The hat. The ditch. The two of us.'

Bastard.

Somewhere outside Preston, at a motorway service station, Ray pointed out that BURMAH, spelled backwards, was HAMRUB.

Aye.

He kept repeating it. Ham Rub. And laughing. And it set him off on some crazy fantasy, the ham rub as a kind of barndance, a country hoedown, all spit and sawdust and jigging fiddles

> Turn your partner doh see doh
> Rub that ham and away we go

By now I was as far gone as he was, and we waved at the next car that passed us, stood there laughing like maniacs at the side of the road in the middle of the night.

Somewhere outside Lancaster I had lost it again. Raw and gritty, snarled up. Nerves jangled, nettlerash stinging on my hand. Stuck on an empty approach road, nothing in sight.

'Bet it was never like this for fucking Kerouac.'

'Bet it was, really.'

And at some point came a numb acceptance. Right. Fine. Here we are.

And Ray must have felt the same.

'I mean, we're out here. We're doing it. This is *it*.'

Aye.

Then came the lorry, roaring up our road and pulling over, stopping for us, its engine running. The door flung open, the driver calling out *London?*

'Great!'

'Magic!'

Chucking up our rucksacks and climbing up after them into the warm fug of the cabin, the welcoming stink of petrol and stubbed-out cigarettes.

And somewhere down the road, first grey light, a stop at some greasy transport place for early breakfast, a glazed fried egg on a roll, a pint mug of dark brown tea to swill it down.

We were utterly content.

Then the last haul down the M1 to London, the sun coming up. The driver dropped us off in Finchley, the nearest he went. The lorry pulled away, butted its way back out into traffic. It was hot. We were wearing too much. Our backpacks dumped beside us blocked the pavement. Folk in a hurry had to check their stride, step round. They glared at us.

'Right.'

Ray dug deep into an inside pocket of his coat, brought out an A to Z and a copy of *International Times*.

'Let's figure out where we are. And where we're going.'

★

This morning I flew down on the 10 o'clock shuttle. Picked at the continental breakfast. Brought some work with me but couldn't settle to it. Had a go at the *Scotsman* crossword. Gave up.

Seven across. *Add it up in your head, that's all.* Eight letters.

The stewardess handing out barleysugar sweets. We are now beginning our descent.

★

With Ray's mapbook we found the station. Finchley Central, we sang the old Temperance Seven number, is only sixpence, diddlydum, from Golder's Green on the Northern Line. Southbound, to Tottenham Court Road, up the escalators and out into the heat and crush of Oxford Street.

We walked the whole length of it, peered in at poster shops, record shops, boutiques. We went into a place called *Indiacraft*, just to look, drawn in by the sweet scent of incense, a shimmer of sitar music. Inside was a glittering cave hung with rugs and drapes, bright saris and silk scarves. Light glinted on mirrors and on images of Hindu gods, Siva dancing in his circle of fire. The woman behind the counter was stunningly beautiful. She wore a red sari embroidered with gold.

Just to look, but I picked something up from a basket on the counter. A child's toy made of wire, bent into the shape of an eight-petal lotus, the petals separated by coloured beads.

The woman leaned over and took it from me.

'Like this.'

And she coaxed and pulled out the lotus into other shapes, a spinning top, a globe. Her thin fingers were graceful and deft. I was mesmerised.

'Is like the Universe,' she said, unfolding it, placing it back in my hand. 'The way it opens out, is all connected.'

I bought it.

'Wasn't she incredible?' I said, back out in the street.

'She saw you coming!' said Ray.

The pavements were hard and hot. At Marble Arch we sat down by the fountain. We pulled off our desert boots, socks, eased our feet in the cool water.

'Oh God!' said Ray. 'Ecstasy!'

Across at Speaker's Corner there was only one wee man ranting, not even up on a soapbox.

These are the last days, my friends. The apocalypse is at hand.

We crossed to Hyde Park. The grass was parched. I was suddenly, completely, exhausted. We lay down flat on our backs and I drifted, dozed, the noise of the city washing over me.

I woke to a jumbo jet roaring across the sky. Diffused hazy light hurt my eyes. I had no idea where I was. Then it came back.

Ray sat up, grinned.

'We're really here!'

London.

★

It took me as long to get in here from Heathrow as it did to fly down. The hotel is comfortable enough, and should be, at the price. My room looks out over a narrow courtyard at the back of an office block. At one window, a man in a dark suit is talking on the phone, swivelling round in his chair. At another, a young girl is typing in front of a computer screen. She stops and turns, responds, perhaps, to something said to her. When she turns back to her keyboard she is laughing.

Down in the courtyard, the day's rubbish has been put out in bins and plastic sacks. A man in an old trenchcoat is rummaging amongst it, lifting the bin-lids to peer in. He stops and looks up, straight at me. He is not old, my own age, maybe less. He mutters something, spits. I step back from the window.

★

We sat in a Lyons tearoom, spending a long time over a pot of tea and two rounds of toast.

'Why *rounds*?' said Ray. 'I mean, the slices are square.'

I'd been poring over the A to Z, looking at where we'd been, the distance we'd covered.

'I reckon we can walk most places.'

'We'll have to,' said Ray. 'Look what we've spent already. That breakfast this morning. The subway in. This stuff.'

'And this!'

I brought the wire lotus out of my inside pocket, opened it up, folded it back.

'Your wee universe!' said Ray, and he laughed.

He picked up the teapot, squeezed the last dregs out of it.

'So anyway,' he said. 'If we walk everywhere.'

'Live on bread and cheese.'

'The odd bar of chocolate.'

'We should be OK.'

'What about a place to stay?'

'If we go to this Arts Lab place,' said Ray, 'we're bound to meet somebody that can put us up.'

'Let us *crash*.'

'Aye, right!' He grinned. 'Hey, maybe we'll get picked up by a couple of gorgeous rich birds and they'll take us back to their place!'

'Oh, sure! Like Jane Asher and Chrissie Shrimpton are gonnae be cruising around looking for a pair of scruffs like us!'

'You never know.'

'Aye. Dream on.'

★

I suppose I should be thinking about lunch, but I still don't have much of an appetite. I pick up the remote control and switch on the TV, flick from channel to channel. Racing from Kempton. A gardening programme. A black and white gangster movie. Australian soap.

Nothing.

I could call down to the desk, get them to send me up another coffee. A cappuccino maybe. Keep me going. Then I should ring the hospital, find out the times of the visiting hours.

★

We had found the address of the Arts Lab in Ray's copy of IT. To get there we'd had to walk back the length of Oxford Street, on past the great empty tower of Centre Point, then down through backstreets towards Soho. At Tottenham Court Road a busker in the underpass had been singing. Baby you're a rich man. Jangled guitar out of tune. How does it feel to be one of the beautiful people?

The Arts Lab was smaller than we'd imagined it. Shabbier. There was a whole programme in the theatre space – music, a film show, a play – but it all cost extra on top of the charge to get in. We contented ourselves with just sitting in the café, eking out a pot of tea, again, making it last, but happy just to be there, to be part of it.

'I bet there's more freaks here than there is in the whole of Glasgow,' said Ray.

'You reckon they're all stoned?'

'Bound to be. Out their skulls. I bet we could score stuff easy. If we had the money.'

'Aye. If.' I looked about. 'Still think Jane and Chrissie'll come cruising by and pick us up?'

'Well, we might have to pitch our sights a *wee* bit lower!'

'Thing is, all the talent's already spoken for. Everybody's *with* somebody.'

'I know. But still. The night's young!' He pointed at my cup. 'More tea?'

★

I think I am remembering these conversations. Not inventing. Maybe reworking a little. Embellishing here and there. The memory does its own editing job.

11

I have been in London thirty, forty times since. But it's
that first time that comes back clear. The exact feel of it.
How it was.

★

It was late. The place would be closing. We would have to
leave and we still had nowhere to stay.

'There's always the park,' said Ray. 'Plenty space!'

'As long as it doesn't rain.'

'Can only hope.'

The guy at the next table came over. I'd noticed him a
few times looking across at us. He was maybe thirty, hair
thin on top but long at the back. He wore cowboy boots, a
buckskin jacket.

He nodded at our rucksacks. 'You guys travelling?'

I liked the sound of that. Travelling.

'That's right,' said Ray.

'Where you from?' said the man, pulling up a chair.

'Scotland,' I said.

'Glasgow,' said Roy.

'Wild place,' said the man. 'Hard.'

Ray shrugged. 'Suppose so.'

'Listen,' said the man. 'Do you need a place to crash?'

'No half,' said Ray. 'Do you know somewhere?'

'Got a place of my own,' said the man. 'You're welcome.'

'Helluva decent of you,' said Ray,

The man leaned over, put his hand on Ray's knee. 'You
can kip with me. Your mate can have the sofa.'

'Aw now, wait a minute.' Ray moved back, scraped his
chair on the floor.

'You guys got something going?' said the man.

'We don't,' said Ray. 'We're not.'

'You mean you're *straight*?'

'Aye.'

The man laughed. 'You don't fancy giving it a try then?'

Ray stood up, grabbed his pack off the floor.

12

'Pity,' said the man. 'A real waste.'

I was still laughing about it half an hour later.

Ray didn't find it so funny. 'Swinging London by fuck.'

He'd been so fazed that he'd misread the map and we'd walked a couple of miles in the wrong direction, found ourselves down on the embankment, looking across the river. We sat on a bench for a while, quiet, just staring.

'Weird feeling,' said Ray. 'Being here.'

'Isn't it.'

'I keep thinking we'd better get moving. Like there's something else we should be doing. Somewhere else we should be.'

'I know what you mean.'

'But there isn't.'

'No.'

'We're just here. And that's all there is to it.'

The park was too far. We were tired. We decided to stay where we were. Take a bench each. Stretch out.

'Luxury!' I said.

I lay back, my rucksack under my head. I was falling up into the night sky. London went out.

More than once I half-woke to some grey limbo, too cold to sleep and too tired to move, the hard bench hurting shoulder and hip, the night chill seeping right deep into me. Then there was bright light shining in my eyes, somebody prodding me awake, a policeman flashing his torch in my face, telling me to get up, shift, get out of it.

There were two of them. The other one had woken up Ray, was giving him the same treatment.

He called over to his friend. 'Right pair of villains, eh?'

'Definitely. Couple of rough customers. Probably carrying drugs, what d'you reckon?'

Again the light was in my eyes, dazzled me. 'Well? Are you?'

I shielded my eyes. 'No.' And it must have sounded so wee and pathetic, so obviously innocent, that he laughed, said, 'Right. Beat it.'

We picked up our bags and started walking, not sure where, just anywhere, away.

'Bastards,' said Ray.

A few blocks on, we stopped to check the map again.

It started to rain.

★

The cappuccino tastes good, if a little tepid under the froth. I swig it down in one go, and the hit is almost immediate, the rush, a sudden sense of wellbeing.

Now.

I ring the operator, get put through to the hospital. Next visiting hour is from three to four.

Fine.

★

The rain was thin and needling, soaked into us. It damped down the dust on the pavement, raised that acrid smell. We kept on walking. The wet streets shone.

We came out at Covent Garden, the market already alive with the shouts of workmen, the thud of crates being loaded onto lorries.

'Now *this* is London,' said Ray.

Through the wet earth smells of vegetables, the ripeness of fruit, the faint stink of something rotten, came a sharper tang, of onions frying, hamburgers. It came from an all night stall, queued out with a weird mix of old tramps and dossers, hippies and nightshift workers, a couple in evening dress slumming it. We joined the queue, drank more sweet tea stewed dark khaki, from paper cups.

'I'll have tea coming out my ears,' I said.

'Out your arse,' said Ray. And he pointed out they were anagrams. Ears and arse. 'Same letters,' he said. 'Rearranged.'

Aye.

But the tea had picked us up. And seeing other folk just hanging about. We shouldered our packs, took our bearings from the A to Z. We set out again, walking.

By the time the sun was up we were back in the park, sprawled flat out on the drying grass. I heard the faraway buzz and drone of the city as it wheeled about us in great concentric circles. I slept.

★

I passed through Covent Garden a year or so back, was down here on business, found myself with time to kill and wandering. The market has been gutted, cleaned up, painted pale shades of cream and beige. I ate a light lunch at an outside table and watched the street theatre, the acrobats and jugglers and buskers. A heavy-set man balanced a bike on his forehead. A young girl ate fire. A boy in a butcher's apron juggled with three meat cleavers. A drum thumped as panpipes played rainforest music. It was all very pleasant. Like Edinburgh at Festival time. Or bits of Glasgow in its Year of Culture. Pleasant and diverting. The bike wavered. The fire was doused in the girl's mouth. The lethal steel blades spun in the air, glinted.

★

At night we found ourselves back at the Arts Lab. Ray hadn't been keen, afraid we'd meet the cowboy again, but we'd walked about all day and didn't know anywhere else to go.

'I'm knackered,' I said.

'Me too.'

There was no sign of the cowboy.

'Thank fuck,' said Ray.

There were a few faces we recognised from the night before. The place was beginning to feel familiar.

'Be good to *do* something,' said Ray. 'Maybe we should go in and see the film.'

'Or the play?' I said.

The play was an adaptation of a story by Kafka. *In the Penal Colony*. We checked our money, decided we could just about afford it.

'What the hell,' said Ray. 'Live a little.'

'Only young once.'

The theatre was a cramped black space, dark except for a sinister-looking structure, a machine in the middle of the floor.

The story was disjointed in the telling. The actors moved around like zombies, spoke in odd jerky phrases, mechanical. And I kept falling asleep, losing the thread, making no sense of it, having to work it out.

The machine was for punishing offenders. The victim was strapped into it and a set of blades, a harrow, came down and carved words on his back, over and over, cut deeper and deeper, till it killed him. But not before he had felt the words, understood their meaning, their message, through the pain.

'Powerful stuff,' said Ray as we came out into the café.

'Intense,' I said.

'They understood the sentence,' said Ray, suddenly seeing it. 'Their sentence!'

The café was crowded. A big bearded guy in a poncho sat down at our table.

'Hi!' he said. 'Enjoy the show?'

He sounded Australian.

'Well,' I said. 'Maybe enjoy's the wrong word.'

He laughed. 'Heavy duty!'

Ray said nothing, wary.

But this time there wasn't a problem. The Australian was called Mike. He was backpacking round Europe, had been in London for a month. He wasn't trying to chat us up, and yes, he did know a place to stay, the place he was staying himself, a kind of hostel, five minutes' walk away, mats on the floor sort of thing, pretty basic but dirt cheap.

'Sounds great,' said Ray. 'Lead us to it!'

★

Downstairs I leave my key at reception, post it through a

kind of brass letterbox set into the desk. With its heavy plastic tag it makes a satisfying thud as it drops. The receptionist smiles up at me, tells me to have a nice day, says it with such an absolute lack of irony it makes me smile back, say Thanks.

Her scent is one of those Calvin Klein potions. Not *Obsession*. Or *Escape*. The other one I've forgotten the name of.

It'll come back to me.

She turns her head and I catch another whiff of it.

Almost.

Have a nice day.

★

The room at the hostel was a big old dusty gym with mats pulled out to sleep on. We staked out our space in the corner, beside Mike. Off the gym was a locker room and a row of ramshackle showers, the fitments rusted. I settled for a cold water wash at the sink.

Back through in the gym, Mike had lit a couple of little candles, nightlights. I understood why when the hall lights were switched off.

'Time to light up!' he said, and he laughed.

'Mike's got some dope,' said Ray, whispering it.

'Quid deal,' said Mike. 'Lebanese Red. Really good shit.'

He unpeeled it from its tinfoil wrapping, held it out, a little cube of resin. Holding it on the foil, he heated it over the candle flame. He took out his cigarette papers, tobacco tin, made a long roll-up and sprinkled the dope along it. He rolled it tight, screwed the paper into a point at one end, tucked in a neat filter at the other, a scrap of card he called a roach.

He held it up for us to admire. 'Perfect!' he said.

Then he lit up and took a long deep drag, sucked in, held, breathed out. He nodded and grinned, passed the joint to Ray, who copied him, the sharp quick intake, the hold, release.

Ray passed it to me and I did the same, gasped in the smoke, choked and gagged but managed not to cough as I gulped it down and it seared my throat and down into my lungs, made my eyes water.

'Don't smoke?' said Mike.

I shook my head. 'Not really.'

'Good time to learn!' he said.

This was us. In London. Doing drugs.

The joint came round again, another quick drag and my head was filled with light, I was laughing for no reason, here we were, this was my old friend Ray I had known forever, and Mike there twinkling away at us in the flickering candlelight like some ancient Red Indian medicine man.

At some point I must have taken out the toy lotus from my bag. I found myself staring into it, a long time. Just a length of wire woven round nothing, making these wonderful simple shapes in space, shapes that opened, unfolded into one another then closed back in on themselves to start the cycle again. The candleflame darted highlights from the gold wire. Everything was just fine.

★

The taxi I flagged down outside the hotel gets caught in a backup of traffic, not even rush hour and we're inching along, grinding through Kensington, nothing to look out at but other cars and their tired angry drivers. Mind numb, I'm drumming with my fingers on my briefcase on the seat beside me, a black executive job with a combination lock. There was absolutely no reason to bring it with me. Just force of habit. Not wanting that uneasy feeling of nowhere to put my hands.

I need to learn to relax. Click open the briefcase. Take out this morning's paper, another look at the crossword. *Add it up in your head. That's all.*

I still don't get it.

Stale and airless, the gym stank of bodies, old mats and bedding, cigarette smoke, manky socks. Grey light filtered in through a single skylight, high up, showed up the thick dust on the floor, the stubbed-out fag ends and spent matches, cardboard roaches from joints, the odd bit of crumpled paper, curled ringpulls and dented empty beer-cans.

'Some place this,' I said, for the first time really seeing it.

'OK for a night or two,' said Ray. 'Better than nothing.'

The way he said it got on my nerves. I felt gritty, irritated.

Mike was heading out to work.

'Work?' I said, not able to hide my astonishment.

'Nothing else for it,' he said. 'I'm signed up with this agency, called Scrubbers.'

'Scrubbers!'

'Temping,' he said. 'Get paid by the hour. No questions asked.'

'Sounds good,' said Ray.

'It is. Especially the perks. All these bored housewives, man. You wouldn't read about it!'

We wanted to hear more. The stuff fantasies were made of. We wanted details. But Mike just laughed, picked up his shoulder bag.

'See you guys later!'

'Right,' said Ray.

'Maybe,' I said.

★

Hospitals always give me that bad feeling, a nervousness twisting in my gut. It's to do with the smells, clinical and metallic, the sharp antiseptic tang that catches at the back of my throat, sets my teeth on edge. Just fear, I suppose, of pain and death. The thought of ending my days in a place like this, dying slow. The best thing would just be to go in your sleep, not wake up. Or fall down dead in the street, like that, finished.

The young nurse at the desk looks tired. Long shifts. Ridiculous hours. Thankless work. Still she manages to be civil, even friendly. She directs me along a corridor to one of the smaller side-rooms, off the main ward.

Right. This is it. Nervous as hell I'm pushing open the door, stepping into the room.

★

Ray was staying on in London. I was heading back. Once we'd decided, we both felt happier, more relaxed, and that last day was the best.

'I just fancy winging it,' he said. 'See what turns up.'

'Sure,' I said.

'Maybe try that cleaning caper with Mike.'

I gave him the clenched fist. 'Woh!'

He laughed. 'I'll tell you what.'

'What?'

'My old man'll have a fit!'

Ray's father was a lawyer, expected a lot of him. They lived in a big house with its own garden, in the West End. I had grown up in a room and kitchen, no bath, no hot water, no inside toilet. And that was it. Ray had something to drop out from. Staying at a place like the hostel was roughing it, had a kind of stupid allure. For me it was different. More squalor I could live without.

'Let's go wild!' said Ray. 'Splash out, you know? Like, travel by bus! Eat at a Wimpy!'

I laughed, caught up in his good mood. 'Why not?'

'I mean, I'll be earning, you're going back, so hey, we might as well blow what we've got, right?'

'Right!'

We took the bus to Notting Hill. That was when Ray saw the sign on the gable end, pointed it out to me as the bus swung past.

BLAND UMBRELLAS.

We walked along Portobello Road, Saturday morning and the market in full swing, antiques and bricabrac and old tat, fruit and vegetable stalls, racks of clothes that smelled of mothballs and dank attics. We bought nothing. I flicked through a few books, picked up a carved wooden Buddha, checked the price, put it back. Ray tried on a green velvet jacket, strutted and posed in it, laughed.

'Maybe next week,' he said. 'If I earn some bread.'

A slogan daubed on a wall read SURRENDER TO THE VOID.

The Electric Cinema was showing the new Warhol. *Lonesome Cowboys.*

Next door, on a closed-up shopfront, was a poster for Donovan in concert at the Albert Hall.

Ray stopped, stared at it. 'Aw man, it's tonight!'

The support band was Tyrannosaurus Rex. That was it. 'We've got to go,' he said.

'You think they'd have tickets left?'

'The Albert Hall's pretty big.'

I sang it. 'Now-they-know-how-many-holes-it-takes-to-fill-the-Albert-Hall.'

Ray laughed. 'And there's that Adrian Mitchell poem about filling it up with custard.'

'The Albert Hall?'

'Yeah. I think it's called *A good idea!*'

I sang again, and Ray joined in, loud.

'I'd love to tu-u-u-urn you-ou-ou-ou on.'

We took the tube back a couple of stops to Kensington, queued at the box office and sure enough there were seats left, the cheapest, up behind the stage.

We bought the tickets and Ray put them away carefully in the deep pocket of his coat.

Outside he ran and jumped up, punched the air, shouted 'Yes!'

★

It's an image of Ray that lingers, that run and jump, the

shout of affirmation.

Yes.

Another image. Ray on our last day at school, up on the platform to collect his prize for English, a dayglo orange shirt shouting down his school uniform. Turning to give a languid wave, the book, the prize, in his hand. He had chosen Genet's *Miracle of the Rose*. Not to be out-posed, I had picked Sartre's *Iron in the Soul* as my Latin prize. I stood in line, waiting my turn, in regulation navy and grey.

Further back, Ray at a party, sometime in fourth year, strutting and lip-synching to the Stones on a scratched 45, *Can't get no satisfaction*, mimicking Jagger, perfect to the last shimmy and pout.

And back again, Ray at the third year dance, trying to choreograph a line of lumbering adolescents to do the Madison and the Shadow-step.

Right back to our first day at school, Ray by pure chance sitting next to me at registration, turning and asking, How long you in for?

Abrupt cut, like changing channels, remote control, to this now, Ray in the hospital bed, wired up and linked to a drip-feed, tubes coming out of his nose, no rewind now, no fast forward, we're here in real time stuck.

His father told me what to expect. His father the judge, coming out of the High Court – only a couple of days ago? – recognised me and stopped to talk, unusual in itself, something he seldom did. *It's Raymond*, he said. *Bad state, I'm afraid. You might want to go down and see him. He was asking after you in fact. In his fashion.*

He filled me in with a few brisk details, the basics, then he had to go. I stood for a while, staring down at the Heart of Midlothian, the shape picked out in cobblestones, its centre covered with gobs of spit, for luck.

A bad state. A bloodclot rising to the base of the brain, affecting his motor functions, leaving him effectively paralysed. His father had told me what to expect, but still I wasn't prepared for this. Ray kept alive by machines, Ray skeletal, wasted, skin drawn tight over the gaunt skull with its thin hair, sunk eyes staring out not knowing me.

I sit down beside the bed. His eyes flicker, get me in focus, and he suddenly sees who I am, recognition in the burnt-out eyes. Yes. And the mouth twisted in a lopsided grimace of a smile. With his eyes he indicates a big square alphabet-card at the foot of the bed. I know about this too. Ray can't speak, but he still has some movement in his hands, spells out words by pointing.

I lift up the card, place it. Ray struggles to hold it flat on his lap, to stop it sliding off the bedclothes. He grunts with the effort of manoeuvering his left hand, skinny and limp, onto the card to hold it still. He slides his right hand across, the bony index finger extended, pointing. It rests on the letter H. Then he slides it across to the E, down to the L, off the card and back again to the L.

HELL.

'Shit, man I know. It must be.'

Ray's eyes register confusion. Then he grunts again, the eyes in spite of everything, amused. And he pushes the bony finger onto the O, to finish the word, to say HELLO.

'Right!' I feel ridiculous, awkward. 'I thought . . .'

That humour in the eyes. He knows fine what I thought. He spells out LONG TIME.

'It is that. A long time.'

He spells out YEARS.

'Christ, aye.'

Christ. Aye.

★

The Albert Hall was a pleasure-dome. The front of the stage was a mass of flowers. There was incense burning – sandalwood – and other scents all about, patchouli and jasmine and from somewhere a waft of hashish.

Marc Bolan and Steve Took strutted their funky acoustic stuff, hunched over guitar and bongos, and we bopped and sang along to *Dug and redug and dug and redug O Deborah*, as if we were in the big front room of somebody's flat, four or five thousand of us sitting round the fire.

Then Donovan was out on stage, a skinny figure dressed all in white. Behind him, just in front of us, was his band, a tight jazz combo of laidback session men, easing through the set, effortless. We drifted off to *Sunshine Superman, Season of the Witch.* We joined in on the chorus of *Mellow Yellow.*

At the end, Donovan threw flowers to the beautiful people in the front two rows. I had felt a warmth at being part of something, through the music, and at the same time a kind of emptiness, a detachment from what was going on.

The show was over, the stage cleared, the audience heading for the exits and all their separate lives. We sat for a while, in no hurry to move.

Ray was still up, euphoric. 'What now?' he said.

A couple of roadies were already dismantling the equipment on stage, ripping up gaffa tape, shifting speakers, winding up lengths of cable and looping it round elbow and thumb.

My clothes smelled. My rucksack, packed, sat squat between my feet.

What now?

★

Ray is exhausted, from spelling out conversation. So I just make small-talk. The wife. The kids. The law practice. Then we sit for a while in silence, listening to the hum and bleep of these machines that monitor his functions, keep him alive. Along the corridor, an orderly pushes a trolley. Two young nurses pass by, their talk a quiet undertone, and one of them suddenly laughs, a flash of brightness, simple joy in the uncomplicated moment.

Ray's eyes register pain at the effort of everything. I start talking again, whatever's in my head.

'I've been remembering that first time we came down here. The two of us. Playing at being hippies. Hanging about the Arts Lab. Going to that Donovan concert! Remember?'

He manages that painful smile. He reaches for the board again, spells out YES.

★

After the concert we went to a Wimpy Bar. I wolfed down a shantyburger, a kind of fishcake on a bun. It tasted of nothing.

'Shanty Shanty Shanty,' said Ray. Then he put on a Dylan voice. 'I think T. S. Eliot said that!'

He was still buzzing, from the concert, from being here, from deciding to stay on. I was numbed at the thought of the journey back home. The song that had stayed in my head from the concert was one of Donovan's. A Saturday night. Feels like a Sunday in some ways. That was the mood.

A little brought down in London.

And just for a moment, Ray must have caught it too.

'Jesus Christ!' he said.

He'd seen an old man at the table across from us. The man seemed to be reading the menu, breathing hard and grunting, one hand deep in the pocket of his greasy raincoat, groping himself.

I looked away. 'Enough to put a man off his shanty-burger.'

Outside, Ray shook his head. 'Wanking over a menu,' he said. 'That's sad. That is sad.'

'Could be you in forty years,' I said. 'Still dossing down in the hostel.'

He looked at me hard. 'Know your trouble, man?'

'Tell me.'

'Because you've never had all that bourgeois crap, you still believe in it.'

'I just want a life.'

He stopped and looked at me, a kind of ironic sympathy in his eyes. 'Me too,' he said. 'Want to shake on it?'

25

We shook hands, the moment absurdly solemn.

'A life,' he said.

'A life.'

I slung up my rucksack and we walked to the tube station. From Ray's A to Z we had worked out my best bet was the Northern Line to Hendon. That meant changing at Tottenham Court Road, where Ray got off for the hostel.

At the point where we went our separate ways we stopped.

'Right, well,' said Ray.

'This is it.'

'Probably be easier hitching on your own,' he said. 'Shouldn't take so long.'

'Hope not.'

It was late and dark, and home felt suddenly so very far.

'Come down and visit,' he said. 'Once I'm fixed up and that.'

'I will. Aye.'

We shook hands again, hugged and backslapped, self-consciously gruff. A last wave and I was gliding out on the escalator, my stride a free-falling moonwalk, down and down, to wait on the bare platform for my train. North-bound.

★

I have no clear recollection of that journey back through the night, just a memory of climbing down from a lorry in Sauchiehall Street sometime the next morning, finding everything familiar and strange. I know when I got home the letter was waiting for me – acceptance to the Law course at University.

From there it was a straight fast road to where I am now.

A life.

Once in a while I'd hear from Ray, always from a different address. Stations on his way, like the phases he moved through. Zen. Agitprop. Street theatre. (Some-where I still have the battered paperback he sent me of

Hesse's *Narziss and Goldmund*. Inside he'd scribbled, *Is this like us or what?*) He dabbled in Divine Light. He was Born Again. (He sent me tracts. I trashed them as so much junkmail.) He wrote advertising copy, but couldn't stick it. (He sent me none of the ads he worked on, wouldn't even tell me what they were.) And through all these changes he was working-on-a-novel. (He sent me a few chapters.) The usual rites-of-passage stuff. Distorted autobiography. Young lad from a good Scottish home flings himself into sixties London.

Some of it I recognised. Some of it surprised me. His father was translated into this surreal vengeful figure, called simply the Judge, who haunts the boy's dreams, rears up in hallucinogenic visions. One scene was set in the Arts Lab. I'd been edited out and the central character had gone on his own, watched the Kafka play, met the cowboy. And he'd ended up going back to the cowboy's place, smoking dope. In the middle of the night he'd woken in the cowboy's bed, sat up and stared at the Judge, standing there in the room. And the Judge had asked him if the prisoner understood his sentence.

In the note Ray sent me with the photocopied chapter, he wrote, *Time I came out. I mean, life's short. Right?*

Right.

Now I'm sitting here at his sickbed, his deathbed maybe. There are complications arising from the stroke. The beginnings of pneumonia. He has fullblown AIDS and the virus has wrecked his immune system. So it's just a matter of time.

So much I want to ask. But I don't have the words. I squeeze his hand and nod. Then I pull the board across towards me, point at the question mark.

?

Ray reaches over with that thin hand. He rests it again on the board, then slides it across to point at the exclamation mark.

!

All there is to say.

★

I feel like walking to clear my head, so I cut back across the park. The drizzle has thinned till it's not much more than a clinging mist. The shapes of the trees fade into the grey, like strokes in a Chinese brush-drawing. I stop at a park bench, but the seat is wet. Run my hand along the slats, wipe the surface water in drops and runnels off the edge. It leaves my hand smeared, mucky. I lay my briefcase on the bench, sit on it. Wipe my hand on my coat. The nap feels damp. My breath clouds in front of me. The dampness in the air is a hush in which sounds are isolated, accentuated. Footsteps along the path. Two figures come out of the mist, huddled under umbrellas. A woodblock print. The floating world.

Bland umbrellas.

Back at the hotel, I collect my key from the same girl. I remember now. Her perfume is called *Eternity*.

Yes.

Up in my room I lie back on the bed for a while. Stare at the ceiling. Sit up again and boil the bedside kettle for tea. I put the black briefcase on the bed, click it open. I sit staring into it, with no idea what I'm looking for. The papers I brought are still neat in their buff folder. There is no way I can even think about working on them. My plane tickets are in their envelope, an ad for car-hire on the back. I notice that AVIS spelled backward is SIVA, like Ray is pointing it out to me.

I flick another glance at the newspaper, look at that crossword I started. Try seven across one more time.

Add it up in your head, that's all.

Right.

Totality.

That's the word.

The smell of eternity. The blandness of umbrellas. The shortness of a life.

Totality. The whole jing-bang. All of it.

SAILMAKER

It was a fine poem my father told me, a poem about a yacht.

> Ah had a *yacht*
> *Y'ought* tae see it
> Put it in the *canal*
> Ye *can all* see it

I thought he had written the poem himself, but he had learned it from his own father. He was simply passing it on.

The poem had a special meaning for me because I did have a yacht. As yet it had no mast, no rigging, no sails, but my father had promised to set that right.

My father was a Sailmaker. The fact that he was working as a credit collector instead made no difference to that. To others he might be no more than the Tick Man, a knock at the door on a Friday night, someone to be avoided when money was short. But that was no part of my reality. He was My Father, and if anyone asked me what he did, I would tell them proudly that he was a Sailmaker, in much the same way I would have answered if he had been a Pirate or an Explorer. The word itself rang, in a way that 'Tick Man' never could. It echoed back across time. For as long as there had been ships there must have been Sailmakers.

My father had inherited a craft, an ancient art. His

sailmaking tools were kept in a canvas bag that he had made himself. There were marlinspikes, some of hard polished wood, and some, wooden-handled, of shining steel; there was a set of thick heavy needles, and for pushing them through, a leather palm with a hole for the thumb. Often I would play with them, wielding the spikes as dagger, sword and club, pretending the needles were arrowheads and the palm some primitive glove worn only by hunters or warriors. In quieter moods I might even pretend to be a Sailmaker myself.

I never played at being a Tick Man. That was a different kind of job altogether. Sailmaking was a trade, and to have a trade was something special. It was to be an initiate, a master of secrets and skills.

To be a Tick Man was to be up and down stairs all day, covering close after close, trying to collect payments on clothes and furniture bought long ago on credit, trying to sell more to keep the whole process going. The never-never. There was nothing in my father's battered briefcase – a set of ledgers, some leaflets, a pen – to compare with those Sailmaker's tools; except perhaps for his torch, heavy and balanced with a shiny metal barrel. My father needed it to find his way up some of the darker, more dismal closes where the stairhead lights were always smashed. And more than once he'd been grateful just for the weight of it when he'd been attacked for the money he was carrying, the little he'd managed to collect. So far he had been lucky, and the worst he had got out of it was a bloody nose. At one end of the torch was a dent where he'd connected with some thick skull in fighting his way clear.

I sometimes used the torch to help me explore the bed-recess in our room. That was where I had found the sailmaking tools. The recess was a clutter of old junk, piled to the ceiling with furniture and clothes, cardboard boxes full of books and toys, the residue and jetsam of years. My mother called it the Glory Hole. I liked nothing better than to wriggle my way in through a tunnel of chairlegs to the very centre of the recess where there was space enough to stand upright. And from there I could climb and rummage and ransack, forever unearthing something new, or something old and long forgotten – an old comic I hadn't read in years, a toy I'd thought was lost. It was the one place that was mine. Once I'd burrowed in there I was safe, I was hidden. I could look out as from deep in the heart of a cave. The Glory Hole.

It was in the Glory Hole too that I found the yacht, wedged under a sideboard. Triumphant, I dragged it out into the light. It was just a hulk, three feet long with an iron keel. The varnished surface was chipped and scraped and scarred. But already I could see it, fresh-painted, with a new set of sails, scudding across the pond at Elder Park. I carried it carefully through to the kitchen, lovingly cleaned it with a wet rag.

'What ye doin wi that auld thing?' asked my mother.

'Ah'm gonnae get ma Daddy tae fix it up.'

'Then we can all sail away in it,' she said, laughing. 'Away tae Never Never Land!'

Never Never Land was where my father was going to take us when he won a lot of money, from the football pools, or from betting on horses and dogs. He had always been trying, as long as I could remember. 'Trying the Pools' was a magical game that in some mysterious way could make us rich. It had once conjured an image of my father fishing in deep pools of water. And although I had later been told that this had no reality, the image, at some level, had remained.

The other betting had less of a magic. Sometimes I would take my father's line to the back-close bookie. And the bookie scared me. His pitch was in a close that was dark and smelly, and there I would have to queue, everybody furtive, looking out for the police. In my young head, bookie was an echo of bogey. He was the back-close bogeyman, sinister and mean. And somehow this bogey could keep our money or give us back more. He had the power.

For writing out his lines, my father used a secret name, a nom de plume, because the whole game was illegal. The name he used was Mainsail, carried over from his sail-making days.

He still had faith that he would one day win a fortune. Then that mainsail would be set, and away we would sail.

There was a song I liked in those days; I used to hear it on the radio:

Red sails in the sunset
Way out on the sea . . .

That was the way I could see my yacht. Red sails. When I asked my father to fix it up for me, he was tired after work. But he said he would rig it out whenever he had time and they could spare the money for materials. I asked him when that would be and he said 'Wait and see.'

My mother told me the yacht had belonged to my cousin Jacky. His family had emigrated to America years before and all the toys he couldn't take with him had been shared out among his cousins. The yacht had been passed on to me, only to lie forgotten until now.

Because the yacht had been Jacky's, I felt that now it was a link with America, where he had gone. And that pleased me. America was a fabled place, like Never Never Land, a place of cowboys and gangsters, prairies and canyons, skyscraper cities and giant cars. From America, at Christmas, I had been sent a parcel, a fat bundle of comics. They were all in colour, not black and white like the ones I could buy here. Superman and Blackhawk, Donald Duck and Mickey Mouse. America was colour.

One Saturday afternoon, my Uncle Billy was visiting and I had the yacht out on the floor. Overturned, with the deck face down, the hulk could be a submarine, or a hill for toy soldiers to climb, or a giant shark, the keel its back fin.

'Where d'ye get the boat?' asked Uncle Billy.

'Used tae be Jacky's,' I said.

'He dragged it out that Glory Hole,' said my mother.

'Ah'm gonnae fix it up,' said my father, 'When ah've got the time.'

'Ah could paint it if ye like,' said Uncle Billy. He worked as a painter's labourer.

He took it away with him that night and brought it back a week or so later. The hull was painted a pure shining white, the deck a light brown, the keel royal blue. I held it, amazed and unbelieving. It was like a whole new boat, unrecognisable, reborn.

After that I must have pestered my father, kept at him to get down to rigging out the yacht. I was aching to see it sail.

But always he was tired from work. Fixing the yacht, he said, was a difficult job. It would take time. Materials were expensive. He didn't have the right tools. But someday he would do it.

'When?' I would ask.

'Wait and see.'

That went on for weeks. And months. And gradually I stopped asking. The yacht went back to being a hulk. A hill for toy soldiers, a submarine, a shark.

In the end I forgot about making it sail, and it found its way back into the Glory Hole.

★

The next time I saw the yacht was long years later. It was a hard time then. My mother had died. My father had no job. A dark time. Across the road from us was a pub on the corner, and next door to that was a betting shop. The street bookie was no longer outlawed and had opened up a place of his own. Between the betting shop and the pub, my father passed most of his days. Afternoons in the shop, mornings and evenings in the pub. Often enough, though, he had no money for either.

This night I remember, the last of our coal had run out. My father's dole money wasn't due till the next day. It must have been January, the bleakest part of winter, miserable and dank, wind shaking the panes, a damp patch spreading on the ceiling.

And there we sat, freezing, wrapped up in coats and scarves, trying to keep warm. We had nothing much to say to each other in those days. He was a middle-aged man, unable to cope with the death of his wife. I was in the first wretched throes of adolescence. We might have come from different universes. We sat facing each other, separate, at either side of the empty hearth, letting the blare of the radio fill the silence between us.

Then my father had an idea. He thought we could dig out some of the old sticks of furniture packed away in the room, break it up and make a fire.

That meant going in again to the Glory Hole. I hadn't been in there in years. I had grown too big to crawl in and under and through. It was more chaotic than ever, darker, more crammed with junk. The dust had settled thicker. I took down the curtain that hung over the doorway and I eased my way in. The front of the recess was blocked with two old kitchen chairs. Piled on top of them were a few tatty cushions, a cardboard box and a stack of old magazines called *Enquire Within*. The chairs and the magazines would burn so I passed them out to my father. The cushions could be thrown out another time. The cardboard box I brought out, to investigate in the light.

My father had the fire going quickly. He tore up a few of the magazines, scrumpled up the pages in the grate. He smashed up the chairs with a cleaver, placed some splintered bits on top of the paper, then he lit it, and we watched it catch and flare and roar; and we grinned at each other as we warmed ourselves.

'That's more like it,' he said. 'That's the stuff!'

In the cardboard box were more old papers, a tartan biscuit tin full of buttons and elastic bands, a few toy soldiers and cars, and my father's old torch. The surface of the torch was dull, had lost its shine. The button was stiff and it wouldn't light.

'Batteries'll be dead,' said my father.

'Pity,' I said. 'Could've used it tae see intae the recess.'

I unscrewed the end of the torch and looked in. The inside had rusted and the batteries were stuck, rotted, covered with pale stuff like green mould.

'What makes it go like that?' I asked.

'Don't know,' said my father. 'Just time. Just . . . time.'

The fire blazed and crackled, but the wood burned quick. So back I went into the recess to bring out more.

This time I took a candle, to see further in. I shifted a mattress and the dust I stirred up made me choke and cough. I passed out a wooden stool, a bagatelle board and the headboard from a bed. And I brought back out with me a little canvas bag.

Again my father set to breaking the wood and stoking the fire.

In the canvas bag were his sailmaking tools, the marlinspikes, the needles, the palm. He looked at them long and he started reminiscing, going back. He had worked on the *Queen Mary*, made awnings and tarpaulins, made guncovers for destroyers during the war. He told me of his apprenticeship when he was my age, how hard those days had been. He looked at the tools and it came back to him. Then he put the wooden marlinspikes on the fire. They were made from lignum vitae, the hardest wood. They were solid and they burned slow.

'Thae other tools can go in the midden sometime,' he said. I put them away and went back once more into the recess. Most of the space was taken up by a sideboard. I tried to shift it and managed to dislodge a mirror that shattered to pieces on the floor.

'Seven years' bad luck,' said my father, then, 'Still. Cannae get much worse than it's been, eh!'

He took the frame from the broken mirror, shook the last bits of glass from it. 'This'll burn,' he said. Then together we struggled and heaved out the sideboard. It was too old to sell, he said, or to be of any use, so it might as well go in the fire with the rest.

As he set to with the cleaver once more, chopping and splitting, he started again to remember back. The sideboard was all that was left of the furniture they'd bought when they were married.

'Got it in Galpern's,' he said. 'That's him that was the Lord Provost. . . . Solid stuff it is too.'

He fingered the carved handle on a door, the fancy beading round the edge. 'Nobody takes the care any more,' he said. 'Nobody's interested in this old stuff.'

He was talking himself back into being sad.

'Seems a shame tae break it up,' he said. 'Still. It's a shame tae freeze as well, isn't it!' He split the door into strips, broke the strips in half to fit the fire.

'Ah remember when we bought this,' he said, his eyes glazing over as he watched it burn. His voice was growing maudlin again, drifting into sentimentality. I couldn't take it, and went back into the room.

All the wood was gone now from the recess. We had stripped it bare. But there on the floor, behind where the sideboard had been, was the hull of that old yacht. I picked it up and dusted it off, carried it through to the kitchen.

'Remember this?' I asked my father.

'Oh aye,' he said. 'Yer uncle Billy painted it.'

'You were always gonnae fix it up for me,' I said. 'Ah could always imagine it. Like that song. Red sails in the sunset.'

'Ah always meant to,' said my father. 'Just . . .'

'Just never did,' I said.

'Story a ma life,' he said.

Then I wedged the yacht into the grate. The flames licked round it. The paint began to blister and bubble. Then the wood of the hull caught and burned. And the yacht had a sail of flame. And it sailed in the fire, like a Viking longboat, out to sea in a blaze with the body of a dead chief. Off to

Valhalla. Up Helly-A!

And the wood burned to embers, and the iron keel clattered onto the hearth.

BIRD OF PARADISE

A reggae version of *White Christmas* tinkled from a radio behind the bar, reminded him again it was December. Winter. He stared out at palm trees in the full heat of the afternoon sun, further out the impossible blue of the Caribbean.

The hotel was called Blue Heaven, named, he supposed, after the song. A turn to the right. A little white light. He had caught himself a few times singing it, mindlessly whistling the tune. Now it would probably be ousted by *White Christmas*. May your days be merry and bright. A benediction.

'Kind of ironic, don't you think?' The American at the next table was addressing him.

'Sorry?'

'The song,' he explained. 'Kind of ironic in this place. White Christmas.'

He hadn't particularly wanted to be drawn into conversation, but cautiously, giving it thought, he replied. 'Aye,' he said. 'Right enough.'

His silence broken, he felt he should say something more.

'Do you think it's conscious?' he asked. 'The irony I mean.'

'Well.' The American paused. 'I haven't seen too much around here that I'd call conscious!'

'It's what you'd call *laid back.*'

'I'd call it goddam comatose!'

The American was about his own age, mid-thirties, wore a red T-shirt, Bermuda shorts and running shoes. He had noticed him earlier with his wife and a daughter he guessed was about eight, chucking a frisbee about the beach. He sat alone now, sipping cold beer. Setting down his glass, he went on. 'You ordered tea, right?'

'Twenty minutes ago.'

'That's what I mean. Fast foods it ain't!'

'Of course, I complicated the issue by asking for toast.'

'Big mistake.'

'They had a conference about whether they could do it or not. Strictly speaking it's for breakfast only.'

'Sure.'

'They decided I could have it. But they're making me wait. That's my part of the bargain. Kind of penance. Mea culpa!'

The American laughed. 'You're English, right?'

'Scottish.'

'Sorry! The difference is important to you guys, huh?'

'Some of us. Sometimes. It's a bit like calling a Texan a Yankee. Or asking a Canadian which part of the States he's from.'

'Jeez, that's serious,' he said. 'Mea maxima culpa!'

'No offence.'

'I went to Scotland once, on vacation. Took in Edinburrow, the Highlands.'

'Very nice.'

'Yeah.'

'I'm from Glasgow myself.' More irony, but the American didn't notice.

'So what brings you to this tropical paradise?'

'You've been reading the same guidebooks as me, eh?'

'Right! Tobago. *An emerald jewel set in an azure sea!*'

'I've actually been working in Trinidad. This is my Christmas holiday.'

40

'What's your line of work?'

'I work for an oil company. American of course!'

'Doing what?'

'Mainly PR stuff. Reports. Articles for the house journals. That sort of thing.'

'So you get to travel with the job.'

He nodded. 'Started out in Aberdeen. Then I spent some time in New York before they sent me down here.'

'Sounds like you got a good deal.'

'Could be worse. What about yourself?'

'I teach high school,' he said. 'This is strictly vacation. A winter break.'

'Following the sun, eh?'

The woman behind the bar brought his tea and toast. He thanked her and she looked through him, sullen. 'Mea cuppa,' he said to the American.

'Very good!' he said, laughing.

The woman was big and heavy, but still moved with a slow lazy grace. She turned up the volume on the radio. White Christmas had given way to a piece of local nonsense, a raucous calypso called *Santa was a black man*.

'Weird,' said the American.

'What is?'

'Black Santa.'

'Makes sense,' he said. 'More sense here than some fat old white guy from the North Pole.'

'Bearing gifts!'

'Santa's obviously a nice old Rastaman with white dreadlocks, stoned out of his head on ganja!'

'Obviously!' said the American, laughing again.

'It's understandable all the same. The way they are.'

'Guess so.'

'They were under the yoke for a long time. British. French. Dutch.'

'We weren't involved for once, huh?'

'Oh, America does its bit. The big corporations. My employers for instance.'

41

'They call it *development.*'

'There's other names for it!'

'Listen,' said the American, 'let's not get into *that*! Can I buy you a drink?'

'No, thanks. I don't.'

'Not even a beer?'

'Been on the wagon for five years. Have to stick to this stuff.' He indicated the tea and poured himself another cup from the pot. To lighten it they'd given him a little jug of condensed milk, sticky and sweet. He spooned some into the tea, stirring it, then he scooped up some more and licked the spoon clean.

'Don't know how you can do that,' said the American. 'I had some of that stuff in my coffee. Disgusting gook!'

'Reminds me of when I was wee,' he said. 'Used to have this on bread for a real treat. If you were lucky you got to lick the spoon, or the drips off the side of the tin.'

'Yich!'

'Of course you can get too much of it, like anything else. Once ate half a tin and was nearly sick.'

'I'm not surprised!'

'Still . . .' he said, dipping his spoon again, winding it. 'Just another wee taste!' The sticky sweetness filled his mouth. 'Nostalgia!' he said.

The American saw his wife and daughter outside, waving to him. He finished his beer and stood up to go. 'Promised I'd take them into town,' he explained. 'Maybe see you again later.'

'Right,' he said. 'Nice talking to you.'

Alone again, he wavered over the milk jug. The woman behind the bar glowered at him. He set down the spoon. He became aware of the radio again, but for once it played something real, Bob Marley, wailing, *No Woman No Cry*. He listened, eyes closed. When the song was over he went back to his room, thought about taking a walk down to the sea.

★

He had hardly spoken to anyone in the week he'd been on the island. He hadn't felt any lack, but talking to the American he had realised it. The sickness had made him insular. He was suffering from a fever, headaches and a watery cough. He had needed the break, away from work. He had looked forward to the trip from Trinidad, and some daft romanticism had decided him to come by boat. But the night crossing had been hell.

He had slept up on deck, lying on top of his bags. When it rained it soaked him, but he couldn't have coped with the jampacked cabins and passageways down below. Once he had woken, convinced he was back in Glasgow on a rowdy late-night bus. Later he had peered out in the grey light, seen a porpoise leaping in the wake of the boat. That had lifted his spirits a bit, but arriving in Tobago he was shivering in spite of the heat. Going back he would fly.

The way from his hotel room down to the beach led through the ruin of an old dance-hall. The paintwork, once skyblue, was flaked and bleached and faded. The place had been part of the hotel in some distant heyday. Blue Heaven. Now it was colonised by bats, hung from the rafters and bannisters. At night they flitted, shrieking, back and forth. The first time he'd gone through he had stopped there, quite still, amazed at the eeriness, the utter strangeness of it. Then something like fear had quickened his step, a creeping unease that he'd laughed off later, putting it down to his fever.

Coming up now in the evening, after his swim, he met the American there, on his way down with his wife and child.

'Hi there!' he waved. 'Been swimming?'

He nodded. 'It's nice at this time. Wee bit cooler.'

'That's where we're going now.' He turned to his wife. 'Honey, this is my Scotch friend I was telling you about. Hey, we didn't even get names! I'm Jack. This is my wife Carol . . .'

'Pleased to meet you. My name's Ian.'

'My daughter Josie . . .'

'Hi!'

They stood for a moment, nothing much to say. A bat squeaked.

'Quite a place,' said Jack, looking about him. 'Like something out of a forties movie. Just see Bogart over there in a white coat.'

'Lauren Bacall,' said his wife.

'It's creepy,' said Josie.

'It would do fine for a horror film,' he said.

'Voodoo,' said Jack. 'And something horrible slithering out of the ocean!'

'It's spooky,' said Josie. 'I bet there's ghosts.'

'Hey, Ian,' said Jack. 'We went down to the Botanic Gardens today, and guess what? There's a couple of your countrymen buried there.'

'Just what I need to hear!' he said. 'The way I've been feeling.'

'You've been sick?' said Carol.

'Just a fever. It'll pass.'

'These guys been there for a while,' said Jack 'Buried back in the 1800s. One was from Glasgow, the other from . . . where was it honey?'

'Lanark.'

'Amazing,' he said. 'They must have been pretty important to be laid out in the Botanics.'

'Important meaning rich!'

'It said they were merchants,' said Carol.

'Probably sugar,' he said. 'Molasses. Rum.'

'Development!' said Jack.

'They were both very young,' said Carol. 'The Glasgow guy was thirty-three and the other one was thirty-seven.'

'Never know the minute,' he said.

A bat flapped past, just above them.

'There really *is* ghosts here,' said Josie.

'Let's go swim,' said Jack, taking her hand. 'See you around, Ian.'

'Bye!' said Carol.

'Cheerio,' he said. 'Or have you noticed what they say around here? Instead of goodbye, they say *Until*.'

Jack laughed. 'Until, man!'

They left the place to its bats and its ghosts.

'Until!'

★

He lay back on his bed, watching a bright green lizard flick and dart across the ceiling, and he thought about the two merchants buried in the Botanic Gardens. Scots in exile. Merchants/mercenaries. Explorers/exploiters.

The part of Glasgow where he'd grown up was called Plantation, near the docks. Plantation Quay. And, not far away, Jamaica Street and Kingston Street and even a Tobago Street. Names brought back by the merchants in the far-off boom days, the opening up of America, the Indies. Cargoes of tobacco, cotton, sugar.

And these two had come here, grown rich and died young. Thirty-three and thirty-seven. He was thirty-five. Nowadays they would probably be working for an oil corporation. And their employers would be milking the North Sea as well as the Caribbean. Development.

'Let's not get into *that*!' the American had said.

He remembered the first time he'd read an article about Scotland in their own house magazine. It had left him irritated for days, just something in the tone of it, the perspective, the viewpoint. Like the kind of thing he might read in *National Geographic* about any small obscure faraway country. Alongside a picture of an oil-rig had been one of Edinburgh Castle and another of a kilted piper. An uneasy memory was coming to the surface.

The first time he'd travelled up to Aberdeen by train. There had been a loud gang of cowboys from Glasgow, on their way up to work on the rigs, listening to Country and Western on a giant stereo radio, singing along. *Honky-tonk angels*. Jean had been with him, tightlipped, unhappy at the

45

move north. The marriage hadn't lasted long after that. One fight too many and she'd packed up, gone to Edinburgh and then to London, left him trying to drink his way into oblivion.

The way things piled up.

His first time on an oil-rig he had almost been killed.

He had been set down from the boat in a personnel basket, hoisted by a crane. But as he'd stepped off, the basket had swung round, hit him in the chest and knocked him over backwards, and he'd plunged forty feet into the North Sea.

It was vivid still, the fall into nothing, the impact as he hit, the water closing over him, bubbles rising. He had thought he was going to die and had felt very calm about it. An acceptance. That was it. Too bad. He had risen to the surface, kept himself afloat. He'd been thrown a lifeline and with difficulty hauled up, coughing and spitting blood. His chest and back were hurt. The old doctor had told him, 'I doubt ye've got a death wish, son. Not content to do it slowly wi the booze. Now yer tryin to do it in one go and swallow the bloody North Sea!'

By the time he recovered his health, he had given up drinking, dried out. Almost five years now but it felt longer, seemed very far away.

His time in America had done that, made things seem small and peripheral. In New York he'd encountered a different sense of scale, an awareness of being centre stage.

That was probably what had annoyed him in the article about Scotland. Small and peripheral. Just another development area.

He was shaken by another fit of coughing that made his eyes water, his head ache. The climate here was killing him, hot and humid, everything rank and lush. It had probably done for those two merchants lying in the Botanics. They were just about his own age. Never know the minute. It's not the cough that carries you off. The fever was making him morbid.

46

He lay down, the spasm past. The lizard had moved from the ceiling, was clinging to the wall above his bed. It seemed to be watching him, lazily, with one glazed eye.

★

He sat, the next evening, on the veranda behind the hotel, sipping some Lucozade he'd bought at the chemist's in town. He heard them come in, laughing, behind him, Jack's voice calling his name.

'Ian! Hi! Oh, man, what a trip we had today! We saw the bird of paradise!'

'For real!' said Carol.

'I saw it first!' said Josie.

'You sure did, honey,' said Jack, laughing and hugging her.

They had been in the sun, had that burnt and bleached look; they were tired but clearly glowing, excited at where they'd been, what they'd seen.

They sat down beside him and Jack told his story.

'We drove to the far end of the island,' he began. 'Decided we'd go see *Little* Tobago. Did you read about it in the brochures?'

'I did,' he said. '*Bird of Paradise Island.*'

'That's it,' said Jack. 'The island's a kind of sanctuary. The birds aren't really indigenous. They brought them in from New Guinea or someplace. But what the hell. They're *there*!'

'It seems there's not too many of them,' said Carol. 'Only a few pairs. And they're very rarely seen.'

'You have to get somebody to take you out by boat,' said Jack. 'They charge a few bucks, give you a guided tour and bring you back.'

'And show you the bird of paradise?'

'This guy *did*,' said Jack. 'He really seemed to have a *feeling* for the bird. An affinity or something. And he took us right to the spot.'

'How long were you there?'

'I guess a couple of hours all told.'

'To tell you the truth', said Carol, 'we almost gave up. We were getting tired and kinda . . . strung out. We wanted to go someplace else. But Josie liked it where we were.'

'I guess she knew,' said Jack. 'And the guy said it too. *This is a good spot*, he said. Then he took himself off someplace. Said he'd be back.'

'Just keeping himself quietly stoned,' said Carol. 'I could smell the dope.'

'So we just settled down and waited,' said Jack. 'Mellowed out. Relaxed. Josie started making herself some kind of den.'

'It was so beautiful,' said Carol. 'We were way deep in the forest and the light was real soft. Like being in a big cathedral.'

'And after a while,' said Jack, 'Josie looked up and said *There's the bird*. She kind of whispered it, real excited. And we looked. And there it was, coming down into the tree. And the guy was there with a big stoned grin on his face. *That's him* he said. *That's the one!*

'The bird didn't stay,' said Carol. 'Just kind of hovered around and then took off again. I guess it knew we were there.'

'What colour was it?'

'Yellow,' she said. 'And orange. With a big crest.'

'Most beautiful goddam thing I ever saw,' said Jack.

'It's a great story to tell,' he said.

The story was already becoming a myth, the journey a quest, the glimpse a vision.

'I have seen the bird of paradise!' Jack intoned the words in a voice like an old-time preacher. Then he laughed. 'Guess I'm just an old hippy at heart!'

Something caught Josie's attention. 'Listen!' she said, turning her head. And they did. And they heard the pulse of a strange rhythm, like some crazed percussion section, passing somewhere near.

'Maybe it's a parade!' said Josie.

They stood up and went to the front of the hotel. A group of men were moving up the driveway, dancing in a straggled circle, beating out the rhythm with drums and maracas, shakers and rattles and coconut shells. At the centre of the circle moved one man, the focus of all their attention. All his clothes were on back to front, a shirt, an old overcoat, a cap. Even his feet were stuffed into a huge pair of wellingtons turned backwards, and he stumbled around, tripping over them, trying not to fall. A few of the others carried sharp sticks and they prodded at him, kept him moving.

There were elements that Ian recognised, could relate to things he knew. Going out guising at Halloween as a child. Dressing up backwards had been an easy one and a favourite, his face blacked with soot. And the procession itself was like the wedding eve ritual he'd seen so often in Glasgow, the girl to be married paraded through the streets.

But the strangeness in what he was watching lay in its intensity. He felt no sense of joy or celebration in it. The man at the centre was scapegoat, sacrificial victim. The rhythm was remorseless. The faces of the others were blank masks. One of them moved away from the edge of the group, came towards the small crowd that had gathered from the hotel to watch. He held out a cap, for money. Ian patted his pockets. Jack shook his head. The man tried another group and collected a few coins.

'It's for Christmas and New Year', said somebody behind them. 'You pay them to take away your bad luck.'

The men were moving on towards the old dance-hall, would dance inside and scatter the bats.

'This place is far out!' said Jack.

The man collecting money turned and spat back in their direction.

★

49

He had a bad night, tortured by the heat and his wheezy cough and a single mosquito that zinged in his ear. Eventually, exhausted, he fell into sleep. He woke at dawn with nothing in his head but the bird of paradise.

He went into town early and hired a car. It didn't even feel like a conscious decision. He simply found himself doing it, as if he had no choice. He would go to the island today, find the bird of paradise, see it for himself. In Scarborough the streets were crowded, even this early. He was always amazed at the number of men just hanging around, on streetcorners, in shop doorways, doing nothing.

The streets were narrow and rutted, the buildings ramshackle. He made his way from shop to shop, bought a few things he would need for his journey; a haversack and a canteen for water, a flashlight, a machete he thought might be useful, some food from a supermarket — bread and cheese, fruit and nuts. He packed everything into the haversack, the handle of the machete jutting out.

From most of the shops, from the bars and cafés, came the loud blare of radio music, all of it reggae, calypso, ska. He heard reggae *Jingle Bells* and *Auld Lang Syne*. And Santa was still a black man.

Somewhere a steel band was rehearsing, playing *Yellow Bird* and *Island in the Sun*. It could have been the background music for a travelogue, Caribbean kitsch, palm trees waving, sand and sea.

In spite of his fever, or perhaps because of it, he felt alert as he wandered, taking it all in. The smell of curry wafted to him from a stall selling hot roti. He thought of buying one but settled instead for something called a snow cone — crushed ice in a paper cup, flavoured with condensed milk. He thought it tasted faintly of paraffin, but the coldness was delight, an ease to his burning throat. Making his way towards the car, he passed a Rastaman sitting cross-legged under a tree, muttering and laughing to himself, shaking his matted dreadlocks. Further along, outside a market, two young boys were fighting, rolling in the dust as a lazy crowd gathered to watch and enjoy.

'Kill him, man,' they encouraged. 'Rip out his gizzard!' Nobody moved to break it up, and the boys fought on, intense and brutal and utterly serious.

He stood a few moments watching, fascinated in spite of himself. Then, remembering his journey, he hurried on.

★

'Gas is so cheap here,' Jack had told him. He remembered now as he filled up the tank for his trip.

'So it should be,' he'd said. 'They drill it just out there.'

By the same reasoning, he thought, it should be cheap in Scotland. He pushed the thought to the back of his mind. He didn't want to think about anything uncomfortable, anything to do with his work. He was going to see the bird of paradise.

Jack had given him specific instructions. He said he should ask for the same man who'd guided them. 'His name's Bishop,' he'd said. 'Big guy with a shark's tooth round his neck.'

He drove carefully, did his best to avoid the potholes that pockmarked the road. It was good to be moving, and although he still felt feverish, and his knuckles and toes itched where he'd been bitten, he felt a lightness, and he sang to himself as he drove along.

> *Yellow bird, up high in banana tree*
> *Yellow bird, you sit all alone like me*

The steel band had been playing it back in town.

> *Did your lady friend leave the nest again?*
> *That is very sad, make you feel so bad*

He remembered the song from his childhood. He would

51

hear it on the radio. Edmundo Ros and his Caribbean Rhythm.

A-one, a-two, a-one,two,three,four . . .

> *You can fly away, to the sky away*
> *You more lucky than me*

Back in the sixties, when they were still students, Jean had given him a postcard of a painting by Paul Klee. *Landscape with Yellow Birds*. When she liked a painting she thought of it as a world, a space she could somehow inhabit. And this one had been her favourite, the world she had wanted them to live in, simple and childlike and bright. Back in the sixties. He still had the postcard, somewhere.

He heard Bob Marley again, from a radio. *No Woman No Cry*. He wondered if the record had been re-released. It was haunting, bittersweet. Times past. *I remember when we used to sit.* But the song itself was a kind of affirmation. Consolation. *No cry.* Marley had died of cancer, aged thirty-six.

Reggae always reminded him of London. They had stayed for a while in Notting Hill, before he took the job in Aberdeen, and everything had moved to the pulse and throb of that same rhythm. It had been a bad time for them, already growing apart. Maybe because of that, the music, for him, had always an edge to it, something brooding behind the easy beat.

He remembered when they used to sit. . . . Evenings in a pub called *The Sun in Splendour*. Drinking too much as the silences grew between them. A long way away from their landscape with yellow birds.

The road wound and twisted, following the coast, wooded slopes on one side, the open sea on the other.

The guidebook had called it Crusoe's Island – claimed it was the original of the island described in the novel.

Crusoe to him meant the illustrated edition he'd read as a boy, the pictures by Dudley Watkins. He remembered it vividly, a yellow cover with Crusoe looking down at that single footprint.

He passed through two or three towns, each one just a straggle of houses, a shop, a bar, between the towns, here and there, a solitary shack by the roadside. The drive took longer than he expected, but at last he crested a rise, turned a bend, saw Little Tobago offshore.

The place was called Speyside. More Scottish merchants, he thought. The village was just as Jack had described it; a little clutter of houses, a modern stone-built pavilion at the road's end with toilets and a parking bay and a clump of men outside.

He parked the car and walked across to them. 'I'm looking for Mr Bishop,' he said.

'Bishop,' said one of them. 'He's home now. You want to find him?'

'I do,' he said. 'But not if it's a problem.'

'No problem, man.' He grinned. 'He's not doin nothin.' He pointed back along the road. 'First street on the right, the house at the end.'

'Thanks.'

'OK, man.'

As he crossed the road he heard one of them mutter something, heard the burst of their laughter behind him. But the feeling from them was friendly, and that made a change.

The street was a narrow dirt track. The house stood in its own patch of ground, built up, like most of them, on pillars of brick, to keep above the floods in the rainy season.

Bishop opened the door to him. He recognised him from Jack's description, a big man, the shark's tooth round his neck on a chain. He wore a sleeveless shirt and trousers cut off ragged at the knee.

'I want to go to the island,' he explained.

'No problem,' said Bishop. 'Twenty dollars, I take you out, show you round, bring you back.'

'That's fine,' he said.

'Give me fifteen minutes,' said Bishop. 'I meet you down there.'

He made his way back towards the shore, headed across to a wooden shack that seemed to be a shop.

An old woman sat inside, working her way through a heap of cocoa pods, deftly, patiently opening them, dropping the beans into a basket at her feet. She looked up and nodded as he came in.

The place seemed not much bigger than a nightwatchman's hut, room for the old woman and maybe two customers at most. The shelves were stacked with bottled drinks, some fruit, a few sweets, packets and cans of this and that.

He bought a can of Fanta orange, some peanuts in what looked like a beerbottle.

'You from England?' she asked.

'Scotland,' he said.

She nodded. 'I got two sons in England. One in London, one in Liverpool. Grandchildren too, but I never seen them. Just pictures.'

London and Liverpool. He had read in the papers about riots through the summer. Gangs of young blacks, out of work and angry. *Uprising.* Looting shops and throwing petrol bombs.

'You goin across to the island?' she asked.

'That's right,' he said. 'I want to see the bird of paradise.'

She smiled. 'It's good you people come,' she said. 'Give something for the men to do. Bring a little bit money.'

He thought of the men back in Scarborough, hanging around. 'Not much work?' he asked.

She shook her head. 'No jobs.'

'How do they manage?'

'Do some fishin,' she said. 'A bit of this, a bit of that.'

'I thought the oil would bring jobs,' he said.

'In Trinidad,' she said. 'Not here.'

He couldn't help smiling to himself at the tone of her voice. She said *Trinidad* the way he would say *England*, the way a Canadian would say *America*.

All the time she spoke her hands kept working, slowly, methodically, opening the pods, taking out the beans. And he watched and was touched by something timeless in it, something enduring, the very rhythm of the place in the movement of an old woman's hands, making do, getting by, accepting her fate and shaping it.

As if she could read his thoughts she looked up at him. 'We live all right,' she said.

'You grow things?' he asked.

She nodded. 'We pick these,' she said, indicating the beans. 'Sell them. Then there's coconuts, and figs.'

'You grow figs?'

'Sure. There's some there, on the counter.'

She was looking at a bunch of very small bananas. The only other fruit on display was a basket of oranges.

'You call these figs?' he said.

'That's figs,' she said, emphatic. 'You try one.'

'I'll buy some,' he said, breaking off a bunch of four. He paid her, told her to keep the change. He couldn't be bothered with coins jingling in his pocket.

'You don't get figs where you come from?'

'Not like these,' he said. He looked at his watch. 'Time I was going.'

'Good luck,' she said. 'I hope you find the bird.'

★

The crossing was short. He felt buoyed up, exhilarated, as the small boat bucked and dipped across the narrow stretch of water.

He was the only passenger. Behind him, steering the boat, was Bishop; two others sat forward, the man who had directed him to Bishop's house, and a young boy about eighteen. The boy was quiet. The two men kept up a constant stream of banter above the noise of the outboard motor.

He loved the rhythm of their talking, the colour and the life of it. When they spoke to each other, there was much he

55

couldn't understand, but often he would catch the drift, make some sense of it. Once or twice Bishop spoke to him direct.

'How come you know to ask for me?' he said.

'I met somebody you took out yesterday.'

'The American?' asked Bishop. 'Wife, little girl?'

'That's right,' he said. 'They recommended you.'

He found that funny. 'Recommended!' he said, grinning. He shouted to his friend. 'You hear that man? I recommended! I first-class tourist guide, you hear now?' They laughed out loud. 'First-class magic-man, find the bird of paradise!'

They were almost at the island now, dense forest above a narrow curve of beach. Bishop cut the engine and they drifted in past a small wooden jetty. The boy was out first, splashing onto the sand, hauling on a rope the other man had thrown to him from the boat.

Now it was his turn. Haversack on his back and trousers rolled up past his knees, he climbed over the side and waded ashore, carrying his sandals in his hand.

The others followed and the three of them dragged the boat up onto the beach.

'OK,' said Bishop, turning to him. 'I show you around. Maybe we get lucky again, see the bird!'

The path was steep and the climb seemed endless. But the view from the top was spectacular. From an observation point they looked out along a sweep of cliffs to the open sea, and far below them seabirds swooped and dived. The going was easier after that, level for a bit and then downhill.

They passed a derelict wooden building. Bishop said it had once been a base for some group studying the bird-life. There was talk, he said, of rebuilding it, making it into a hostel, but so far it had come to nothing.

'Does anybody ever stay here?' he asked.

'Sometimes. Scientists, birdwatchers. They camp out in the clearing there, by the building.'

Further on, deeper in, the path grew fainter, overgrown. At last Bishop stopped.

'This is where we come yesterday,' he said. 'That's the tree.' They both looked up.

'I got to go in an hour,' he went on. 'You got to be pretty lucky to see that bird. Yesterday he come here. Now who knows, maybe nobody see him for a month.'

'I've been thinking' he said. 'Maybe you could leave me here, come back for me.'

'Later?'

'Tomorrow.'

'You want to stay here all night?'

He nodded. 'I've got some food. I can sleep back at that clearing.'

Bishop thought about it, finally said, 'OK. But that's another trip for us. Be more money.'

'Another twenty?'

'All right.'

'We pick you up at noon. You come down to the boat.'

'Sure. That's great. Thanks!'

'So,' said Bishop, turning to go. 'Take it easy man. Enjoy yourself.'

'Right,' he said. As Bishop headed off, he called after him, 'Until!'

Bishop turned, grinned back at him. 'Until!'

★

He was weaker than he'd realised. The trek had left him tired and shaky. Left to himself now, he ate some of his food, drank the can of orange; then he lay back, his head on his haversack, gazing up into the green of the trees, here and there a fleck of blue sky showing through.

Lying still, he noticed every sound, every movement: rustling in the undergrowth, shrill birdsong, the buzz and creak of insects. Turning his head he saw a lizard, bigger than any he had seen, a miniature dragon, yellow patterns along its back. Two bright butterflies flickered between the trees, and far above a small blue bird hovered and settled on a branch. A sanctuary.

Like a big cathedral, Carol had said. But this was brighter than any stained glass, a living tapestry that changed from moment to moment.

When he felt rested, he decided to go exploring, follow his instinct and see where it led him.

★

The further he went, the more tangled and overgrown the path became. Now and again he had to use his machete, hack his way through. His course led downhill and he gradually realised he was heading towards the sea. He could hear it, caught a glimpse from time to time. And finally he reached it. He cut through another clump of bush, slithered down a slope and found himself in a rocky inlet with a tiny arc of beach. Three or four palm trees bordered the sand and a scatter of coconuts lay beneath them. He picked up two, put them in his haversack. They would add to his stock of food and drink for later.

The realisation came to him, suddenly amazed him, that at this moment he was the only human being on the island. The thought frightened and excited him at the same time. He felt an emptiness in the pit of his stomach. What if Bishop and the others didn't come back? What if he was injured here, far away from where they'd left him? Morbid again. *I doubt ye've got a death wish, son.* Maybe the old doctor had been right.

He looked about him at the sea and the palm trees, the unbelievable blue of the sky, and it all felt dreamlike, unreal. He laughed at it, and somehow nothing mattered. He decided to go for a swim.

He piled up his clothes and his bag behind the trees and waded, naked, into the water. When the waves started breaking over his head, he struck out for a rock, a little way offshore.

It was further than he'd thought, and hard against the tide. At times he felt as if he wasn't moving forward. But he made it, clambered up, exhausted, onto the rock and lay there drying off in the sun. He felt like some great slow lizard himself, coiled in the warmth.

He sat up and was overwhelmed again with that sense of unreality. He saw himself sitting there, on a rock, in the ocean. He had come from the mainland, to Trinidad, to Tobago, to Little Tobago, to this rock. Stepping stones, getting smaller and smaller.

He noticed he had forgotten to take off his watch. Its digital face was completely black, showed nothing. It must be late afternoon. He should think about heading back to his base before it started to get dark. He felt like Crusoe, like the character in a million cartoons, alone on his desert island.

Once, in Aberdeen, he had gone to his bookcase looking for that Crusoe book with the pictures. He had fully expected to find it. But the book had been gone some fifteen years, given away for jumble in Glasgow. He would probably ask for it on his deathbed, like Orson Welles in *Citizen Kane*, muttering 'Rosebud'. He licked his lips, tasted salt. He remembered from somewhere the story of a salt doll that made a pilgrimage to the ocean. Afraid to go in, it had hesitated, then finally rushed in and dissolved, losing its separate identity, becoming the ocean itself.

Sometimes he was amazed at the stuff stored up in his brain.

He stood up and stretched himself, dived cleanly into the water.

At first he moved easily, then he felt himself tire; about halfway back he knew he was in difficulty. A swell seemed to carry him backwards, an undercurrent. His arms ached as he thrashed and pushed against it. The water closed over his head.

He grabbed a breath and pushed once more, made no headway and went under again. He felt afraid now, but overriding it came the same acceptance he'd felt when he fell from the rig. This is it. Too bad.

He even saw some kind of pattern to it, as if he had

known all along: his morbid brooding, his crazy quest for the bird of paradise, the sense of not being in control, of being pushed along by whatever force had driven him out here on his own, from stepping stone to stepping stone and finally off into nothing.

He struggled again, depleted, spent. He went under for a third time.

A stream of images bubbled up; a salt doll, a yellow book, a Paul Klee postcard, a street in Glasgow long ago. He felt himself already moving out. He watched himself, the small pale body, frail like a baby, struggling to be born. The body was a tiny creature, wriggling in the sea, something he had once been. He felt himself plunging. He was a lizard, trying to rise, to be clear of the sea, to breathe in air. Bubbles rose in the strange green light. He felt his body turning, something he had once been. He floated, seemed to fly. He soared on yellow wings. He was bird of paradise coming home to himself.

A wave must have carried him, thrown him headlong. He groped forward, found himself in the shallows. His feet touched bottom. Half-conscious, he stumbled from the water and collapsed onto the sand.

★

He felt as if he had lain a long time, though it wasn't yet dark when he woke. He tried to dust off the sand. He put on his clothes. He picked up his bag. Still in a dream he headed back the way he had come, barely able to haul himself up the slope and stagger, uphill, along the rough path. But somehow, as if guided, he found the spot where he had rested, where Bishop had left him. He pushed further on to the clearing. He slumped down on the grass and fell into a deep sleep. He was wakened, some time in the night, by the rain battering his face. He remembered who he was, and where. He picked up his bag, fumbled for the flashlight and found his way into the wooden building through a door

60

that hung open on one hinge. He lay down on the floor and slept again.

He was looking for the bird in his dream. He was in the ruined dance-hall, back at Blue Heaven, but he knew that outside were familiar Glasgow streets. A crowd came in and formed a circle around him, laughing and playing drums. One or two poked him with sharp sticks. He saw Jean's face among them, a moment then gone. He realised his clothes were on backwards and he tore them off, stood naked. The crowd howled. A voice he thought he knew shouted out. *Let's show him the bird of paradise.* Then a bat flapped in his face and he fell over backwards. He picked himself up. He was on a rock surrounded by water. He stepped onto another rock, smaller, and another, smaller again. They led on and out, each one smaller, till the last was only a point. He tried to keep his balance on it. He felt himself fall. . . .

The rain had stopped and he went outside, breathed in the smell of the wet vegetation. He looked up at a clear circle of sky. He had never seen so many stars. He felt the spaces between them, the immensity of the night sky. It made him feel small, and yet, at the same time, close to it all. Fevered, half-dead, all alone on a tiny island; to him at that moment, ridiculously, the universe looked friendly. He smiled to himself and to the stars. He lay down on the porch, slept again and had no more dreams.

★

In the morning he woke late. He felt it though he couldn't be sure without his watch. His body was still tired, but strangely, he felt his fever was passing. He ate the rest of his food, bread and cheese, bananas. He was hungry and ate like an animal. He opened one of the coconuts, splitting it with the machete; he drank the milk and ate some of the flesh.

He splashed his face at a stream, drank water from cupped hands. And as he leaned forward to refill his canteen, he saw a snake moving away from him into the

61

bushes. He felt no fear, just watched, hypnotised by the movement as it slithered out of sight. He had never seen one before, except in a zoo. Encouraged, he went back to the tree where the others had seen the bird. The grasses were already dried out by the sun, and he lay down on his back again and waited.

He was weak, his body heavy. He was happy just to laze there, at peace with the world, and he drifted into a doze.

He woke to a flutter of wings, looked up and saw the bird. He felt no excitement, no exhilaration. It all seemed perfectly natural, matter-of-fact. He didn't even sit up, just lay back and watched the beautiful golden bird settle on the topmost branch. It had orange markings and a crest, the way Carol had described it. It was real. It perched there a minute or two, maybe more. He didn't know; had lost his sense of time. It flurried off and he closed his eyes again, perfectly content.

When he woke again it was to a voice calling. Bishop. It must be noon. He gathered up his things and headed as fast as he was able, back towards the landing point. Halfway down he met Bishop.

'Hey, man!' he shouted. 'It's noon.'

'I'm sorry,' he said. 'My watch got broken. I didn't know the time.'

'That's all right, man. It's just we got fishin to do.'

'Hey listen,' he said. 'I saw the bird!'

'You did?'

'This morning. Back there.'

'That's great,' said Bishop. 'But you lookin kinda tired now. You sure you didn't dream it? See it in your sleep?'

'Oh no,' he said. 'It was real.'

'Great!' said Bishop, laughing. 'You know, you lookin good, even though you tired. Yesterday you was wound up tight. Today you hangin more loose.'

'Loose.' He felt himself grinning.

'Bird of paradise done you good!'

Back at the jetty, the other man was arguing with the

boy. 'Don't vex me now,' he was saying. 'Don't you vex me man!' The boy looked angry.

Bishop spoke to them, tried to bring them round, but the boy turned away. Then Bishop seemed to notice something. He went across to a tree and called the others over, excited.

'You got machete?' he asked Ian.

'Sure,' he said, and he took off his haversack, handed him the knife.

Bishop started chopping and hacking at the tree, a few feet above the ground. A flurry of bees swarmed about his head.

He kept on chopping till he'd cut right through and the top of the tree toppled over. They whooped and yelled, delighted, as he scooped something out of the tree. Ian came closer, wary of the angry bees, saw that he held what looked like a lump of black wax. A golden liquid dripped from it. Bishop motioned him to hold out his hand and he poured some into it.

'Honey,' he explained.

Ian licked his hand, rolled his eyes in appreciation. He had never tasted anything so good. The sweetness was intoxicating. Bishop gave him more, shared it out among them. They laughed like children. Time was unimportant, fishing forgotten. And when the honey was finished, they washed their sticky hands in the sea and climbed into the boat.

'Did I see you got a coconut there?' asked Bishop as they moved out.

'Aye,' he said. 'That's right. Do you want some?'

Bishop shook his head. 'You drink the milk,' he said. 'Then you know that place is a land of milk and honey! That really Paradise you been to. That's why the bird live there!' He laughed and repeated the joke to his friend. 'The land of milk and honey!'

'Oh, man!' said his friend. 'We been in Paradise today!'

He realised now they had been smoking ganja, were

63

flying. Only the boy seemed inside himself, brooding again.

Ian looked back at the island, diminishing now, fading. Less than a day he had been there. It felt much longer.

He looked at his watch. Its blank face still registered nothing.

They were nearing Tobago. He could see the stone pavilion, the tiny wooden shop, his car, parked, waiting for him.

The two men were still laughing at Bishop's joke, his blinding vision. The boy sat sullen, stared straight ahead.

CHRISTIAN ENDEAVOUR

I had been a religious fanatic for only a few weeks.

'What is it the night then?' asked my father. 'The bandy hope?' I caught the mockery, but he meant no harm.

'Christian Endeavour,' I said, drying my face with a towel and stretching up to peer at myself in the cracked mirror above the sink. 'Band a Hope's on Thursday.'

The two halves of my face in the mirror didn't quite match because of the crack, were slightly out of alignment. It was an old shaving mirror of my father's with an aluminium rim, hung squint from a nail in the window frame.

'Ah thought Christian Endeavour was last night?'

'That was just the Juniors,' I said. 'Tonight's the real one.'

'Are ye no too young?' said my father.

'The minister says ah can come.'

'Is that because ye were top in the bible exam?'

'Top equal,' I said. 'Ah don't know if that's why. He just said ah could come.'

'Ach well,' said my father, going back behind his newspaper. 'Keeps ye aff the streets.'

'Ah'll be the youngest there,' I said, proud of myself and wanting to share it.

'Mind yer heid in the door,' he said. 'It's that big ye'll get stuck.'

65

I pulled on my jacket and was ready to go.

'Seen ma Bible?' I asked.

'Try lookin where ye left it,' he said.

I found it on the table with another book, *The Life of David Livingstone*, under the past week's heap of newspapers and comics. The book had been my prize in the Bible exam.

The exam had been easy. Questions like *Who carried Christ's cross on the way to Calvary?* And from the Shorter Catechism, *Into what estate did the fall bring mankind?*

It was just a matter of remembering.

The label gummed in the book read FIRST PRIZE, with EQUAL penned in above BIBLE KNOWLEDGE, and then my name.

My father remembered reading the same book as a boy. He had been a sergeant in the Boys' Brigade, and the book had made him want to be a missionary himself.

'Great White Doctor an that,' he said. 'Off tae darkest Africa.'

But somehow he had drifted away from it all. 'Wound up in darkest Govan instead,' he said.

For the years he had been in the Boys' Brigade, he had been given a long-service badge. I still kept it in a drawer with a hoard of other badges I had gathered over the years. Most of them were cheap tin things, button badges: ABC Minors, Keep Britain Tidy. But the BB badge was special, heavier metal in the shape of an anchor. I had polished it with Brasso till it shone. There were two other treasures in the drawer: an army badge an uncle had given me, shaped like a flame, and a Rangers supporter's badge, a silver shield with the lion rampant in red.

Christian Endeavour had a badge of its own. A dark blue circle with a gold rim, and CE in gold letters. The Sunday school teachers at the Mission all wore it. I had been disappointed that there wasn't one for the Juniors. But now that I was moving up, I would be entitled to wear the badge. CE. In gold.

'Is there gonnae be any other youngsters there the night?' asked my father.

'Just Norman,' I said. Norman was the minister's son. He was twelve, a year older than me.

'Ye don't like him, do ye?'

'He's a big snotter,' I said. 'Thinks he's great.'

'Wis he top in the bible exam as well?'

'Top equal,' I said. My father laughed.

'That minister's quite a nice wee fella,' he said. 'That time he came up here, after yer mother died, we had quite a wee chat.'

'Aye, ye told me,' I said.

'Ah think he got a surprise. Wi me no goin tae church an that, he musta thought ah was a bitty a heathen. Expected tae find me aw bitter, crackin up y'know.'

'Aye, ah know.'

'But ah wisnae. Ah showed um ma long-service badge fae the BB. Even quoted scripture at him!'

'Aye.'

'In my father's house there are many mansions, ah said. That's the text they read at the funeral.'

'Time ah was goin,' I said.

'He wanted me tae come tae church,' said my father. 'But ah cannae be bothered wi aw that. Anywey, you're goin enough for the two ae us these days, eh?'

'Aye. Cheerio, Da.'

'See ye after, son.'

I took a last look at my reflection in the squinty mirror.

'Right,' I said.

★

I took the shortcut to the Mission, across the back-courts. It was already dark, and in the light from the windows I could make out five or six boys in the distance. From their noise I could recognise them as my friends, and I hurried on, not really wanting them to see me. If they asked where I was going, they would only mock.

I hadn't been out with them this week, except for playing football after school. They thought I was soft in the head for going so much to the Mission. They couldn't understand. I felt a glow. It was good to feel good. It had come on stronger since my mother had died. The Mission was a refuge from the empty feeling.

But part of me was always drawn back to my friends, to their rampaging and their madness.

I heard a midden bin being overturned, a bottle being smashed, and the gang of boys scattered laughing through the backs as somebody shouted after them from a third storey window. Head down, I hurried through a close and out into the street.

Now that I was almost at the Mission, I felt nervous and a little afraid. I had never been to an adult meeting before. I thought of the lapel-badge with the gold letters. CE. Perhaps I would even be given one tonight. Initiated. There was another badge I had seen the teachers wearing. It was green with a gold lamp, an oil lamp like Aladdin's. But maybe that was only for ministers and teachers.

> Give me oil in my lamp, keep me burning.
> Give me oil in my lamp I pray,
> Halleluja!

The Mission hall was an old converted shop, the windows covered over with corrugated iron. A handwritten sign on the door read CHRISTIAN ENDEAVOUR. Tonight. 7.30. I stood for a moment, hesitating, outside. Then I pushed open the door and went in to the brightness and warmth.

I was early, and only a handful of people had arrived. They sat, talking, in a group near the front of the hall, and nobody seemed to have noticed me come in.

Norman was busy stacking hymn-books. Looking up, he saw me and nodded, then went out into the back room.

The minister saw me then and waved me over. There were two or three earnest conversations going on. The minister introduced me to a middle-aged African couple.

'These are our very special guests,' he said. 'Mr and Mrs Lutula. From Africa.'

'How do you do,' we all said, and very formally shook hands. There was a momentary lull, then the conversations picked up again. But I could feel the big black woman looking at me.

'And tell me,' she said, her voice deep like a man's. 'When did the Lord Jesus come into your heart?'

'Pardon?' I said, terrified.

'Ah said, when did the Lord Jesus come into your heart, child?'

That was what I thought she had said. And she wanted an answer. From me. I looked up at the broad face smiling at me, the dark eyes shining. I looked down at the floor. I could feel myself blush. What kind of question was that to ask? How was I supposed to answer it?

Why didn't she ask me something straightforward?

Who carried Christ's cross on the way to Calvary?
Simon of Cyrene.
Into what estate did the fall bring mankind?
The fall brought mankind into an estate of sin and misery.

I sat, tense and rigid, on the hard wooden seat. Now my face was really hot and flushed. I cleared my throat. In a squeak of a voice I said, 'I don't know if . . .'

I looked at the floor.

She leaned over and patted my arm. 'Bless you, child,' she said, smiling, and turned to talk to her husband.

I stood up, still looking at the floor. I made my way, conscious of every step, clumsy and awkward, to the back of the hall and out into the street. I walked faster, I began to run, away from the Mission, along the street, through the close into the back-court.

The night air cooled me. I stopped and leaned against a midden wall. I was in absolute misery, tortured by my own sense of foolishness. It wasn't just the question, it was what it had opened up; a realm where I knew nothing, could say nothing.

When did the Lord Jesus come into my heart? I could have said it was when my mother died. That would have sounded pious. But I didn't think it was true. I didn't know. That was it: I didn't know. If the Lord Jesus had come into my heart, I should know.

And how could I go back in now? It was all too much for me. I would tell the minister on Sunday I had felt hot and flushed, had gone outside for some air. That much was true. I would say I had felt sick and gone home.

The back-court was quiet. There was no sound, except for the TV from this house or that. Bright lit windows in the dark tenement blocks. I walked on, slow, across the back, and as I passed another midden, I kicked over a bin, and ran.

Nearer home I slowed down again.

My father would ask why I was back so early.

MILAN CATHEDRAL AT
THE BOTTOM OF THE SEA

They had to get out of the city.

Milan in winter had been bad enough, the dank cold, thick fogs, acrid air. *Una brutta citta*. An ugly city. But this was where the work was. A living to be made. Teaching English to students not much younger than themselves. They had eked it out for a year, happy to be away from Glasgow.

Spring had been a respite. But this summer heat was unbearable. Heavy and humid, it mugged you in the street. The constant haze of pollution diffused the light so it hurt your eyes. And the air itself had a rank smell, a taste at the back of the throat, like burning rubber.

Andrew remembered asking, early on. What's that smell in the air?

Sorry pal, Kathleen had said. I think it *is* the air!

Brutta.

August was the worst.

'Even the locals can't take it,' he said. 'The whole place shuts down dead. Half the population buggers off to the mountains.'

He looked out the window as he spoke. Their apartment was on the outskirts where rents were cheap. The window faced north, and once in a while, when the fug cleared, it was possible to see in the far distance the jagged line of the Alps. He stared in that direction above the rows of rooftiles, the clusters of TV aerials, but today he could see nothing, screwed up his eyes against the fuzzy glare, the aching mustard-yellow haze.

'So let's go the other way,' she said. 'Head south.'

'Like where?'

'Not too far. I thought maybe Florence.'

'*Ei!*' he said, affecting an Italian shrug. '*Che bella!*'

'We won't even have to hitch,' she said. 'We've saved a wee bit from the teaching. We can take the train.'

'Right. Aye. Beautiful,' he said. 'Let's do it. *Andiamo!*'

★

They stood a long time waiting for a bus into town.

Across the road from the bus stop a man dropped his trousers, matter-of-fact, and sat hunkered down, crapping into the gutter. Nobody paid him any heed, and he glared over at them when they glanced in his direction.

An old gypsy woman, head to toe in thick black clothes, came up and started hustling them for money. Wary of the evil eye, they gave her a few coins. As she moved away she turned, and back across her shoulder said, '*Sciopero.*'

They should have realised. A strike.

It happened all the time. Two or three times a week. They would be in a bank, a post office, even just a shop. They would barely be inside the door, or they'd just get to the counter, and the shutters would come down. Bang. Like that. *Sciopero.* Usually it lasted a couple of hours. The staff would head for the nearest bar, or just hang out where they were, drink coffee, read the papers, smoke cigarettes, argue, wait. Then the word would go round, some mysterious agreement had been reached. Shutters, doors, were flung open. The strike was over.

But when it hit transport, like this, it was rough. They were miles from the city centre, the train station. It was hot. They were carrying backpacks. The few taxis that sped past were full, or unwilling to stop.

'I'm beginning to take this personal,' he said.

'You don't want to do that,' she said. 'Not ever.'

'All these strikes and everything. It's like we're being singled out for special attention.'

'You shouldn't take *anything* personal,' she said. 'Even when it's meant. *Especially* when it's meant.'

He laughed. 'Should put that on button-badges. T-shirts.' He placed the words with his hand, in the air, laid them out. *'Don't take it personal!'*

'Good philosophy,' she said.

'Right!'

She pulled her long hair back into a ponytail, caught and held it at the nape of her neck, tugged it twice through a doubled elastic band.

'OK,' she said, picking up her backpack. 'Let's walk.'

Halfway in, they managed to flag down a taxi. They were jolted back in their seats as the cab screeched and roared off, bumped up on the pavement to overtake a van, shouldered its way into traffic.

'I guess Mario was right,' she said. 'About the driving.'

Mario was one of their students. He'd said with some pride that Italian drivers were the worst in Europe. And Milanese drivers were the worst in Italy. And the taxi drivers were the worst in Milan.

This one had a shrine set up on his dashboard. A rosary. A garland of plastic flowers. Plaster Madonna. A Sacred Heart postcard. A picture of Padre Pio, bearded and serious, hands in fingerless gloves to hide his stigmata.

The driver was conducting his own litany, directed at everything else on the road.

'Madonna! Santa Maria! Madre di Dio!' He thumped the wheel, waved both hands, slapped his forehead. A cartoon Italian.

A bus eased alongside, jampacked with passengers. Whatever the dispute, it had been resolved.

'Porca miseria!' said the taxi driver, to no one in particular. Then he asked over his shoulder, *'Americani?'*

They shook their heads, both said, 'No.'

73

'Ah!' said the driver. '*Inglesi.*' It was a statement.

They shook their heads more vigorously. No. Definitely not.

Now the driver was puzzled. '*Tedeschi?*' Hearing maybe something guttural in their accent.

No. Not German.

The driver gave up.

'*Scozzesi,*' they said.

'*Si?*' He turned right round, delighted. 'Glasgow Celtic!'

'Aye. *Si!*'

And suddenly they were swerving off the main road, careering down cobblestoned backstreets in what turned out to be a shortcut.

Bobbi Murdoc!' the driver shouted out, catching his eye in the mirror. 'Jimi Jonson!'

At the station he helped them out with their rucksacks, shook hands, waved and called back *Ciao!* as he drove off.

'Bizarre!' said Andrew, as they climbed the station steps.

'Such an ugly place this,' said Kathleen, looking up at the huge pillars, the dark heavy stone. 'So oppressive.'

'Mustabeen Mussolini,' he said.

They had missed the train they'd planned to get, and the next one wasn't for a couple of hours. It wasn't a queue at the ticket desk, more a scrum, a loose maul. They elbowed to the front, bought two returns. The train was listed as *Doppio Rapido*.

'Double quick!' he said. 'Sounds good!'

'Super Express.'

'Means we should make up some time.'

Back outside, they wandered round the square, down a sidestreet, found a little café-bar. They were drawn in by the smell of coffee. Inside was cool and dark. They dumped their bags, sat down.

'I'm knackered already,' he said.

'Me too.'

They ordered coffee and crusty rolls, *panini*. A small boy, maybe nine or ten years old, came in and looked around, made straight for their table. Skinny and ragged, he stood there, said nothing, just stared at them, held up a sheet of card with a message scrawled in felt-tip. It said he was hungry and sick and homeless and orphaned. His whole family had been wiped out in an earthquake. He was all alone in the world.

'*Niente moneta,*' she said, the corners of her mouth dropping in a clown mask of regret. And it was true, they had no change. The gypsy woman had begged the last of it.

The boy shrugged, unconcerned. Then he turned to the man behind the counter and ordered an ice cream, a huge double cone with extra toppings. He scooped out a handful of coins from his pocket, counted out enough to pay, stuffed the rest back in the pocket. He folded up the card and tucked it under his arm, held the cone up carefully in front of him. At the open door he threw a last quick glance back at them, then stepped out, licking at the ice cream with absolute seriousness, total concentration.

'Amazing!' she said.

The man behind the counter called over, 'He make good business!'

They laughed. 'That'll be his commission,' said Andrew.

'The wee devil,' said Kathleen, and she shook her head. 'This whole country is mad!' She caught the eye of the man again, spread her hands in a stage gesture of non-comprehension. 'Crazy!' she said. '*Pazzo!*'

'*Si,*' said the man. '*Tutto!*'

Everything.

★

Now there was a strike at the station. Their train had been cancelled. There might be another one later. There might not.

'Christ!' she said, dropping her rucksack.

'Maybe it's not meant,' he said. 'Maybe we should just go home. Try again tomorrow.'

'I don't know,' she said. 'I just hate the thought of it.

Traipsing all the way back. Unpacking our bags.'

'It would be kind of miserable right enough.'

'I mean we are in Milan. It's not like it's a problem killing time!'

They stuffed their bags in a luggage locker, took the subway, four stops, to Piazza Duomo. Whenever they came in to the city, they usually ended up here. And no matter how many times they saw the Cathedral itself, they were impressed, even moved, by the sheer scale of it, the massive buttressed façade, the intricacies of its carving, the flourish of arches and spires. Often they would take refuge inside, happy just to sit in the cool high-vaulted space. But they'd never climbed to the roof. So today, with this time to kill, they did.

The climb was hard going, up hundreds of steep stone steps. The last flight, right up to the roof, was outside in the open air, exposed and windblown, a stone balustrade on one side, a metal railing on the other. At the top he turned back and saw her stuck halfway up, shaky, half-laughing, clinging to the railing.

'Heights!' she called to him. 'Legs like rubber!'

He climbed down and took her hand, led her up a step at a time.

'It's just when I can see the sheer drop,' she said. 'Something about that flimsy wee railing! But I'm OK now.' She nodded, too vigorously. 'I'm fine.'

All the same, she stayed away from the edge, kept in towards the last spire with its gold statue, the *Madonnina*. It was hard to look at the statue too long against that harsh hazy yellow of the sky. And the figure itself seemed to gather the light, shimmer in it. He shielded his eyes, turned away. He half-ran across the terrace to the edge where he could lean on the balustrade, look down at the square. She followed him across, taking her own time, each step tentative.

'You all right?' he asked.

'Fine. Well, sort of. Gives me sweaty palms just watching you lean out.' She wiped her hands on her jeans, pressed against the solid stone, steadied herself. 'It's just, when I'm up high I can imagine myself falling. Or jumping. I mean, it's really strong, like I can actually visualise it.'

'Jeez.'

'I'm sure it's just vertigo. The form it takes.'

'I guess so.'

'Still. It's scary!'

She braced herself, breathed deep, looked down.

He unfolded a leaflet he'd picked up downstairs. 'It says here!' He tapped the page. 'On a clear day.'

'You can see forever?'

'Just about!' He read it out. 'The snowcapped Alps, hills of the Po Valley, Mont Blanc, the Matterhorn, the mountains of Bergamo, the cupolas of Pavia Cathedral, the Appenines towards Genoa.' He waved the leaflet. 'And what can we see? Piazza Duomo! And an endless sulphurous haze!'

Far below in the square, groups of tourists were hustled and cajoled by street photographers, by pushers selling balloons and trinkets and birdseed. Now and again some noise would startle the pigeons and they'd flurry up, hundreds of them, spiral round and settle again, get back to their strutting and pecking.

They had just passed through all this, been down there amongst it. Now from up here it was all so tiny, so unreal. In the corner nearest, across from the Galleria Vittorio Emmanuele, was a bright postage stamp of colour. Even from this height, they could see it was a copy of a Raphael Madonna, done by a pavement artist in coloured chalks.

Something else caught, tugged at their attention, insistent. They had been aware of voices in the distance, shouting, a rhythmic chant. Now it came closer, louder, and looking across to the far side, they saw the marchers swing round into the square, their red and black banners raised, voices echoing, drifting up.

Continua la lotta!

Carry on the struggle.

The procession was marshalled across the square, off in the direction of Piazza della Repubblica, by a posse of *carabinieri*, motorcycle outriders at the back. A single male voice, distorted by a megaphone, kept up constant exhortation. This high they couldn't make it out. The words bounced back off the buildings, ended up dissipated, lost. Except for the odd clear call. *Liberta! L'Unita!* And the response once more. *Continua la Lotta!*

★

The *Doppio Rapido* stopped at every station. Because of the delay it was packed. They had to stand in the corridor the whole way, four hours, wedged in beside a Born Again Christian who wanted to save them in Italian. By the time they stepped off the train at Florence they were worn out, wrecked. It was late afternoon.

'Today's been about four days long,' said Kathleen.

'I know what you mean.'

Out of the station they walked, no idea where, just anywhere, to clear their heads, ease the stiff tired deadness in their legs. They followed narrow sidestreets, to see where they led. Kids on scooters and mopeds buzzed past, zipped through, all innocent bravado, full of itself.

'It's different already,' she said. 'It *smells* different.'

They emerged into a square, stood there facing the great dome of the Cathedral.

'God,' she said. 'It's so beautiful.'

Warm sunlight on old stone, white red green marble.

'I read about all this,' she said. 'That over there's the baptistry. And this is the *campanile*. The belltower.'

The tower was picked out in the same coloured marble as the Duomo. Here and there it glinted.

'Isn't it magic?' she said. 'I think that was designed by Giotto. You know, he could just sit down and draw a perfect circle. I mean *freehand*!'

'Incredible!'

'There's some great stuff inside the main building,' she said. 'Like there's an amazing *Pietá* by Michelangelo.'

'Lead me to it!'

They found it in a small chapel, next to the sacristy. They put down their bags, just sat for a while simply in front of it. A lump of stone made flesh, imbued with grace and pity. The dead Christ cradled in his mother's lap, nativity come to this. And yet.

'It's really something,' he said.

She nodded, smiled.

They wandered round the rest of the Cathedral, stood finally under the cupola and looked directly up.

'God!' she said. 'You could fall up into it.'

The murals rose in great concentric circles, scenes from the Last Judgement, sweeping round and up towards the central light.

'Like a mandala,' he said, turning round to take it all in.

She spun round with her arms out, her head thrown back. She staggered a step, dizzy, and she laughed.

'Back down to earth,' he said. 'We need a place to eat and a place to stay.'

'Sounds good!' she said.

'And what do you reckon now?' he said. 'Today's been *five* days long?'

'Definitely.'

They stepped out into the sunlit square.

It was just a flicker out the corner of the eye as they turned away a sense of something moving in the air then a loud bang like a gunshot and a terrible highpitched scream a young girl screaming and crying and running away from that heap of clothes at the foot of the belltower the heap of clothes with the legs jutting out the heap that was a woman's body and what had happened was she'd climbed to the top of the tower and thrown herself off and what they'd heard was her head exploding on impact as it hit the ground.

★

79

They both reran the whole thing, replayed it, not able to believe it had really happened. The blur of movement, the bang, the scream, the young girl running. Another couple had been standing nearby, a bearded man, a thin fairhaired girl, and the man had been the first to react, ran across and threw down his jacket, to cover the mess that had been this woman's head.

Andrew and Kathleen had moved away, nothing to be done, no way to help, down the first street they came to, into the first bar. They had to sit down, that was all. Ordered tea. Sat numbed and blank.

'Hard to take in,' he said.

She nodded. 'Shakes you.'

'Just the starkness of it.'

'Makes everything kind of unreal.'

A burst of noise behind the bar, laughter and loud bantering talk, gush of the cappuccino machine. Noise and froth.

The door opened and the couple from the square came in, the bearded man, the blonde girl. As they looked around there was momentary eye contact, recognition, and the couple came over, indicated the empty seats at their table.

'*Permesso?*' said the man.

'*Si,*' said Andrew. '*Prego.*'

'*Una cosa terribile,*' said the man when they'd sat down.

'*Si.*' said Andrew. A terrible thing right enough.

The man held out his hand to Andrew, introducing himself. 'Carlo.'

'Anna,' said the girl.

'Andrew.'

'Kathleen.'

They all shook hands, each to each.

'*Inglesi?*' asked Anna.

Kathleen smiled. '*Scozzesi.*'

'Ah,' said Carlo. '*Mi piace molto.* I like very much Scotland.' And he ordered some wine, filled their glasses.

By the end of the evening they were old friends, had

exchanged life stories. Carlo was a painter, making his way. Anna wanted to write, but for now she was working in an office, typing to earn a wage, to keep them going.

When they got up to leave, Carlo was insisting they come back home with them to eat, stay the night, stay the week, move in. Then for a moment he seemed confused, looking for something behind his chair.

'Lost something?' asked Andrew.

But Carlo had stopped looking, shook his head. 'Is OK,' he said, and he mimed pulling something over his shoulders. 'My jacket.' He looked serious again, pained. 'I forgot.' Then he had to explain. 'It was . . . spoiled. I didn't want to take it back.' He shrugged, hands spread. 'It was old. Anna been telling me for years to get rid of it.' Outside it was dark, but the night air was mild. 'You know *l'Induismo?*'

'Hinduism?' said Andrew. 'I've read a bit. And some Buddhism. Zen.'

'Ei!' Carlo stopped, called to Anna. 'We are *meant* to meet these people!'

Turning back to Andrew, he said, 'You know the Gita?'

'Some.'

'What Krishna say to Arjuna about death. When the soul leave the body.' They had stopped at the corner. Carlo had Andrew by the shoulders, talked right at him, intense. 'Is like a man leave off an old worn-out coat.' He mimed taking off a jacket, chucking it away. 'Like that.'

Their route to the bus stop took them back across Piazza del Duomo, different now. They were all of them quiet, subdued, aware of the bad thing that had happened. As they crossed the square there was a sudden loud bang, an explosion, and this couldn't be happening, not again, they all turned to look at the *campanile*, and Kathleen had grabbed Andrew's arm and Anna's hands were up covering her ears, her mouth open in a little stifled scream, but this time it was nothing, just a backfiring car, and taking the edge off the rush of relief was a sense of something malevolent in the coincidence, like a mean sick joke had been played on them.

★

The bus took them out of town, up into the hills. They got off at the last stop, came in at the gate of an old villa built round a central courtyard. The villa had been broken up into flats and bedsits. Through open windows the noises from different rooms made a kind of crazy soundtrack to the strange movie this endless day had become. The clatter of dishes. A TV gameshow. A woman yelling *Basta!* Enough. John Lennon's *Imagine* fighting it out with Gigli singing from *Lucia di Lammermoor*.

Imagine there's no heaven. *Giusto Cielo, Rispondete . . .*

Carlo and Anna led them along a narrow corridor, up steep stairs to their second floor apartment.

The main room had a kind of messy warmth about it. An old couch, couple of comfortable chairs. Books and papers, a typewriter. Smell of turpentine, oil paints, from the canvases stacked facing one wall. An easel set up by the window, a canvas propped up on it, draped with an old sheet spattered with paint.

'*Allora!*' said Carlo, making for the little kitchen, through an open doorway off the room. They watched as he moved around in the small space, banged an old blackened frying pan onto the gas, poured in olive oil, chopped up garlic and scraped it in to fry, filling the whole place with its smell. Then he took a heavy pot, upended its contents onto the chopping board.

'*Polenta*,' said Anna. 'We made today. I hope you like.'

'It's great,' said Andrew.

She smiled. 'It's cheap.'

The thick cornmeal porridge had congealed and set, was firm enough to cut. Carlo sliced it into inch-thick slabs and slid them into the hot oil.

'Now I help!' said Anna, standing up. And she moved deftly round Carlo, with quick brisk strokes rinsed and

82

chopped up vegetables, conjured up a salad. Then she came back through, unfolded a dropleaf table, set four places, cut bread, poured wine.

Carlo dished out the browned *polenta* slices, brought through a small pot that had been heating on the gas, poured from it a fragrant tomato sauce, a little over each slice.

They sat down to eat.

'Good appetite!' said Carlo.

'This is incredible!' said Andrew. 'Delicious. *Squisito!*'

He smiled and turned to Kathleen, saw right away something was wrong. Her shoulders were hunched and shaking, eyes closed, mouth drawn tight with the effort of not breaking down into tears.

'Hey!' Andrew reached out, touched her arm. 'What is it?'

It was too much and she broke, sobbed, tears running down her face.

Anna put a hand on her shoulder, stroked her hair, made soothing, mothering noises.

'Feel so . . . stupid!' she said through her sobs. 'It's just . . .' But she'd lost it, couldn't say.

They let her be, let her cry it out, subside.

'Ei!' said Carlo, choosing his moment. 'I guess the *polenta* was pretty bad!'

And that set her off again as she laughed, cried, laughed again, cried. Eventually, she was calm enough, secure enough, to try again to say it.

'It's just . . .' She wiped her face with a napkin. 'It's just *this.*' Her gesture took in the room and all of them in it. 'Just the kindness of it. The simple . . . *goodness.*' Her lip quivered a bit, but she gathered herself, went on. 'That poor woman. To do that to herself. To destroy herself. She must have just got so far away from it. The simplicity. The *ordinariness* of what's good.' She looked round the table at them, gave a self-conscious little shrug. 'That's all.'

Andrew was about to try to explain, to translate, but

Carlo stopped him with a look.

'*Capito*,' he said.

Understood.

★

The day had been a whole week long. They slept on the pulled-down couch, in the warm close dark, in the friendly cluttered room among the smells of garlic and oil paints and turps. They held each other, suddenly, completely, exhausted, fell immediately into deep sleep.

They woke in the middle of the night, Kathleen sitting bolt upright and shouting out, Andrew dragged up out of a dream by the noise.

'I was falling,' she said, still living it, not quite awake. 'Off the roof of the Duomo in Milan. I tried to stop myself but I couldn't. I went right over the edge.'

'I was lost,' he said. 'I couldn't find my jacket. And somehow it was really important. I knew if I found it I could stop that woman killing herself. And everything would be all right. But I just kept running through all these wee backstreets, getting further and further away.'

'It was so real,' she said. 'The falling. And the ground was covered with those frescoes of the Last Judgement, like the pavement artists had done them. But somebody had drawn a perfect circle right in the centre. Only instead of light, it led into this deep deep dark. And I was falling into it.'

'I kept going into cafés and bars,' he said, 'looking for the jacket. But I couldn't remember any Italian. And all these faces kept leering at me. And the further I went, the more lost I got. And I started looking for you. But I couldn't find you. Then I heard you shout. And I rushed up out of it. Woke up. And you really had shouted. In your sleep.'

'It was so real,' she said. 'Real as anything.'

When they woke again it was morning, first light. That sense of unreality, themselves here in this strange room. Without thinking about it they tidied up, made a neat pile of their bedding, folded up the couch. They moved tentatively, tried not to make too much noise. Then they heard the others moving about, talking in the next room.

Carlo knocked at the door, came through, calling out, 'All right?'

'Fine,' they both said, still feeling the strangeness of it all, a strangeness denied by Carlo's easy familiarity.

'*Dormito bene?*' he asked.

'*Si*' said Andrew. Yes, they'd slept well enough. 'Except for a couple of bad dreams.'

'*Si?*'

'She was falling. I was lost.'

Isolated like that, the words sounded stark and absolute. Falling and lost.

'*Capito,*' said Carlo, nodding.

'And you?' asked Andrew.

'Sorry?'

'You slept well?'

'You say, *like a log?*'

'That's right!'

'*Out like the light,*' said Anna, the image fresh the way she said it.

'Good!' said Andrew. 'Great!'

★

Anna had to go to work, ended up leaving in a rush, a quick swig of coffee and out the door, a bright *Ciao!* thrown back over her shoulder as she went.

'*Ci vediamo!*'

See you later. But in the Italian somehow warmer, more inclusive. We'll see each other.

Carlo said he'd be back in a minute, went out. Reappeared with fresh *panini*, some cheese.

'Breakfast!' he said, and set more coffee to brew.

He had also bought a paper, *La Nazione*, chucked it down on the couch.

'Christ!' said Andrew, picking it up. The whole front

85

page was given over to the story of a bomb blast on a train, near Bologna. Twelve dead, over a hundred injured.

'*La lotta continua,*' said Andrew.

Carlo looked at him a moment strangely, as if across a great gulf in comprehension. And he said quietly, 'But maybe is not the Left who do this. Is more likely the *fascisti.*'

'But why?'

'They want to make trouble. Chaos. Then everybody blame the Left and nobody vote for the *comunisti.*'

'Jesus,' said Andrew, shaking his head at the enormity, the complexity of it. 'What a mess.'

'*Si,*' said Carlo. 'Our whole country is a mess.'

Kathleen had taken the newspaper, was searching through it.

'Here,' she said. 'There's something about that woman.' She folded the paper, folded it again. 'Just a tiny wee paragraph. Jumped to her death. Says her name was Laura Bagnoli. Age forty-two. Married. Three kids. Her family said she'd been depressed. And that's it. That's all. Nothing else.'

'Is sad,' said Carlo. 'But the life goes on. We carry on the struggle, eh?'

'*La lotta,*' said Andrew.

'*Ma questa e la lotta,*' said Carlo. '*Questa qui!*' His eyes were wide, real passion in his voice. '*This* is the struggle. To make something. To be a little kind. To keep ourselves from dying. *Non e vero?*'

'*Si,*' said Kathleen. '*E vero.*' Yes. It was true. Absolutely.

'So!' said Carlo, brightening again. 'We eat!'

When they'd finished the rolls, the cheese, the coffee, Carlo stood at the window. 'Is a good view,' he said.

They stood beside him, looking out past the low buildings opposite, over cypress trees to the city in the distance.

'*Piu bello che si puo,*' said Carlo. 'As beautiful as possible. That was how they wanted the city. Can you imagine? Leonardo and Michelangelo and Dante and Galileo walking about those streets. You know Amerigo Vespucci lived in this villa? Is true. Right here. And he found the New World with the maps of Toscanelli. You know Toscanelli? He was astronomer. Measured the whole heaven from inside the Duomo. This place was the centre of the universe!'

The city shone in the morning light, like some dream of perfection. Warm sun on the Dome, the baptistry, the *campanile*.

Kathleen breathed out hard through her nose, half-ironic half-sad.

'What?' said Andrew.

'Giotto,' she said. 'Designing the belltower. For Laura Bagnoli to throw herself off, five hundred years later.'

'I don't suppose she was the first.'

'No. I'm sure she wasn't.'

'And I don't think Giotto would have taken it personal!'

'No.' She looked out again at the skyline. '*Piu bello che si puo.*'

'Is a good *credo*,' said Carlo.

'Listen,' said Andrew, turning to him. 'Can we see some of your work? Your paintings?

'Work?' said Carlo, delighted at the word. '*Si*, is work. But is also play! Is important, no?'

He pointed at the easel by the window, the canvas draped with the old sheet.

'This is the latest,' he said. 'So is also the best! Is almost finished.'

And he took the sheet, whipped it off with a flourish, unveiled the painting.

'*Ecco!*'

It was an underwater scene, play of light in the bluegreen depth of some tropical sea. Looking close they could make out weird rock formations, patterns of coral, a shimmer of rainbow fish through fronds of vegetation. And there, small and white in the middle distance, not obvious at first but just emerging, catching the eye, was the shape of Milan Cathedral, painted in precise detail, resting on the sea bed.

Carlo grinned, sharing the mystery, the joke.

'*Il Duomo di Milano nel fondo del mare!*'

Milan Cathedral at the bottom of the sea.

They looked at it a long time.

'It's amazing,' said Kathleen.

'Magic,' said Andrew. 'The way you just suddenly *see* it!'

'Make you laugh!' she said. 'The surprise of it.'

'Then something else happens. At first you think it's a nice wee piece of surrealism, you know, the dislocation. Then your mind does a kind of double-take, makes a leap. Like you're maybe looking at some possible future.'

'When the waters have risen,' she said. 'Covered the globe.'

'Apocalyptic!' he said.

She nodded, looked closely again at the picture, the detail on the Cathedral façade, then she stepped back to take in the whole thing.

After a while she said, quietly, 'It changes your sense of scale. Puts things in perspective.'

'*Si,*' said Carlo. '*Giusto!*'

The three of them stood there, just looking at it.

Milan Cathedral. At the bottom of the sea.

WONDERFUL LAND

The patterns on the battered desktop made a whole world. Its varnished surface had been notched and carved by generations of boys, nicked and scraped and inked, initialled as far back as 1948. But in behind the names, behind the markings, were the forms, the shapes, that drew me in, the texture and grain of the wood itself. Here was a flow like tidemarks on sand, here a swirl like a great eye, here a knot with a ripple of ellipses round it, like a stone dropped in a pool, like Saturn with its rings.

Doug nudged me under the desk, brought me back. Where we were. Last period of the day. Geography. Three o'clock on a Wednesday afternoon. Grey Glasgow light, out there, already growing dark.

There was a strange quiet, one or two boys fidgeting, turning round to look in my direction. Old Bryce was staring straight at me. Waiting.

'Well?'

He must have asked me a direct question. I hadn't even heard, and now he wanted his answer.

'Could you repeat the question sir. I didn't quite catch it.'

'You what?'

'Didn't quite catch the question, sir.'

'Didn't *quite* catch it!' He leaned forward. 'Right. I'll repeat it very, very slowly. You're listening now? Quite sure? Right. Tell-me-the-names-of-the-six-rivers-that-flow-into-the-Humber.'

He might as well have asked me to list the principal exports of Outer Mongolia, name all the canals in Mars.

No idea.

Doug tried to whisper something to me, his lips tight, a hand over his mouth. It sounded like *someone*. He changed it to a cough when he thought the teacher had heard him.

'Well?'

'*Someone!*' (Cough).

'Don't know sir.'

Silence.

'How about *one* of the rivers?'

Doug had given up on me, left me to my fate.

'Does this look at all familiar to you?' said Bryce, indicating a word chalked on the blackboard in square block capitals. The word was SUNWAD.

Sun. Wad. A wad of sun. No sense.

Not a place name either. Too strange, even for the North of England. Could be East European, Slav. But we hadn't travelled that far. Began with the British Isles and moved round the world in time for the O-Levels in fourth year. Europe, Africa, North and South America. Sunwad. Might have been a moon of Jupiter for all I knew.

Sunwad the Sailor.

The way a word could just look wrong on the page. It had happened the other day with *the*. Turned it this way and that, but the separate letters had come adrift, meant nothing. The same now with this *sunwad*. No meaning. Maybe old Bryce had written it wrong, meant *sunward*.

Sunward the Great Ships. Sunward Ho!

'Well?'

'No sir.'

'Ever heard of a *mnemonic*?'

Every Good Boy Deserves Favour.

'Yes sir.'

'Well that's what this is. Something to help you remember. Right?'

'Sir.'

'Write this down. *The six rivers that flow into the Humber are: Swale, Ure, Nidd, Wharfe, Aire, Don.*'

S.U.N.W.A.D.

'Got that? Good. I want you to write it out five hundred times for tomorrow morning.' He turned his attention to the class. 'Right. Take out your notebooks.'

'Hard cheese' said Doug, under his breath.

'Thanks for trying to tell me,' I said.

Bryce started drawing a map on the board. 'Copy this.'

Across the back page of my book I pencilled B.A.S.T.A.R.D. And underneath, Baldy Auld Shity Turdy Arsed Rotten Diddy. I showed it to Doug and he grinned.

'A mnemonic!' I said.

'In case we forget!'

I turned to the front of the book, made a start on copying the map.

★

After school I walked down through town, the shop windows bright, the streetlights on early, shrill din of starlings above the noise of traffic. I could have taken the subway from Buchanan Street, but I carried on instead to St Enoch. I was taking my time, putting off going home. My father would be working late. He had to take all the overtime he could get. Two nights and a Sunday. The house would be empty and cold.

Our close was at the end of the street. We lived on the top flat, a room and kitchen, three up right. The building still had gas lamps, outside toilets. It had been condemned, would eventually be knocked down, and we would be rehoused in one of the schemes. I turned the key in the door, flicked the light switch in the lobby. But nothing happened. No light. I switched it off then on again, off, on. Still nothing. I thought a fuse must have blown. Then in the light from the stairhead I saw the card on the floor. It was from the Electricity Board. Red lettering. We had disregarded the Reminder and the Final Notice. Now we had been disconnected, cut off.

Through in the kitchen I stumbled around in the darkness, found matches by the cooker, a stub of candle in a drawer. I cleared a space on the table, set the candle down and lit it. The flicker of light brought a kind of warmth. In its soft glow the things on the table stood illumined like objects in some strange painting. Still life with grubby cups, saltcellar, milkbottle, plain loaf, bag of sugar and pile of newspapers. Outside the pool of light, the room faded out to dark in the corners, shadows wavering up the walls.

At least my transistor radio ran on batteries. I switched it on, found Luxembourg, moved the set around till the reception came clear. The Beatles were singing *Money*. The best things in life are free. It held back the bleakness I'd felt closing in. Things could be worse. The cooker was gas. On the mantelpiece was a single shilling for the meter. I could still heat the pie I had bought for my tea. Have it with sixpenceworth of chips. Couple of slices of bread. Wash the lot down with tea.

I checked the coal in the brown paper bag beside the fireplace, a 28 pound bag from the corner shop. It was two-thirds full. If I didn't light the fire till after I'd eaten, I should be able to eke out the coal, make it last the night.

I went to the window and leaned over the sink, looked out across the dark back-courts. In the tenement opposite, the windows were bright squares, lights burning in other kitchens. I stepped back, saw my own silhouette reflected. I had read somewhere it was bad luck to see your own reflection by candlelight – an omen, like seeing the full moon through glass. I pulled the curtains shut.

★

I cut across the wasteground to the chip shop, bought my sixpenceworth, headed back. I held the bag of chips inside my jacket. The heat of it against my stomach was comfort, like a hot water bottle. My jersey would stink of chipfat and vinegar but I didn't care. I stopped at the corner shop to buy another candle.

'No something we sell a lot of,' said old Norrie behind the counter.

'Lights have fused,' I said.

'Oh aye.'

'My Da's working late. He'll fix it when he gets in.'

'That's terrible that. Boy like you. Supposed to be educated. Canny even fix a fuse.'

I said nothing, managed a stupid embarrassed grin.

'They chips smell good,' he said.

'Aye. I better get up the house before they get cold.'

I turned to go and almost walked into Cathy coming in the door. Cathy had been in my class at primary school. She was fifteen, the same age as me, but already looked older, had a boyfriend at least eighteen. For years I had sat beside this girl every day. Now being close to her turned me inside out, the half-smile she flashed at me, passing, the scent of her, the way her black hair hung straight and shiny, swung as she turned her head.

'Hiya.'

'Hi.'

Outside I was glad of the cold. It cooled the flush I could feel in my face. In the middle of the wasteground, a group of men had broken up bits of wood to light a fire. They stood huddled round it, waiting for it to catch, passed a bottle from hand to hand. They came from the Wine Alley, the scheme where Cathy lived. But the wasteground was their territory, the place they hung about, all hours. There had once been a lemonade factory here. Cantrell and Cochrane. And a row of houses we'd called the Buggy Lawn. All of it had been bulldozed. Highrise blocks were planned for the site. But for years it had been left like this, a gap, an empty space.

By some kind of sideways connection, I remembered I had a composition to write for English. As if the lines for

93

Bryce weren't enough. The composition was on a poem. Something about windy spaces. And those that toiled in the sweat of their faces.

One of the men was breaking up an orange box for the fire, stamping it with the heel of his boot, then splitting it, ripping the slats apart. He looked across and saw me. He turned and said something to his friend, and they both laughed. The last few yards to my close were suddenly difficult. But concentrating, eyes down, one foot after the other I made it. Home.

★

While the pie was heating in the oven I buttered the two slices of bread, put the kettle on for tea. There was interference on Luxembourg – crackling, a highpitched whine, snatches of a man's voice talking German. So I couldn't hear what music was being played. I cleared a space on the table for my plate, shifted the pile of newspapers. The bottom paper had stuck to something spilled. It tore and left a patch from the back page glued to the red formica. On the torn scrap, two letters from a headline read IF. I tried to scrape it off but it wouldn't come away. I would have to take hot water to it, use a knife. But later. After I'd eaten.

The chips were still just hot enough. I laid a row of them on the first slice of bread, folded it over, bit into it. This was the best thing. The butter melting over the chips, the soft bread, the taste of it all together far back in my throat, on the roof of my mouth. The piecrust was crisp, almost burnt, the way I liked it. The tea was hot, sweet. I swilled it down, poured out more.

The crackling static on the radio suddenly cut. The noises from outer space faded. The German voice shut up. Luxembourg was coming through clear again. Twanging guitars soared over a string section. The Shadows playing *Wonderful Land*. The record was an old one, at least a couple of years. But I still loved it. I stood up and strutted, did the

Shadow-step. Forward, crossover, back, side. I had all the moves down tight, exact, as I played the melody on Hank Marvin's red Stratocaster, bending those notes with the tremolo arm, just the way. I had been a big Shadows fan, knew all their records. I had kept the tunes in my head by putting words to them. *There is a Frightened Ci-ty.* Or *This is a Won-der-ful Land.*

The record stopped. The red guitar vanished. The disc jockey was lost again in a wash of noise, waves of signals drowning him. I was standing in our cold kitchen, in the weird light from a stub of candle guttering on the cluttered table.

Somewhere, at the back of a school jotter, I had Hank Marvin's autograph. Back in the summer, the Shadows had been playing at the Odeon. I couldn't afford a ticket, but on my way home from school I'd taken a wander past. Just on the off chance. And there he'd been at the side door, surrounded by people shoving books and scraps of paper at him, to sign.

He looked sharp, in a short leather coat belted at the waist, the collar turned up. Hair slicked back and those Buddy Holly glasses with the thick black frames. I hurried over, rummaging in my haversack, pulling out the jotter. It was all I had, my notebook for Geography. Hank signed his name, wrote *Best Wishes* inside the back cover, opposite a diagram of the Planetary Wind System.

Bryce had given me a hard time about the autograph. Told me I'd lose marks for defacing the notebook. Asked me who was Honk Mervin anyway. Just showing his ignorance. I didn't care. The autograph was precious.

The only other autograph I had was Jim Baxter's. Slim Jim had signed a photo of himself I'd won in a competition. It had been in the *Evening Citizen*, had really been aimed at adults. I'd only been twelve but I'd entered it anyway, and won. My father had said I was a genius, I took after my mother God rest her, if only she could see me, she'd be proud, I had brains, I'd get on, get a good education, get out.

The way Slim Jim could stroke the ball with his left foot, flight it accurately over sixty yards, was pure grace, perfection. In the photo he had the ball at his feet, in soft-toed lowcut black adidas boots, the blue Rangers jersey tucked into his shorts at the back but hanging outside at the front. His right arm was stretched out for balance, that left foot poised, drawn back. The picture had been taken in his first game, against Partick Thistle at Ibrox. I had been at the game, in fact I was there in that section of terracing, the blurred background.

The picture was in a frame, still hung on the wall beside the fireplace. I looked across but couldn't see it clearly for the candlelight flickering off the glass.

The competition had been to make up a slogan. Jim Baxter had just joined Rangers from Raith Rovers, but he still had time to serve in the army. Every Saturday they would let him out on leave to play. The words of the slogan had to begin with the initial letters of SOLDIER. An acrostic. Like Bryce's mnemonic. SUNWAD, to remind me. I had lines to write, and a composition, but later. My slogan had been *Soldier On Leave Devastates In Every Raid*, and I couldn't believe how good it was. But still I'd been amazed at seeing my name in the list of winners. My name in the paper, in print. And a few days later my name again, typed, on the long brown stiffbacked envelope that dropped through the door. The postman never brought us anything but bills, no letters, no packages, nothing. So when I heard it hit the floor, I knew it couldn't be anything else. The photo was full colour, glossy, covered with a sheet of tissue paper to keep it good.

I'd taken it to Rangers' next home game. I'd waited afterwards, outside the marble entranceway to the stadium. When Jim Baxter had come out I'd pushed my way forward and handed him the photo. And he'd looked at it and smiled, signed his name, with *Best Wishes*. The same as Hank Marvin had written in my notebook. As I'd turned away with the photo, sliding it back in its envelope, a man had grabbed me by the arm.

'I'll buy that off you son. Give you ten bob.'

He'd held out the ten shilling note. A fortune.

I'd shaken my head. This was mine, my prize. I had won it. And now it was autographed, it was priceless.

'No.'

'Twelve and a tanner. And that's my last offer.'

He had no idea.

'No.'

The glass on the picture frame was dusty. I lifted it down, breathed on it, gave it a wipe with my sleeve. Where it had hung, a rectangle of wallpaper had been left pale, its colours fresher than the rest.

★

Down on my knees I raked out the ashes from the grate, shovelled them into the grey metal bucket to be emptied, sometime, in the midden. Then I set the fire. First a few sheets of newspaper, crumpled. Then more sheets rolled up tight, curled and tucked into shapes like doughnuts. Then the layer of coal, shaken out from the bag, spread out carefully, any bigger lumps placed on top. Touch a match to the corners, the edges of the crumpled paper, and watch it catch.

One or two gusts made blowdowns, beat back smoke down the chimney and billowed it into the room. I covered the front of the fire with the blower, a square sheet of soot-blacked iron. Across it I spread another sheet of newspaper, a double page, and the sudden updraught sucked it from my hands as the fire took with a roar. When the sheet of paper started to brown, I peeled it off, folded it small and used it to lift off the blower. The coal had caught and the flames settled back to a steady comforting dance, another source of light as well as warmth.

The knock at the door made me jump.

Nobody ever came to visit. The same way we never had

97

any letters.

The knock was hard, a loud hammering.

My hands were black from the coal, smudged with soot and ash.

It came again. Batter.

I managed to turn the handle with the heels of my hands, so as not to cover it with coaldust.

There were three men standing there in overcoats and soft hats, like the police.

'Your father in?' said the one nearest the door.

'No. He's working late.'

'Well. We'll have to come in anyway.' He held up a sheet of paper. 'Sherriff's Officers. Your father's facing a warrant sale. For debt. We've got to make a list of all his goods. Put a price on them.'

'What goods?'

'That's what we're here to find out.'

I was aware I was holding my hands up awkwardly in front of me, keeping them away from my jersey.

'Been lighting the fire,' I explained.

'Aye.' Deadpan.

'Well. I suppose you'd better come in.'

'We were planning to.'

Their bulk filled the whole kitchen, made it small. The candle threw their shadows, huge, up the walls and onto the ceiling.

'Light been cut off?'

'Just fused,' I said.

'Oh aye?'

The noise from the radio was suddenly an irritant, a whine. I switched it off.

'Got that down?' said the man to one of the others who was scribbling in a notebook.

'The radio? Aye.'

'But the radio's mine,' I said.

'Household goods, son. Got to go down.' He looked about him. 'Formica-top table. Four matching chairs.

Kitchen cabinet. Two old armchairs.' He slapped one of them, raised dust. 'Worth damn all.' He pointed to the corner. 'One TV. Eighteen inch.'

'That's no ours,' I said. 'It's rented.'

He picked up the candle to look closer. 'One of these coin in the slot jobs, eh? I couldnae see it right in the dark.' He held the candle up higher. 'Bed in the recess. We canny touch that. Or the cooker. That's about it for in here.'

He turned to me again. 'Anything through in the room?'

'Nothing much.'

'We'll take a look.'

He had put the candle back down on the table. I picked it up and led them through. The draught caught the flame and it flickered, almost went out. A dribble of melted wax ran down onto my finger, hot at first but quick to cool and congeal, form a skin.

Seen in this candlelight, seen by these three men, here, taking up space, the room was a familiar place made strange. My bed unmade. Books and papers on the floor. Cold linoleum. A two-bar electric fire, unplugged. A few pictures cut from magazines tacked up on the wall. Jim Baxter again. The Beatles. The Shadows. Jane Asher.

'No much right enough,' said the man in charge. 'Sideboard. Chest of drawers. Another manky old armchair. Put down a tenner for the lot.'

The man with the notebook wrote it all down. The third man stood looking out the window, across to the wasteground where that fire was burning, the dark figures gathered round it.

I took a step to the side so I couldn't see my reflection.

The room was freezing.

'Right,' said the first man. 'That's it. Tell your father he'll be hearing from us.'

I shut the door behind them and stood for a moment listening. They were talking to each other on their way down the stairs, but I couldn't make out any of it.

Through in the kitchen I put the stub of candle back on

the table. I peeled the skin of wax from my fingertip. Looking close I could see the wax had taken an impression. My finger had left its print, its unique pattern of loops and whorls. I pressed the wax, rolled it into a tiny ball and flicked it into the fire where it flared with a quick hiss, a spurt of yellow flame.

I raked over the glowing coals, a first layer. I shook on more coal from the bag, rationing it out. My hands were still grubby with dust and ash. I washed them at the sink. The rush of tapwater was icy cold.

★

I had cleared more space on the table. I had laid out a fresh sheet of newspaper to lean on, so nothing would stick to my papers and books. I had scribbled on the edge of the newspaper with my blue biro, to make sure the ink was flowing. I thought about lighting the new candle. The stub I'd been using had burned low. But I decided to leave it. Might as well use up the last of it.

I would start with the composition. The lines for Bryce were mechanical, dull repetition. I would leave them till later, maybe even do half of them in the morning. The six rivers that flow into the Humber. The composition would take more effort. It would have to be done now. But I couldn't settle to it. I couldn't focus. I sat staring at the candle flame, thinking nothing, mind empty and numb.

Write about the thoughts and feelings evoked by the following.

> This is my country
> The land that begat me.
> These windy spaces
> Are surely my own,
> And those that here toil
> In the sweat of their faces
> Are flesh of my flesh,
> And bone of my bone.

No thoughts and no feelings. The only windy spaces I knew were the gap-sites like the one across the road where the men from the Wine Alley were standing round their fire. The poem was about another world.

I picked up my Geography notebook. Inside the back cover was Hank Marvin's autograph. Best Wishes. And on the facing page, the Planetary Wind System. The rotation of the earth on its axis from west to east causes different parts of its surface to move at different rates. Winds are deflected to the right in the northern hemisphere and to the left in the southern hemisphere. Ferrel's Law.

Because we were in the Northern Temperate Zone, the prevailing winds were from the south west. The windows rattled. A draught came under the door. The candle flame wavered. Another gust blew more smoke back down the chimney. The winds came off the Atlantic. On my map they were blue arrows, drawn in coloured pencil.

I shut the notebook and pushed it away.

The poem was called *Scotland*. I had nothing to say about it.

I should at least make a start on the five hundred lines, do something. But I couldn't face it. I was suddenly weary.

The core of the fire now was a good red glow. If I poked it and stacked coal on top, it would build to a fine blaze in no time. But it had to last out the night. I shook the bag, picked out a few more lumps and threw them on. Again I had to wash my hands at the cold tap. I sat down in the armchair, held out my hands to warm them. The sherriff's man had said the chairs were manky, worth nothing. I leaned over and switched on the radio.

On Luxembourg, Garner Ted Armstrong was preaching hellfire and damnation, previewing his full-length show on Sunday. Telling the Plain Truth. He faded out in another wash of noise, and when it cleared there was music coming through. A couple called Miki and Grif singing I don't want to go to a party with you. I don't want to go to a dance. Sweet country harmonies. I just want to stay here and love you. I stretched out in the chair. I thought about Cathy, pictured her.

The details were unimportant. What mattered was, somehow, she was here, and that half-smile, and the way her hair, black and shiny, and through to the cold room, the flickering candlelight, the unmade bed, and a sudden draught that blew the candle out and left us in the cold dark, close then touching and clinging together. I lay back in the manky armchair in front of the fire imagining it, working myself up.

★

I shivered and sat up, not sure where I was. Dark and freezing cold, a hissing noise, a strange acrid smell. My eyes felt gritty. My neck was stiff. Then I remembered. The kitchen. No light. We had been cut off. My father was working late.

The fire was almost out. I must have fallen asleep. The hiss was the radio, the music gone again, lost in space. The last inch of candle must have burned down. I still couldn't place the smell, sharp and burnt and faintly chemical. I stood up and fumbled on the table, I found the other candle, the new one, and lit it. Then I saw the mess, where the smell was coming from. Where the first stub of candle had been. I hadn't thought to rest it on anything. In burning right down it had scorched the table top. It had made a round hole, the formica cracked and buckled round about it, like a volcanic crater.

Krakatoa. East of Java.

'No,' I said, picking off the melted wax. 'Shit. No.'

★

I had done my best to revive the fire. It flickered away, feebly. The coal in the bag was just about down to the last dross. When my father came home he tried the light switch, not thinking.

'What's happened?' he said. 'No light?'

The way he said it, he knew.

'Been cut off,' I said. 'They left a card.'

He nodded. He rubbed his face. He looked tired.

'And these men came,' I said. 'Sherriff's Officers. Talked about a warrant sale. Made a list of the furniture. The radio and everything. Said there wasn't much.'

He made a noise in his throat, very quiet, a soft groan, a kind of sigh. He sat down in the other armchair, across from me. We sat there in the unreal light.

'Listen,' I said. 'I'm sorry.'

'What are you sorry about? It's no your fault.'

'No, I don't mean that. It's something else.'

'Eh?'

'I lit this wee bit candle that was in the drawer. I put it on the table so I could see to do my homework. Only I sat here in front of the fire and I must have dozed off.'

He still didn't understand.

'It's burned a hole.'

He stood up and stared at the damage. It was one thing too many.

'It's wasted,' he said. His voice was desolate. 'It's spoiled.

★

All of this was years back. My father died long ago. The street we lived in no longer exists.

★

'What are you thinking?' says my wife.

A few days in London and now we are driving north, back home to Scotland, through the night in this rented car. My wife is driving. My job is to stay awake, make conversation. But it's dark outside and raining hard. The windscreen wipers beat and swish, a steady rhythm. The warmth of the car keeps lulling me.

'You're away in your own head. Haven't said a word for half an hour.'

Half an hour ago I wound down my window to let in a

blast of cold air. We happened to be passing a road sign that read RIVER SWALE.

'What are you thinking?'

★

SUNWAD.

★

I am back there standing in the room again, in the dark, looking out the window across that wasteground. The place is empty now, deserted. The fire there has been left to burn out. The wind rakes across its ashes, raises a last smouldering glow, a wisp of smoke. The first few drops of rain spatter the window.

The prevailing wind is from the south west, coming off the Atlantic. Blue arrows on my map of the Planetary Wind System. Best Wishes from Hank Marvin. This is a Wonder-ful Land. These windy spaces are surely my own. I haven't written my essay, or done my five hundred lines. I'll have to take a day off school. Dog it. I'll write a note in my father's handwriting. Please excuse. And oblige. Yours sincerely. His writing is fluid and cursive, copperplate, with here and there a flourish of his own. My father is through in the miserable kitchen, in the candlelight. I imagine him sitting with his head in his hands, wondering how his life could have come to this.

THAT AND A DOLLAR

He made up his mind.

'I'll take the spinach and feta omelette. Side order of french fries. Butter roll.'

Laura wrote it down on her pad. 'Tea? Coffee?'

'Cup of tea,' he said. 'But bring it after.'

'You got it.'

He closed the menu, handed it to her. 'Oh and hey.'

'I know. I know. Vinegar for the fries.' She wrinkled her nose. 'Gross!'

'Only way to eat chips,' he said. 'Dripping with vinegar. Nothing to beat it.'

She shook her head, turned and called his order through the hatch. 'Omelette for Scotty. Spinach and feta. Side order fries.'

She laid the menu on the pile beside the cash register, tore off his tab and slapped it on the counter, put her notepad in the pocket of her apron, tucked the stub of pencil behind her ear. He realised he was watching her, not thinking, his concentration total and mindless. Something bland, synthesised, oozed from the sound system. Easy listening.

From out in the street came the howl of a car alarm. He wondered if it had been going for a while and he just hadn't noticed. The kind of thing he'd learned to shut out. His seat was by the window. He looked out at the parking lot, the sign that read DINER, vertical in red neon. Traffic passed along the street, endless headlights. He still couldn't get used to how quickly the night came down, the fast fade to dark, no half-light in between.

Each window table had its own miniature jukebox. He turned the knob on the side to flip through the titles. A mix of old sixties hits, country and western, recent pop, rap. Nothing he specially wanted to hear. Laura brought him water in a smoky-yellow glass, ice-cubes clunking the sides as she set it down. Then she brought his knife and fork wrapped in a napkin, his buttered roll cut in half, and finally the vinegar in a red plastic bottle.

She made a face again. 'What can I say?'

'Hey, this is America, right? Land of the free?'

'Right! Whatever you want.'

He looked out the window again, across to where his own car was parked, and something caught his eye, a movement. He leaned closer to the glass, shielding his eyes. And sure enough, a figure was crouched there, seemed to be tampering with the radiator grill.

His car.

He was up and out of his seat, almost crashing into Laura. She called after him. 'What's the problem?' But he was out the door.

The kid was already up on his feet, facing him. Maybe fourteen, fifteen. Baseball cap on backwards. Public Enemy T-shirt. White white Reeboks. A screwdriver in his hand.

'What's the story here?'

'What you talking about?'

'This is my car.'

'So what?'

He couldn't believe this. 'So what the fuck were you doing to it?'

'Back off man. I never touched your fucking car.' He checked the front of the car. No obvious damage. The kid started moving away, casual. 'I don't need this shit man. I'm out of here.'

'That's right,' he said. 'Beat it.'

'Asshole,' the kid said, then broke into a jog, light on his feet in those white sneakers.

Looking closer he saw what looked like scratchmarks round the badge, the VW logo, as if the boy had tried to prise it off. Down the street that car alarm kept on wailing.

Back inside, Laura had his order ready, laid it on the table. 'So. Was it something I said?'

'Some kid. Messing with my car.'

Arnie the manager stuck his head through the hatch. 'He get anything?'

'Nothing to get. Somebody already took the radio, tape deck, must be six months ago.'

'I remember.'

'I even put one of those NO RADIO signs in the window.'

'Didn't do no good, huh?' Arnie's shrug was a whole attitude. Long suffering.

'The funny thing is, it looks as if he was trying to get the badge off the front.'

'Don't tell me!' said Arnie. 'You got a Volks?'

'That's right.'

'Well that's it!' said Arnie. 'That's it right there!'

'How do you mean?'

'I read about it. Some rock group. They wear these things round their necks.'

'VW badges?'

'Right! So these kids go round ripping them off cars.'

'Can you believe it?'

'Hey!' Again that shrug. Seen it all. And then some. This is America. 'Last week I heard about a kid getting killed for the sneakers he was wearing. Right here in the neighbourhood.'

'You gonna eat this or what?' said Laura. 'It's getting cold.'

'Sure,' he said. 'Thanks.'

'Enjoy,' she said.

Arnie called over. 'Hey Scotty!'

'What?'

'Beam me up!'

'Right,' he said, as always. 'Phasers on stun.'

★

Back at his apartment he listened to his answering machine.

The first message was a hustle from some insurance company.

If you would spare us an hour of your time to answer some questions about your insurance cover, we'll pay you fifty dollars for your trouble. Plus expenses. Call toll free 1-800-SAVE.

Americans never could get the hang of the subjunctive. If you would, we will.

Now Julie's voice was on the machine.

Hi baby. Sorry I have to be out of town on the weekend. Got to head out to the Coast, talk to some guys about a new line. Could be really big. Tell you all about it when I get back. So, be good! I'll call.

The only other message was from Nathan, his agent. No pressure, man, but that magazine wants the illustration by Monday, remember? The one with the kids and the car? I told them no problem. The kind of thing you can do with your eyes closed! They want the usual stuff. Kind of Rockwell. Like the kids should be cute, squeaky clean. And the car should be a little beat-up, but friendly. I mean these kids are not going out wilding! But why am I telling you this? You know, right! So just do it!

A click and a bleep and that was it. No more messages. He reset the machine and went through to the kitchen to get himself a beer.

Stuck to the fridge door was a cartoon he had cut from the *New Yorker*, held in place with little magnets shaped like ladybirds. The cartoon still made him smile, every time. A fat balding middle-aged businessman was talking to this svelte elegant woman, straight out of Bloomingdale's. They had met in the street, as in Fifth Avenue, maybe Wall Street. Her look was tightlipped, total distaste. Oblivious,

108

he was grinning, pleased to see her.

Hey! he was saying. I haven't seen you since Woodstock! Do you still make your own shoes?

The first time he'd read it he'd laughed out loud. Julie had managed a smile, said Yeah. Neat.

Now she was out on the West Coast, hustling. She ran her own company, selling health, marketing the New Age. Last year she had packaged a diet drink made from lemon juice and maple syrup, given it the name Bittersweet. He had done the artwork, that was how they had met.

He opened his can of beer, nudged the fridge door shut with his hip.

Do you still make your own shoes!

In the fruitbasket on the table was a single apple, rotting. A week or so back he had noticed it was starting to shrivel. He had meant to throw it out but hadn't. It had turned brown, bruised. Mugged by the central heating. It had grown fur, dissolved in on itself. He caught the sick–sweet smell of it fermenting, faintly alcoholic. Change and decay. The kind of thing he might once have tried to paint. A sequence, from the full red shiny fruit, to this dull mush stuck to the basket.

These days he would more likely photograph it, take polaroid snaps at each stage, tack them up on his notice-board. He could even film it, in time-lapse. Set it up. A whole bowlful of fresh fruit, arranged just so. Still life. A nice irony. Fix the timer on the camera, a frame every three or four minutes. Adjust the lighting. Crank up the heat. Let it roll.

He picked up the basket and shook the rotten fruit into the plastic bin under the sink. He knocked the basket against the rim of the bin, trying to shake off the residue, but it stayed, a sticky mess coating the wicker, mulched into the weave. He knew it would be awkward to clean, so he ditched it in the bin. He could buy a new one for a few cents.

Hey, this is America!

109

★

The illustration was almost complete. The car was a red Thunderbird, airbrushed to perfection, all smooth curves and gleaming chrome. He had worked from photographs and a diagram in an old manual, so it was anatomically accurate, photorealistically exact.

The airbrush was just right for these shiny surfaces, sharp edges and bright clear colours, glints of highlight, metallic sheen. He liked the way he had caught the glass of the windscreen, suggested its reflectiveness, without obscuring the two kids in behind.

The boy had his right hand on the wheel, his left elbow out the rolled-down window. He wore a baseball cap, back to front. He was grinning, pleased with himself. The girl was flushed and laughing, both hands raised, pushing back the tangle of her thick blonde hair.

The kind of thing he could do with his eyes closed.

But deep in his guts was a niggling discomfort, an irritation as he stood looking at it, the technically perfect car, the bland happy faces.

Still. Bland was what they wanted, bland was what they got. Hey!

From nowhere came the memory of a toy car he'd had as a child. A cheap tin shell with all the detail just painted on its surface, including the windows and the two figures supposed to be inside. Their faces were painted on the windscreen, their profiles on the side windows, the backs of their heads on the rear.

He remembered exactly the feeling of unease. Holding the car at an angle, to see the front and side at the same time, two views of the same face but not connecting up. Or turning it round, to see the back and side views, separate. Somehow it had disturbed him, made him feel uncomfortable, like this. The way he felt now.

He sipped more beer. This Bud's for you. He didn't really like drinking straight from the can. The touch of it on

110

his lips and tongue made the drink taste metallic. Something he felt in his teeth just thinking about it. There was maybe half the can left. He picked up a mug from the draining-board, set it the right way up. The inside of the mug was stained dark tan from tea and coffee. He poured in the beer and threw the can in the bin, on top of the wasted basket, the squished apple.

He went back through with his cup of beer and stood looking again at the picture he had painted, the sleek lines of the car, light glancing off the windscreen, those faces seen through the glass. Nathan had said the car should be a little beat-up. Maybe a dent in the fender, some rust on the bodywork. And maybe after that he'd do something about the faces.

Maybe not.

For a moment he saw again the face of the kid back at the diner, the one who had tried to rip the logo off his car. And what he remembered was the blankness in the boy's eyes, the expression that had registered nothing beyond a routine defensiveness, a vague annoyance at being stopped.

The room felt suddenly stuffy, too hot. He turned down the heating a few degrees, opened the window to let in some air.

The streetnoise had only been background, so much a constant that he hardly noticed it. Now it rushed in, amplified. Traffic along Grand Central Parkway, the endless electric buzz of the city, shot through with the specific, rising clear. A ghettoblaster pumping out rap, young voices yelling, laughing loud, a shriek, breaking glass, waft of cool jazz, a guard dog barking at some passer-by, the scream of an ambulance, a jingle on TV, and gathering it all up, drowning it out for a moment, the swallowing roar of a jet out of La Guardia.

Every time he went back home, to Scotland, it took him days to get used to the quiet, the moments of almost silence when he felt the hush, the wash of it against his ears.

Here there was never a silence, anywhere, ever.

Across the street shone the bright lights of the Allnite Deli, open twenty-four hours. Outside it, as always, a bunch of kids hung out, goofed, clowned, made noise. Neon advertised Millerlite, Colt 45, and a handwritten sign read *Hero's Soda's Beer's*. He always wanted to take out those apostrophes, white them out. His reaction to them was unreasoning, almost physical, a twist of irritation. He knew it was ridiculous. But.

Next to the deli was a vacant lot, overgrown. Once it had been fenced off with wire mesh, but the fence had been torn down bit by bit and never replaced. In the centre of the lot was the burned-out carcass of what had once been a car, probably stolen and dumped there, picked clean as if by jackals. He had seen it happen before. A car would be abandoned down some sidestreet, or left, broken-down, beside the highway, and overnight it would be stripped down to nothing.

Now that *would* be worth filming in time-lapse. Never mind rotting fruit or flowers opening. Film the total disintegration of a car over a few days. The problem would be setting it up, finding a car at an early enough stage in the process, figuring out where to place the camera so it wouldn't be damaged or stolen. It would have to be a matter of chance, something that would just happen. Right place right time. The randomness of it appealed to him. It meant he wouldn't have to plan it, just be ready. He could even work that up into a philosophy.

But he knew that like most of his ideas it would stay just that, something to be kicked around, talked about, never actually realised. He looked across at the wasteground, the gutted chassis. He looked down below at his own car. It was badly parked, at an angle, squeezed into a tight space, the right front wheel bumped up onto the kerb. The space was the one he always tried to get, right out front, directly under the streetlamp for safety, visibility. But even here, how safe was it? If some kid started dismantling it, would anybody take any notice? Would anybody care? He had lived in this apartment block three years and didn't know another soul in the building. If he dropped dead tonight he would lie and rot for days and not be missed. The messages would pile up on his answering machine. No pressure, man. Be good. Call toll free. If you would we will. This is America.

The telephone wire from his building crossed the street just above his window. It sagged in the middle, swayed a little, catching the streetlight. Dangling from it was a pair of old beat-up sneakers, tied together by their laces. They'd been tossed up, spun like *bolas*, to catch on the wire and hang there, a street mobile. He hadn't noticed them before. They could have been there for years, could stay for years more, not rotting, nonbiodegradable.

★

He couldn't get the pattern of rusting right. He had scraped away at the surface of the painting with a hard eraser, made a ragged patch of rough texture along the edge of the fender. He had mixed his colour – russet, burnt umber, a touch of ochre. He had stippled it with a sponge, grinding it in. He had flecked it with the tip of a fine brush to finish. But still it looked wrong, a blotch on the paper instead of on the painted car.

He took his airbrush again, adjusted the nozzle, did a quick respray to restore the smooth finish, the surface sheen. It was good enough. The customer would buy it.

He sprayed off the last dregs of paint onto a scrap of paper, kept spraying till the air jet was clear. Then he rinsed out the fluid chamber, filled it with water and again kept spraying till all the colour was gone, the jet of water clear. He unscrewed the handle, eased out the needle and drew it across the palm of his hand to dry. He put away the whole apparatus, dismantled, in its case. Another job done.

★

'Shark cartilage,' said Julie. 'It's the greatest thing.'

They'd met for coffee in the basement of Trump Tower. Julie had suggested it as a meeting place. It was convenient, fitted in with the rest of her day, and he didn't really mind. Even if the coffee cost two fifty and came in a paper cup. Visually he enjoyed the excesses of the place, the red marble, burnished mirror glass, brass handrails. He'd been watching the shoppers glide up and down on the escalators, zigzagging past each other at forty-five degrees, gently numbed by piped Gershwin, an ambience from discreet speakers.

'So tell me about it.'

'We'll make it into powder,' she said. 'Freeze-dried. Sell it in capsules.'

'Easy to swallow.'

'Exactly.' If she'd caught his irony she was ignoring it.

'So what's it good for?'

'You name it.'

'Anything that ails you.'

'Don't tell me!' she said, waving her hands. '*Pennies from Heaven*, right? The guy was Steve Martin, the girl was, don't tell me, Bernadette Peters!'

'Got it in one.' He sang it. 'Love is good for anything that ails you.'

She laughed. 'That's the one!'

'So this stuff is a regular cure-all?'

She nodded. 'Speeds up the healing process. It makes sense when you think about it. I mean, when did you ever hear of a sick shark?'

He thought about it.

'When did I ever hear of a sick aardvark? A sick okapi?'

'Come on! You know what I'm saying!'

He knew what she was saying.

'What are you going to call it? *Jaws*?'

'Neat!' she said. 'Wrong, but neat!'

This time she could definitely sense it, his *attitude*. But she kept talking. 'The really exciting thing about it, I mean for like *now* is it strengthens the immune system. And what with this whole AIDS thing.'

'There's a market out there.'

'Not just that.'

No. Of course not.

He looked up through the slanted glass roof, let his gaze follow the flow of water, lit from below, cascading down the sheer marble wall from four floors up.

'I feel like a character in a Woody Allen movie,' he said.

'Which one?'

'Any one!'

He sipped the last of his coffee, dark and bitter through the froth. The dusting of chocolate left a sweet aftertaste. He licked it from his top lip. 'So. Are you coming over tonight, or should I come round to yours?'

'Actually,' she said, 'I'm seriously jetlagged. Still catching up with myself.'

'It's always worse coming in this direction.'

'So give me a couple of days, I'll call, OK?'

'OK.'

Outside in the street she waved down a taxi.

'So,' she said, and she kissed him full on the mouth with a real warmth, and she stepped into the yellow cab, a scene from so many movies, she waved to him as the cab pulled out into Fifth Avenue traffic, she mouthed *I'll call* behind glass.

Turning he almost fell over a supermarket trolley being pushed along the sidewalk by some skidrow down-and-out. The man stared at him, eyes hard and bleak. The face was a grey death's-head, the greyness ground in, ingrained in the hollows and crevices, grey skin stretched taut over the skull, the caved-in cheeks covered with rough stubble. In the trolley were the man's belongings. Worldly goods. A cardboard box. A couple of plastic carrier bags stuffed with old clothes. A blue camping gas stove resting inside a saucepan, beside it a tin of baked beans and, crazily, a sixpack of Coke. Propped on top of it all was a scrap of card, the flap ripped from a carton, and printed on it in black felt-tip, in careful block capitals, was the man's story. HOMELESS NO JOB HIV+ PLEASE HELP.

He felt for the money in his pocket. The notes were all the same size, twenties, tens, fives, singles, so there was no way of telling by touch. He pulled out a bill, relieved it was a dollar, and handed it to the man.

The man took the dollar and looked at it, looked him up and down, looked in the direction the cab had gone, looked up at the gleaming tower, looked again at the dollar, said *Shit!*

★

He hadn't bought a new fruitbasket so he set up the still life on a dinnerplate, cleared a space for it in the middle of the table. Two apples. An orange. A pear. Green grapes. A plum. He turned the spot so the light fell directly on it. Good. He clicked the polaroid, watched the picture materialise, the colours bright and artificial, the plate of fruit reduced, small in the centre of the frame. He held the print by the corner, carefully between finger and thumb, waved it to dry. Then he placed it on the fridge door, held on by two of the tiny magnets. A message on the answering machine, from Nathan, said the illustration was fine, great, just what they wanted, they loved it, they would put more work his way, more of the same.

Another memory came to him, for no reason, his first day at Art School in Glasgow, the best part of twenty years back, the sheer grace and elegance of the Mackintosh building, the throat-catching smells of oilpaints and linseed and turps, an atmosphere you could taste.

For years he'd had two Mackintosh postcards tacked up on the wall of his bedsit, one a reproduction of a watercolour, withered flowers in a vase, the other an aphorism, lettered by the artist.

THERE IS HOPE IN HONEST ERROR. NONE IN

But the way the words ran on, the fall of the line endings, meant he'd read it as *merest ylist*, and he'd wondered what in God's name was an *ylist*. The ring of it had been vaguely Chaucerian. Merest ylist. Then one day he'd just been staring at it, vacant, and it had fallen into place, was just there. The mere stylist! The ludicrous illumination had made him laugh. Now he would read it as a jibe, what he'd become.

He readjusted the little polaroid still life, smiled at it. A memo to himself. A note.

From out in the street came a long sustained blast on a car horn. Nathan called it the Mexican doorbell. Another alarm started up its amplified whoop whoop.

Somehow he had to make this film, make it happen.

★

'A Zee and Two Noughts,' said Julie. 'By that British guy, Peter Greenaway.

'I've seen it,' he said. 'And it's *zed*. A *zed* and two noughts.'

'Whatever. Well, it's full of that time-lapse stuff. Rotting carcasses and everything.'

'Same technique,' he said. 'That's the beauty of the thing, applying it to a car!'

'And you'd want to show it in a gallery?'

He nodded. 'Could be worked up into a fullblown installation. I could airbrush some big panels, like billboard ads for cars. Fit in some potent quotes, you know, advertising copy, statements from the Futurists, lines from rock songs.'

'Riding along in my automobile.'

'Right. That kind of thing.'

'You could have the songs playing on a tape.'

'Instal a jukebox!'

'Wow!' She was finally warming to the idea. 'It's a great

117

concept.' Then she hesitated. 'There's only one thing.'

'What?'

'Money.'

'Can I quote you on that?'

'Sorry?'

'What you just said. *There's only one thing – money*.'

Here it was again, his attitude. 'You know what I mean.'

'Sure.'

'I mean, with an exhibition, the gallery sells the paintings or whatever, it takes its cut.'

'Fifty percent.'

'That much, huh? But with stuff like this, who pays? Could you charge admission?'

He shrugged. 'What about National Endowment grants?'

'I could ask Edward.' Edward was her ex, was involved in running a gallery in TriBeCa. 'I know he sometimes puts on weird stuff.'

'Weird!'

'All right, unusual. Unclassifiable.'

'Uncommercial?'

'Now that I don't know!'

'But you'd ask him for me?'

'No problem. Maybe we could meet with him.'

'Soon?'

'This week would be good. Next week I'll be out on the Coast again.'

'Catching more sharks?'

'Something like that, yeah.'

He laughed, did the threatening music from *Jaws*.

★

'Conceptually it's great,' said Edward. 'I like the *irony* of it, setting up all these glossy images then undercutting it all with the *reality* of this car being picked to bits. It's a very strong motif.'

He nodded, waited. 'But?'

'There's a few difficulties,' said Edward.

'I thought there might be!'

'The first thing is the sheer practicality of it. I mean, it reminds me of some site-specific stuff I've seen. The location is all-important, and so is the record of the event, the documentation.'

'Right.'

'But how would this work? You just going to carry your camera around and hope you come on the right car in the right place?'

'In this city? I see two or three a week!'

'OK. So where do you set up your camera? And how do you stay unobtrusive while you're filming?'

'We talked about this,' said Julie.

'And?'

'Details,' he said. 'It'll work out. I'll set up on a roof or something. Use a telefoto lens.'

'There is another possibility. You could set the whole thing up in a gallery. Bring in a car then abandon it to the public. Let *them* tear it to bits.'

'Wow!' said Julie.

'It changes the whole context, you see. Underscores that irony even more. By placing it *here* in the sacred space of the gallery, you're saying *This is Art*.'

'It's a nice comment on consumerism in the art world,' said Julie. 'Everybody grabbing a piece.'

'You could call it an exercise in deconstruction!' said Edward. 'Add to your conceptual streetcred.'

'I don't know,' he said. 'I'm not sure. It's not how I'd seen it, a bit of designer vandalism for middleclass wankers.'

'You should write a manifesto!' said Edward. 'No, I'm serious. And with that accent of yours it would sound great read on tape. Or be there yourself, declaiming it!'

'Performance,' he said.

'A star is born!' said Julie.

'Scotland is fashionable right now,' said Edward.

'Marketable. Especially Glasgow.'

'Flavour of the month.'

'Some of your countrymen have been making it big. These young guys. Campbell. Wysznewski.'

'I like their stuff.'

'You don't have any giant canvases with cryptic titles?' He shook his head.

'Actually,' said Edward, 'that brings in something else. I mean these guys are names.'

'And I'm not.'

'Being a magazine illustrator just doesn't cut it.'

'Thanks.'

'It comes down to finance. With a name I could get funding. Maybe even for an event like this.'

'What about National Endowment grants?'

'Tell me about it! Our grants have been slashed. Because of the whole AIDS thing, the anti-gay backlash.'

'Moral Majority,' said Julie.

'I don't follow.'

'Well, there's no money for any work that could even remotely be interpreted as promoting homosexuality.'

'But this isn't.'

'No, but *galleries* that have been guilty of this *wickedness* in the *past* are finding their budgets *cut*. Just in case!'

'And that's been happening to you?'

'Systematically.' Edward flicked out his cuffs, sneaked a look at his watch. A busy man.

'I guess there's always sponsorship,' said Julie.

'Who do you suggest?' he said. 'Ford Motors? Have them donate a little number from their showroom?'

Edward laughed, stood up. A *very* busy man. The audience was over. 'Anyway. I hope you can work something out. But I wouldn't be too hopeful.'

'Don't give up my day job.'

'Right!'

★

120

'Smug bastard!' he said, as he tried to start up his car.

'Come on!' said Julie. 'He was really nice!'

'Oh sure.' The engine coughed, hacked. 'He was *very* nice. Charming. Told me I'd sold out.'

'When did he say that?'

'*Being an illustrator doesn't cut it.* That's as near as dammit.'

'He's talking product, and how to sell it. That's his job.'

'Exactly.' He tried the engine again. It growled and spluttered. 'Exactly! All that talk about the sacred space of the gallery. That's all it was. Talk. Well, fuck his gallery. The sacred space is here, inside my head.'

'Another line for your manifesto!'

The car stuttered again, packed up. 'Jesus Christ!' he said, thumping the dashboard.

'You'll end up like John Cleese in that Fawlty Towers thing!'

'Give me a break!'

'Screaming at the car! Whipping it!'

'OK,' he said, spreading his hands. 'Let's be calm about this.' He took a deep breath, tried again.

Nothing.

'Bastard!'

One. Last. Time.

It kicked and spurted, sparked into life.

'Yes!' he shouted.

'All *right*!' said Julie.

The exhilaration was ridiculous. But just to be moving was enough, was good.

Half a mile down the road there was steam coming out from under the bonnet. Julie made him pull over, said she'd take a cab. 'I'm already running late,' she said. 'I don't need this.'

Halfway across the Queensboro Bridge, the 59th Street, *feeling groovy*, stuck in a backup of traffic, *slow down you move too fast*, all the cheap bastards who came this way to avoid the toll, he should have taken the Midtown, the steam now billowing out of the engine, some kids in the next car laughing and giving him the finger, *life I love you*, fuck Paul Simon.

Inching forward and finally, finally, off the bridge at the other side and crawling along at twenty in clouds of steam in angry traffic and only-just-making-it to a garage two blocks from where he lived. The mechanic was young, greasemonkey in blue overalls. He had a walkman clipped to his belt. The noise jangled and buzzed through the headphones, guitar solo that must be searing his ears. 'Yeah?' he shouted, and switched off the walkman but kept the headphones in place.

He told him about the overheating, the not starting, the steam.

'So what's the exact problem?' said the boy.

'I thought *you* could tell *me*.'

The boy stared at him, hard. 'I'm kind of busy right now. If you leave it here I'll check it out in the morning.'

'You can't give me any idea?'

The boy shrugged. 'Sounds like maybe it's ready to blow a gasket.'

'I know the feeling.'

'Huh?'

'Forget it.' He got back in the car and slammed the door shut. The boy shook his head and laughed, switched on his music again, turned it up louder.

The last two blocks the car juddered and stalled every few yards, convulsed and hissed out more steam. He could smell burning rubber. He made it back on willpower alone.

★

The still life was in the first stages of dissolution, the grapes brown and puckered, the orange skin hard and flecked with mould, the apple dull and bruised, the plum turning liquid, dissolving in its own juice. He took another polaroid, from the same place, the same angle as before. He wafted the snapshot dry and put it on the fridge door beside the first one. He placed them edge to edge, moved one of the magnets over the join, borrowed another from the *New Yorker* cartoon. In a few more days he would take another shot, complete the sequence. A Polaroid triptych. He moved the cartoon to one side, to make space for it.

He called Julie, found himself listening to her answering machine. For her message she had taped a line from Laurie Anderson's *O Superman*, taken it straight from the record.

Hi! I'm not home right now, but if you want to leave a message, just start talking at the sound of the tone.

He hung up.

★

There was a line from Laurie Anderson he could use in his manifesto.

I am in my body the way I am in my car.

He wrote it on a file card, a three by five, added it to the growing pile on his desk.

Riding along in my automobile,
My baby beside me at the wheel.

A roaring motor car is more beautiful than the Victory of Samothrace

Baby you can drive my car.

Vorsprung durch Technik.

★

Somewhere in the middle of the night he woke up with a sense of absolute certainty. He knew exactly what he had to do.

He checked his watch. Five to three. He pulled on his trackpants and training shoes, his sweatshirt and padded jacket. He picked up his keys from the kitchen table. He went down quietly by the stairs and out into the street. The front door clicked shut behind him, closed by its own

123

weight. The night air was cold. He was wide awake, keenly alert.

His usual space was taken by another car, an old red Chevy. On its windscreen was a sticker that read, *This car is protected by party animals.* His own car was where he'd had to leave it, the only one on the other side of the street. Nobody ever parked there, it was too close to the wasteground, the empty lot. He'd had no choice, but now he was glad, it had worked out well, as if he'd planned it.

He opened the car door and leaned inside. Kneeling on the passenger seat he cleared his bits and pieces from the dashboard and the glove compartment – a pencil and a fibretip pen, a nickel, a subway token, a few crumpled receipts. He shoved them all in his jacket pocket, backed out and moved round to the driver's side, climbed in.

He released the handbrake, turned the key in the ignition. It started first time, a last ironic joke, with a racket he thought would wake up half the neighbourhood. But it didn't matter. Nobody else cared, so why should he? Hey!

He turned the steering wheel hard right, pressed the accelerator, bumped up onto the sidewalk and across it, lurched straight onto the empty lot, crunched over garbage and debris, cardboard, tin cans, broken glass. He came to a stop in front of the derelict hulk, the picked-over remains of that other car, the one that had given him the idea.

He got out and locked the doors, a reflex. He patted the car on the roof with a kind of affection. He caught himself doing it and laughed. A heavy truck went growling past. An old man, hunkered down in a doorway, stared out at him, and through him, intent but uninterested.

Back in the apartment he worked quickly, set up the camera on its tripod by the open window, adjusted the lens so his car filled most of the frame. He set the timer, a shot every three minutes. He was ready.

Then he thought about the petrol left in the gas tank, he pictured some crazy kid torching it and blowing himself skyhigh. He rummaged in his junk-cluttered cupbᵣard for a plastic canister. Now he needed a length of tube and he had nothing. He was pulling open drawers, scrabbling through papers, looking for something he didn't have in places it couldn't possibly be.

He had just about given up when he remembered the rubber tube on his washing machine. He dragged it out. He took the scalpel from his drawing-board and sliced the tube from the machine, cut off the nozzle. He ran downstairs with the tube and the canister, out again into the street. Across to the car. Unscrew the cap. Feed the tube into the tank. Siphon off the petrol, suck it up and stop the tube with his thumb. Something from the science lab at school. Titration, using a pipette. Somewhere a dog barked. A phone rang and rang, unanswered. His concentration slipped and he took a mouthful of petrol, spat it out and gagged, spat again, kept spitting out the taste.

A voice called across to him. 'Yo man! Good buzz?'

Some deadhead coming out of the deli.

He shouted back. 'Get a life!'

The man half-snarled half-laughed.

The taste was still in his mouth. He had done enough. There couldn't be any more than dregs left in the tank.

Back upstairs he gargled with mouthwash, swilled away the taste. He washed the smell of petrol from his hands. He checked that everything was still set. The timer. The angle. The focus. The frame.

Now. This was it. This time.

Hit the switch.

Lights. Camera. Action.

★

First to go was the logo and with it the whole radiator grill prised off with a crowbar a quick blur of movement and gone and likewise the numberplates then all the windows dematerialised smashed in the headlamps shattered then the wheels off the car jacked up on bricks and the doors one by one and the seats ripped out and the steering wheel and the bricks kicked away the chassis slumped to the ground the hood up and the whole engine grappled out surgically removed and the roof dented hammered in the body folding in on itself the light constantly shifting from night through day and back again the quick flicker of shadow figures one of them himself when he'd gone across to take a closer look stood there long enough to pose to be in the picture himself doing a Hitchcock ghosting through the frame and the last image to end it was a fire started up some garbage set alight and what was left of the car his car going up in a blaze the paint burning the battered metal framework wavering in the flames.

★

He watched it four times straight through, projected onto the bare white wall. He tried to call Julie but was still getting only her answering machine. He should record a message, set it up so his machine was calling her machine.

> – Hi, I'm not home right now
> – Too bad, neither am I
> – But if you want to leave a message
> – That's exactly what I'm doing
> – Just start talking at the sound of the tone
> – Bleep
> – Hi
> – Bleep
> – Hi

He called Nathan, who said he'd *love* to see the film, could he put it on VHS? And he didn't expect him to *place* it, did he? But keep in touch, there was more magazine stuff coming up.

He found the card Edward had given him, tried calling him at the gallery and at home. But both lines were engaged. Busy.

He watched the film another four times, with the same

excitement, the way he used to feel when he painted just for himself, for the love of it.

He would have to think about a soundtrack, music. And maybe titles. At the very least a closing credit, with the name he'd decided to use.

Merest Ylist Productions.

★

'So what's it to be?' said Laura.

'I'll go for the silver dollar pancakes,' he said. 'And a brewed decaff.'

'Don't tell me,' she said. 'You want vinegar on the pancakes.'

He laughed. 'Just the butter and the maple syrup!'

She called through his order. 'Silver dollar for Scotty.'

Arnie stuck his head through. 'Hey! Where you been?'

He shrugged. 'You know. Working on something.'

'We thought you'd deserted us.'

'Never!'

Arnie liked that. He disappeared through the hatch, reappeared with the plate, piled high. 'One order of pancakes to beam up.'

'I'm locking onto the coordinates!'

When Laura brought them over, he said, 'Maybe you can help me with something.'

'Ask.'

'Do you know any songs with lines about cars?'

'Cars?'

'You know, like *Riding along in my automobile*.'

She thought about it, scratched her head with her pencil. 'There's *American Pie*.' She sang, 'Took my Chevy to the levee but the levee was dry.'

'That's great!' He wrote it down, on a napkin.

'What's it for anyway?'

'This thing I've been working on. I'm writing a manifesto.'

'I'm glad I asked!' She called through the hatch. 'Hey,

Arnie! Scotty needs some pop songs about cars!'

Again Arnie's head appeared. 'Cars?'

'Yeah,' said Laura. 'Chuck Berry, stuff like that.'

'There's all these old Beach Boys numbers,' said Arnie. '*Little Deuce Coupe.*'

'Yeah!' He wrote it down.

Arnie tried singing, a ragged cracked falsetto. 'And we'll have fun fun fun till her daddy takes her T-bird away.'

'Great!'

Laura put her hands over her ears.

'What's it for?' said Arnie, ignoring her.

'He's writing a manifesto,' she said.

'Oh yeah? That and a dollar will get you on the subway!'

'A dollar?' said Laura. 'Listen to him! It's a dollar fifteen.'

'I know how much it costs,' said Arnie. 'I ride the subway every day. But it just doesn't have the same ring to it. That and a dollar fifteen. Am I right or am I right?'

'You're right,' he said. 'Absolutely.'

'See! There's a man who knows what he's talking about! And listen. I just thought of something else you can use. From the man himself. The Boss.'

'Springsteen?'

Arnie nodded. 'You know *Thunder Road*?'

'I've heard it.'

'Well, there's a great line about, what is it? Roll down the window. Let the wind blow back your hair.'

'Right! I remember it. One last chance to make it real. Trade in these wings for some wheels.'

'Yeah! And how does the next bit go? You hear their engines roaring on, da-da-ra-da, you know they're gone.'

'Nice.'

It was hard to write fast with his fibretip on the napkin. The ink blotched on the soft surface and the letters spread. He had to write large and leave space. He covered the first napkin, moved on to a second.

Arnie had the tune now, sang it in that cracked voice. 'The skeleton frames of burnt-out Chevrolets.'

'That's just right,' he said. 'That's exactly right.'

'Hey,' said Arnie. 'Just cut me in for a percentage!'

'I'll list you in the credits,' he said.

'Fame!' said Arnie. 'I'm gonna live forever!'

'Don't give up your day job!'

'Ha!'

He finished the last of his pancakes, wiping up the syrup. 'Great,' he said.

Laura took his plate. 'Anything else?'

'Actually. You know what I'd like?'

'Surprise me.'

'Just a piece of fresh fruit. An apple, a pear, anything.'

'Apples we got.'

And she brought him one, huge and red with a waxy shine. It almost looked artificial, too rich and lush to be real. He picked it up, felt the weight of it in his hand. He looked at the writing on the two napkins, not seeing the words, just the random shapes of the blotched letters, like detail from some action painting, a spidery calligraphy.

Arnie called over. 'One more line from that song. You ready?'

'Sure.' And Arnie sang again. 'All the redemption I can offer is beneath this dirty hood.'

'Hey!' he said. 'That and a dollar!'

'Dollar fifteen,' said Laura.

He laughed. He polished the apple on his sleeve. He bit into it. It tasted good.

129

I'll be Han-Shan,
You be Shih-te

I was sick of logic. An hour of it had ground me down. The lecturer's voice was a bored drone, with just enough whining edge to prevent it being shut out. Through the high windows I could see the shapes of trees in the park, fading into mist. The trees looked bare still, but I knew they were already in bud. A girl, two rows in front, had a delicate way, with her middle finger, of pushing her dark hair back behind her ear to stop it falling across her face as she bent forward, writing. Every word. Scribble.

It follows that universality and generality are not attributes of things, but of ideas and words. Of course any idea or word is also particular. But.

Scribble. It seemed mad that she was writing it down. Mad that I was listening to it. On my blank notepad I had jotted random words and phrases. In a week I would find them vague shapes in a mist.

Space. Duration. Infinity. Simple ideas – the scent and whiteness of a lily. Universality. Language. A sort of thing.

In a corner of the page I had sketched a tree. Across the top I had written TINY MENTAL PHILOSOPHY RULES OK

By the time the lecturer closed his notes I was yawning, felt drained. I was to go direct to a tutorial on the Metaphysical Poets. But I'd had enough. Even though we would be reading Herbert.

I struck the board and cry'd, No more.

130

That was the mood. No more. I skipped the tutorial, decided to go and see Doug instead.

★

I ran down to Byres Road, took a bus across the city. Banged on Doug's door but he wasn't home. He might be at his lock-up though, working on his motorbike.

The lock-up garage was one of three, set back from the main road, in the grounds of a big house that had been burned out and left to rot. Doug was hunkered down in the doorway, polishing a bit of metal. He let out a roar when he saw me, by way of greeting. We shook hands, hugged, pummeled each other on the back.

'Great to see you, man!' he said. 'Dogging classes?'

'Had enough for one day,' I said.

We had been friends for a long time, all the way through school. After the Highers, Doug had left. He had worked from time to time, but these days was content to be signing on and drawing dole.

'Philosophy was it?' he asked.

'Logic this morning.'

'Say no more,' said Doug. 'Here, I've got the very thing.'

The very thing was half a flagon of cider, left over from the weekend.

'The very thing,' I said. 'The thing in itself.'

'No more philosophy,' said Doug. 'It's a bad habit. Makes you deaf.'

He uncorked the bottle and crooked his finger through the handle, tilting it to his lips in a way we'd seen John Wayne do it, years ago, in *The Alamo*. He passed it to me and I tried drinking the same way, but only succeeded in dribbling it down the front of my jersey. That set us both laughing as we passed it back and forward between us, swig for swig.

When the bottle was drained, Doug set it down empty beside him.

'Another dead soldier.'

131

I saluted. 'Remember the Alamo.'

We grinned at each other, happy in our nonsense.

'Couple of old cronies,' said Doug.

'Ancient Trusty Drouthy.'

I remembered the book I had meant to show him. Digging into my haversack, I discarded an anthology of the Metaphysical Poets and volume five of a History of Philosophy, brought out instead a battered paperback called *Cold Mountain: Poems of Han-Shan*.

I passed it over to Doug. 'Have a swatch at that,' I said. 'It's great stuff.'

He opened at the frontispiece, a drawing of Han-Shan with his old friend Shih-Te, crazy Zen hermits, wild-eyed and ragged, mad smiles on their crinkled faces. Doug laughed out loud.

'Right out their heads!'

'The poems are really beautiful,' I said.

'Really knew the score did they?'

'Absolutely.'

Doug turned the pages, taking in one and another of the poems, now and again nodding and smiling. The book looked small in his big hands, the palms mucky and shiny, dirt ingrained from working on the bike. It was still chilly, and the thought of working with grimy hands on the cold metal set my teeth on edge.

'You can borrow the book when I've finished with it,' I said. He nodded thanks and handed it carefully back to me, then picked up again the bit of metal he'd been polishing. It was a small flat disc with a hole at its centre. Holding it up to his eye, he squinted at me through it.

We were beginning to feel mellow, and we talked again of going away. We talked about it often. Doug fancied going to America. I liked the idea of Japan. As yet we had got no further than London. Today what he had in mind was even closer to home.

'Last summer,' he said, 'me and Jenny took the tent and went up to Loch Lomond.' Doug and Jenny would

probably be married in the summer, though for the
moment she was back staying with her parents. 'We found
a great wee place. Right up on the side of Ben Lomond.'
'Cold Mountain!'
'Right!'
We agreed to go.
'I've got to sign on on Friday morning,' he said. 'We can
go right after that.'
He chucked the bit of metal to me. It was warm from his
hands and from the polishing. I could see my face reflected
in its shine. I held it up to my eye and peered at the world
through it, and it looked good.

*

'Bastard!' said Doug. 'Look at that!'
He had dragged out the tent, assembled it on the floor of
his room. The tent had a square base, four sides curving up
to meet at a peak. The frame was solid, the groundsheet
intact, but two of the four sides were mildewed and rotted.
Doug scowled at it.
'Listen man,' he said after a while. 'I was up the
Corporation dump yesterday. Just moseying about. And I
saw these big blinds. Eight feet long they were. Must've
been out a school. Good thick stuff.'
'Thinking we could use them to patch up the tent?'
'Fancy it?'
'Worth a try.'
We drove to the dump on Doug's bike, me on the pillion,
nervous without a helmet. We climbed over the fence,
scrambled about the rubbish till Doug came on the blinds
again. He unrolled them to make sure they were still good.
And he was right about the size. Eight feet long by five feet
wide. We rolled them up tight, made it back over the fence
just as a workman started shouting at us from away across
the dump. But by then it was too late. We were on our way.
As we roared along, I played at being Jack Nicholson in *Easy
Rider*, singing *If ya wanna be a bird*. But I couldn't flap my

arms for clutching our booty, the blinds jutting high in the air like banners.

★

Back at Doug's place we ripped the tent apart, made templates and cut out two new sides from the blinds. The side with the entrance-flap was still whole, so all we had to do was stitch the pieces together.

'My mother's got a sewing machine,' he said. 'She'll be out at work, so we can nip down and use it.'

His mother lived about five minutes walk away. It was a ground floor flat, and Doug let himself in through the back window, then opened the door to me from the inside.

'Breaking and entering,' I said.

'Oh I know,' said Doug. 'Terrible!'

The sewing machine sat on its own table in a corner of the room. Doug set to work right away. I settled down in an armchair, content and at ease, lulled by the clatter and whirr of the machine.

I realised I had been dozing when the noise stopped and I sat up, startled, not sure where I was. Doug was holding up the tent, its two new sections stitched firmly in place.

'Broke a couple of needles,' he said. 'But I think they were duff anyway. All it needs now's waterproofing and we're away.'

'We're away!' I said, and we both laughed, delighted with it all.

★

Friday morning was bright and dry as I stood in George Square, waiting for Doug to arrive on his bike. In my backpack was a sleeping-bag and a change of clothes, a borrowed axe, tin plates and plastic bowls, a spoon, a tin-opener and one sharp knife, a new pen, a blank jotter and the book of Han-Shan's poems. We had stocked up on food – bread and cheese, cereals and fruit, tea and sugar, an assortment of stuff in packets and tins. Doug would be bringing that, somehow, on the back of the bike, along with the tent and his own pack, and an extra helmet for me.

He was twenty minutes late, but that was nothing. I sat down on a bench with my feet up on my rucksack, watched the pigeons and the passers-by. Forty minutes though and I was starting to worry. Then I looked up and saw him across the square, struggling off a bus with his gear and the food and the tent.

I waved and hurried over.

'Bastardn bike!' he said. 'Broke down on me. We'll have to take the train to Balloch and then hitch it.'

'Never mind,' I said. 'Would've been pretty hard to get all this stuff on the back of the bike anyway.'

'Suppose so.'

We shared out the load. Doug took the tent, I carried its frame, and we split up the food into two plastic bags. He'd had a hard morning, wasn't in a good mood. But once we were on the train he cheered up. We ate the first of our food, a Mars bar each, sat back happy as the blue train rattled out through Bowling and Dumbarton, Renton and Alexandria.

'Like going your holidays!' said Doug.

It was good to be moving.

★

At Balloch we set down our things and breathed the clear air. We felt the pace change, ourselves slow down. We took our bearings from Doug's map, fixed our route through Balmaha to Rowardennan. At the neck of the loch, yachts and dinghies and motorboats bobbed at their moorings. We stopped to look, to take it all in, then moved on again, Doug walking out in front along the narrow pavement. An oil-lamp, hung from his rucksack, swung from side to side. To the same rhythm the rods of the tent-frame, tied in a bundle and slung over my shoulder, clanked together at every step.

At the edge of town, on the Balmaha road, we picked our

spot and started to hitch. There was little traffic, mostly private cars, the odd commercial van, but no lorries.

An hour of it and nothing had stopped.

'Think we were Martians,' I said.

'Scotland can be like that,' said Doug. 'One time we were trying to get to Oban, we got stuck at some wee dump for three hours.'

I tried not to think about it. I watched a sparrow, bellyflopped in a tiny puddle, flipping water up and over itself. It flurried off as another car went past.

Doug glowered along the empty road. 'Bastardn bike.'

Up ahead we heard the noise of another engine, and a bus came nosing over a hump in the road. The destination board, tantalising, read *Balmaha*. We looked at each other, agreed, with a shrug, to cut our losses, and flagged it down.

★

This was it. The real thing. The deep of the loch and the blue hills, the furthest peak still covered in snow. We sat on the shingle beach at Balmaha, gazing out at it. We had eaten the first of our bread and cheese, were sharing a bottle of lemonade.

'It's even better up there,' said Doug. 'Where we're going. Thing is, there's even less traffic going to Rowardennan. We're best to start walking, try hitching anything that comes along. It's only about four or five miles.'

The first stretch of road was a steep slope that had us sweating, an irritating prickly itch on the scalp and down the back. But it soon levelled out and we settled to our rhythm, the swing of the oil-lamp, the clank of the tent-frame, the sound of our feet on the road. We took it slow and the rhythm kept us going, we only paused to shift our bundles, switch a bag from hand to hand, or just to look down at the loch away on our left, glimpsed through trees, a level stretch of blue, a glimmer in the sun.

We had gone maybe three miles, stopped to rest at the roadside.

'Not so far now,' said Doug, easing off his pack.

We had seen only five cars, and two of those had been going the opposite way, back to Balmaha. Another came towards us now, a landrover. The driver passed us, then slowed to a stop and backed up.

'Where you off to?' he called out to us, that note of authority in his tone.

'Further up the loch,' said Doug.

'Rowardennan?' said the man.

'Aye.'

'Looks like you're going camping,' said the man, looking straight at the rolled-up tent.

'That's right,' said Doug.

The man shook his head. 'There's no campsite up there. Just the Youth Hostel.'

'Can we not just camp up on the hill?' I asked.

'Not at all,' said the man. 'This is all Forestry Commission land. You'll get fined if you try that caper.'

'Where can we camp then?' asked Doug.

'Nearest site's at Luss,' said the man. 'Across the loch.'

'That's miles away!' said Doug.

'Sorry about that, lads. You'll have to go back. Either that or stay at the hostel. OK?'

'Aye,' said Doug. 'OK.'

The man closed his window, the conversation over, his job done, and the landrover moved on, down the road and out of sight.

'Bastard!' said Doug.

'What now?'

'Well, we're no going to Luss anyway. That's for sure. It's all the way back to Balloch and nine miles up the other side. I think the best thing is to keep going. Nick over the fence a bit further up and camp down at the loch. There's lots of bits hidden away from the road. And if buggerlugs comes back while we're still walking, we'll say we're going to the hostel.'

Half a mile on, we climbed the fence, rounded the base of a hill and laid down our things in a thicket of trees.

'You wait here and watch the stuff,' said Doug. 'I'll see if I can find a good place.'

I watched him go and lay back in the grass, staring up at the sky through a tangle of branches. It wasn't long before I heard him whistle, like a Red Indian. I sat up and saw him loping back towards me.

'Brilliant wee place down there,' he said. 'Right down at the loch. Magic it is.'

We loaded up again and I followed him down.

The spot he'd found was perfect, a little clearing, a hollow carpeted with grass and dead leaves. It was sheltered on two sides by trees and at the back by a steep rock slope. Where the trees stopped, another outcrop of rock ran down to the water's edge a few yards away. The view across the loch was unobstructed, clear.

'This place was just waiting for us,' I said.

'Told you, man,' said Doug. 'Pure magic.'

As quickly as we could, we pitched the tent, then we fetched water from the loch and gathered wood for a fire.

Pure. Magic. Just what the words meant.

★

Doug thought it best to wait till it was dark before lighting the fire.

'Somebody could see the smoke from the road.' So we agreed to have our one cooked meal at night.

'Real boy scout stuff!' I said, as Doug cooked up bacon and beans in the lid of his camping pot. With the dark had come the cold, and we were glad of the fire, its comfort and warmth.

'What's that over there?' I asked, pointing towards the far shore where a line of lights shimmered between the water and the dark bulk of the hills.

'Probably Luss,' said Doug. 'I'll check the map later.'

'I used to go there when I was wee,' I said. 'The-Prettiest-

Village-In-Scotland. That's what it said on the postcards. My auntie had a wee ramshackle hut on the beach, and we went there in the summer for our holidays.'

The endlessness of those summers, myself a tiny skinny boy in khaki shorts, running daft with my cousin Jack. He was a year younger, but bigger and stronger than me. We were friends and enemies a hundred times in a day. Holidays. Holy days. We floated on the loch in an old rubber tyre.

'What happened to the hut?' said Doug.

'There were tons of them,' I said. 'Lots of families had them. But the council bought them all and knocked them down. Said they were an eyesore.'

'That's a real shame,' said Doug. 'Wish you still had it now.'

As the fire faded down and the night grew deeper, we looked up in utter amazement at the stars.

'Look at them,' said Doug. 'Hundreds and thousands. You don't see a tenth of that lot when you're in Glasgow.'

'There's the Plough,' I said. 'And there's Cassiopeia. Big W.'

'There's Orion,' said Doug.

'O'Ryan,' I said, with an Irish accent.

'Aren't the constellations weird?' said Doug. 'I mean, who says that's the way they are?'

'That's what philosophy's like,' I said. 'Making maps of the stars. And arguing about them.'

'We could make up our own!' said Doug.

'Orion looks like a goalkeeper!' I said.

'That up there's a motorbike!'

'There's a sailing ship!'

'An electric guitar!'

And on we went, mapping out the heavens, making our own constellations and giving them names.

The Marie Celeste. The Ice Cream Cone. Bob Dylan. The Wellington Boot. The Holy Grail. O'Ryan the Irish Goalie. The Harley-Davidson. The Buddha. The Hell's

Angel. Han-Shan and Shih-Te.

The fire died out and we raked the ashes with a stick. The constellations moved above us. The prettiest-village-in-Scotland twinkled at us, miles away. We crawled into our sleeping-bags, closed over the tent-flap, doused the oil-lamp, and slept.

★

Neither of us had a watch. 'Living the timeless life,' Doug had said. But it felt early when we woke, a mistiness over the loch and no sound. We splashed our faces, shocked ourselves awake with the icy cold of it. For breakfast we ate cereal, with evaporated milk from a tin.

Doug wanted to go exploring, and moving would keep us warm. So we set out first to climb the hill that sloped up behind the tent. The climb was hard in places, loose soil underfoot, tangled bush and branch that snagged on clothes and hair. But the view from the top made up for it, a wide clear vista down the loch.

'Look at that!' said Doug. And we sat down just to look. At that.

The sun was warmer now, the mist breaking up. It would be a fine day. Over the tops of the trees we could see a section of the road, and away back, a white house we'd passed yesterday, on the way.

'Imagine living up here,' said Doug.

'Be brilliant,' I said. 'You could stay in the city for winter. Make some money and move out here in the spring.'

'Build a log cabin!' said Doug.

We lazed there the whole morning, enjoying the peace, solving all the ills of the universe. We only came down when we felt it was time to eat. The afternoon passed as quickly. Doug went roaming again, along the edge of the loch. I read Han-Shan for a bit, then did some rough drawings in my notebook – the shapes of the hills, the rocks down by the water, the patchwork tent, its friendly comic shape under the trees.

★

Doug had come on a rowing boat tethered to a wooden jetty. He'd been tempted to borrow it, but it was near the white house on the road and he'd been afraid of being seen.

'Pity,' he said. 'We could have gone out to the islands and had a wander about.'

I showed him my sketches and told him a bit more about Han-Shan.

'Him and Shih-Te were mad! This guy came to them, looking for spiritual instruction, and they ran away into the hills. He followed them and they kept popping up behind rocks and shouting *Thief!* at him.'

'Did he catch them?'

'No. They finally disappeared altogether. And the guy gathered up all the poems Han-Shan had left lying about.'

'So he got his instruction after all?'

'In a way.'

'Imagine us up here being like them!' said Doug. 'Scudding about in that wee boat. Running away from the Forestry Commissioner!'

'I don't think it's spiritual instruction he'd be after!'

When it started to get dark we lit the fire again, heated up a pot of packet-soup.

'Remember when we were about twelve we wanted to be beatniks!' said Doug.

'Right!' I said. 'Read about them in *Mad* magazine. Beads and sandals and bongo drums!'

'And after that we were going to be Druids!'

'Seemed like a good idea!'

'And here we are.'

'Here we are.'

'Listen!' said Doug, shooshing me. 'Did you hear that?'

'Voices?' I said.

'They must be coming right across the loch. From Luss.'

141

We listened to bits of a conversation, carried across the water.

– *Ach Moira, you're daft.*

– *No me, I'm no daft.*

– *Coulda fooled me!*

– *Wouldnae be hard.*

'Amazing we can hear it so clear,' said Doug. 'So far away.'

We listened again.

– *I don't know. What's it aboot?*

– *Apples.*

– *I don't know.*

– *Daft apples!*

The voices faded, grew indistinct. Then a last shout.

– *Nothing!*

Laughter. A soft splash, the size of an apple.

– *Nothing!*

'Remember a bit in *Huckleberry Finn* where that happens?' I said.

'That's right!' said Doug. 'Huck's drifting in a canoe and he hears guys talking miles away.'

We stared into the fire, watched it smoulder down.

Voices in the dark. Daft apples. Nothing.

'Must go exploring again tomorrow,' said Doug.

'Right,' I said. 'I'll be Tom Sawyer, you be Huck Finn.'

★

The next day the weather was even better, bright sun in a clear sky, warm enough to lay off our jackets and roll up our sleeves. Late morning found us once more at the crest of our hill. Far off we could see a tiny dark shape, a small boat with a figure in it, moving slowly, slowly across the massive backdrop of the loch and the hazy hills.

'Fishing,' said Doug.

'It's just so much like a Japanese painting I can't believe it. The hills and the wee boat.'

'Wonder if it's the same boat I saw yesterday,' said Doug. 'Down at the jetty.'

We looked over at the white house, saw two children playing, heard their shouts and their laughing carried faintly on the air. A wind sent a ripple over the surface of the water, and the sunlight set it sparkling.

'Aw man!' said Doug, pointing. 'Isn't that just . . .'

He had no words for what it was. Neither did I. We laughed at it. Sun on the water. It sparkled inside us.

★

Later we went wandering, further up the lochside. When we reached a point that looked too difficult to pass, thick bushes blocking us, we headed back, gathering up firewood as we went.

As Doug set to kindling the fire, I read more of Han-Shan.

> *I settled at Cold Mountain long ago.*
> *Already it seems like years.*

'Cold Mountain was his own name,' I told Doug, 'That's what Han-Shan means. Getting back to Cold Mountain means getting back to himself.'

> *Drifting, I prowl the woods and streams.*
> *Linger, watching things themselves.*

'That's us man,' said Doug.

> *The blue sky makes a good cover,*
> *Let heaven and earth go about their changes.*

'Have you thought about when we'll go back?' said Doug.

'How long's the food going to last?'

'Another couple of days. Suppose we could go back then, or else one of us could go to Balmaha and get some more food.'

'Sounds fine,' I said.

After we'd eaten, I took up my notebook and wrote two haiku about the morning up on the hill.

small boat on the loch,
a still black speck
far off hills
faintly blue through mist

trying to talk,
we can only laugh and point –
sun glinting on the loch

★

The third morning I woke feeling bad, a tightness and pressure above the eyes, the beginnings of a headache.

'I'm not feeling too great myself,' said Doug. 'A bit queasy in the stomach. Maybe that cheese is starting to go off. Tasted a bit strong last night.'

The day looked as grey as I was feeling inside, heavy and clouded, a dullness over everything.

Doug must have had more resilience than me. While I hung about the tent feeling miserable, he was off climbing a tree. It seemed like a stupid thing to do. From where I was, it all looked stupid, the whole trip, the pair of us playing at being Red Indians, or Zen men. But the only thing worse than staying here would be going back to Glasgow.

I saw it all through a grey film, separate. The ache got worse and I curled inside my sleeping-bag. I wanted the dark. I wanted to disappear, to be nothing. I got up and moved about, lay down again, slept and woke. My head was splitting in half, down the middle, cleaved in two by the pain. I lay as still as I could.

It started to rain then. I heard it on the leaves outside, then a steady drip and patter on the roof of the tent. That brought a momentary ease. I felt almost peaceful, drawn up inside myself.

Doug came into the tent to shelter, brought a few sticks of wood to keep them dry for later.

'Still feeling bad, man?' he asked.

'Just lying feeling sorry for myself,' I said. 'You know

144

what it's like. Everything's so total.'

'End of the world!' he said.

'Worse!'

We lay on our backs, heard the rain beat harder on the tent.

'That sound always makes me remember being a baby in my pram,' I said. 'Nobody ever believes me. But I really remember it. The pram shoogling along and the rain on the hood, me tucked up safe.'

'I believe you,' said Doug.

'Do you know that Zen question?' I asked. '*What was your original face, before you were born?* It's possible to remember further back than being a baby. Further back than being conceived.'

Back to nothing. Or everything.

'I believe you.'

★

I couldn't eat. By evening the pain was moving towards nausea. I could feel its deep root, knotted.

It was dark now and the rain had stopped. Doug was heating a tin of spaghetti over a smoky, hissing fire. I went in under the trees and I felt the sickness rise in my throat. I watched, with a kind of detached wretchedness, my own vomit spatter the wet leaves. I wiped my watery eyes. I felt weak and shaky, but purged.

Up behind the hill there was a lightness in the sky. The moon must be rising. The hill had hidden it from us the other nights, and we hadn't been up there in the dark. I wanted to see, and I set out to climb it.

The day's rain made the going harder. Branches stung my face and caught my hair. My feet slipped on the wet soil. But I made it to the top, mud on my hands, a scratch on my forehead, my knuckles scraped. I stood and looked up at the full bright moon.

I wiped my hands on my denims and sat down on a rock. The silence and the peace were palpable. I might have been the last man on earth. Everything sat still in that clear light. It touched the contours of the hills, silvered the dripping trees. And down below, the same moon floated in the waters of the loch. I strained to remember bits of Han-Shan's poems.

On top of Cold Mountain, the lone round moon.

This was where he had been, what he had seen. My back seemed to straighten of itself, and I felt the last of the sickness and pain being drawn up out of me. The cold was delight. I breathed it in. I felt a smile come from deep, felt it in my eyes and the corners of my mouth. I smiled at nothing, and the moon smiled back at me with a face I had known forever.

I know the pearl, a boundless perfect sphere.

I heard a movement in the bushes, but felt no fear.
'Thought you might be up here,' said Doug. 'Feeling better?'
'Much.'
'Some night, eh?'
'Look at the moon.'
'Big smiling face!' he said.
We sat, sharing it. We were ancient friends. We had known each other for lifetimes.
'Do you remember when you were wee', said Doug, 'there used to be this advert for Cremola custard? A wee boy spooning it into the mouth on the moon's face?'
'I do!' I said, laughing. 'I remember!'
'I used to find that face really disturbing,' said Doug.
'Me too!' I said. 'Sort of comical and frightening at the same time.'
'That's it,' said Doug. 'I've always remembered it.'
We laughed and looked again at the smiling moon.

★

Next morning we decided to go. Our food was almost finished, and we both felt the need of a hot bath and clean clothes. Taking a chance, we lit one more fire and boiled up water for tea, drank it, sweet, with the last of the evaporated milk.

It was almost sad to see the tent dismantled and packed away. It left a square depression in the leaves underneath. That and the ashes from the fire were the only traces of our stay.

★

On the road, we both felt slightly unreal to be going back.

'Isn't it amazing!' said Doug. 'Best part of a week wi no dope no bevvy no nookie no nothing!'

'Sometimes it's good to stay clear,' I said.

'Sometimes I think you should have been a monk!' said Doug, laughing. 'But listen, man. Seriously. We've got to do this again.'

'Absolutely,' I said.

★

We never did. The way things happen.

★

The sun came out, shimmered again on the loch.

'Look at that,' said Doug. 'Isn't it just . . .'

'Isn't it!'

At Balmaha we stopped, took a last look back at the mountain we didn't reach.

147

STONE GARDEN

He was drifting, jetlagged.

He looked about the room, stared blankly at a map of the world on the wall behind the desk. Then he realised what was different about it. The scale and proportions were what he was used to. The same old Mercator Projection he remembered from battered school textbooks in Geography. Only the point of view had changed. At the right hand edge, the far east, was the Atlantic coast of America. Furthest west was little Britain, the seaboard of Spain and Portugal, Africa. The centre of the map, the focal point, was Japan. Nippon. Sun-origin. Forget the Greenwich Meridian. Time starts and stops here.

The desktop was an uncluttered expanse of immaculate black hardwood, polished to an even sheen. Looking down at it was like gazing into deep dark water. Shining black.

On the desk's perfect surface only a single object rested. It looked like a glass paperweight, a clear globe on a wooden base. He stood up to take a closer look. Inside the globe, as if suspended there, floating, were four smaller globes, each about the size of a child's marble. He reached across to pick the thing up, was surprised that the glass ball came away from the base, had only been cradled in it. From the weight, it didn't even feel like glass, more like perspex. The four little marbles had a rough unfinished look, not perfect spheres, opaque and faintly grey.

Probably some exclusive designer desk-sculpture. Executive Zen. He replaced the globe in its base, gave it a wipe with the cuff of his jacket. He had just sat back down when the door opened and Yamamoto came in. He stood up again and bowed. Yamamoto held out his hand.

'So sorry to keep you waiting.'

'Not at all.'

They exchanged cards.

Yamamoto was fiftyish, short, stocky-built. Gave an impression of contained strength. Expensive double-breasted suit. Greying hair brushed back neat.

'Please.' Motioning him to sit down.

'Thank you.' He noticed him flick a glance at the perspex globe. Perhaps it had been replaced a millimetre out of position. 'I was just admiring your paperweight.'

'Really?' said Yamamoto. 'There's a story behind it. Perhaps I'll tell you sometime.'

'Sounds interesting.'

'It is.' Yamamoto smiled. 'So. You are Scottish.'

'That's right.'

'Do you play golf?'

He said it *pray goruf.*

'Afraid not.'

'Pity.' A brief pause, a beat or two. 'I went to your country once. Just to pray.'

Play.

'Where did you go?'

'Everywhere!' He picked his way through the thicket of names. 'Muirfield. Gleneagles. St Andrews. For me was a kind of pilgrimage.'

So maybe he did mean *pray.*

'I can't believe it. You live there and you don't play.'

'Wrong social class,' he said. 'Too poor as a kid. My game was football.'

'Ah!' Yamamoto laughed. 'This is the Scottish passion!'

'Right!'

'In Japan too this game is, you say catching on? Or taking off?'

'Either. Both.'

'We are going to qualify for World Cup in America.'

'I've been following it on TV. Tonight's the big one, isn't it? You just have to beat Iraq.'

'We will do it. We are strong.'

The drunk he had encountered in the street the night before. Salaryman in a crumpled suit, shirtcollar open, tie loosened. A long day at the office and drinking hard till late. Unsteady on his feet. Face screwed up at the effort of bringing things into focus. Then homing in.

'*Gaijin* no good! Foreigner no good! Specially American! Japan number one nation!'

'Sure,' he had said, '*Ichiban*. Number one.'

Yamamoto was still smiling politeness. 'This is your first time in Kyoto?'

He nodded. 'Last time I was just in Tokyo.'

'Is different here. I think you like it.'

'I'm sure I will.'

A concrete poem he remembered from years ago in some magazine. The Tokyo-Kyoto Express. *Tokyotokyoto-Kyoto* . . .

'So.' Yamamoto looked at his watch. 'Let us talk little business.'

'Fine.'

'Of course, in many ways is difficult time. Like you we have recession'.

Even a year ago he wouldn't have believed that, would have thought it was just a line. But now there were signs. Businesses closing. Empty office blocks. At Shinjuku station he had even seen homeless folk, sleeping rough, sheltered in doorways.

'But this has been interesting week,' said Yamamoto. 'There are signs of important changes. You say, straws in the wind?'

He nodded, heard the words as very Japanese, like a line from a haiku. Straws in the wind.

Yamamoto continued. 'You know about the failure of our rice crop?'

'I read about it.'

'So we have to agree to import rice from America, Australia. Is a big step for us. Does not come easy! And I think is thin end of wedge.'

Again, the way he said it made the image tangible, physical. A wedge of solid wood forced in, hammered home.

'Most likely America will make condition. That we drop tariff on other things. Reduce trade barrier.' He paused a moment. 'This is good news I think for all foreign companies. Should make things easier. More open. Now. You have presentation to show me?'

'Yes, of course.' He brought out the portfolio, handed it to Yamamoto who took it with a slight nod of the head. For what seemed a long time he turned the pages, fingered each fabric sample, made little noises that could be approval, once or twice a kind of grunt. Then with another nod he said, 'Very fine.' And he placed the portfolio on that vast black desk. 'The colours are like your Scottish Highlands.'

'That's it,' he said. 'That's it exactly!'

A telephone rang somewhere close, a muted highpitched warble.

'Excuse me.' Yamamoto flipped open the armrest on his chair and the sound became fractionally louder. He lifted out a miniature cordless handset from its niche, spoke briskly into it.

'*Hai, moshi moshi, Yamamoto san . . .*'

The exchange was brief. Talking Japanese, Yamamoto seemed more aggressive, his voice more guttural and gruff. When he had finished, he clicked the phone back in its place, shut the armrest, glanced at his watch.

'So sorry. Is something very crucial I have to deal with. I have to cut our meeting short.'

'I understand.'

'Perhaps we can meet later?'

'I'd appreciate that.'

'You are free this evening?'

'Of course. Yes. Absolutely.'

'Good. If you tell my secretary where you are staying, we will have you picked up. Say 7.30?'

The meeting was over.

Out in the street he grinned at nothing in particular. The sun was warm. He took off his jacket, slung it over his shoulder, hooked on his finger. He started walking just anywhere, down the street. He didn't mind the noise, the crowds, the traffic. He was in Kyoto, had a free afternoon, nowhere he had to be. Life could be worse.

★

The stone garden at Ryoan-ji Temple was what he wanted to see. No matter that it was the tourist thing to do. He wanted to feel that sense of space he had read about, that emptiness. On the map it didn't look too far, a short bus trip.

The ticket system was a miracle of efficiency. Take a ticket when you get on the bus. The number on it is the fare stage. When it's time to get off check the lit-up display at the front. Under your number is what you owe. And next to the white-gloved driver, a machine that gives change.

Perfection.

At the temple he had to queue, pay to get in. His ticket had a drawing of the rocks, the raked sand. He would keep it to use as a bookmark.

The path to the garden was signposted. He followed it, breathing deep the clear air. Walking along he kept hearing a sound, repeated at regular intervals. A deep beat – *thunk* – like wood on hollow wood. He could hear it more clearly as he came up to a wooden bridge over a running stream. Above the ripple of the running water came that same beat repeated, every ten or twelve seconds. *Thunk.* He stopped on the bridge and looked down. In midstream a length of bamboo had been set in place, angled over a rock.

One end, open, faced upstream, so it gradually filled with water, till the weight tipped it over and it emptied out again. Empty, it dropped back, hit the rock underneath. *Thunk.* The whole thing was a kind of kinetic sculpture, designed just to make that noise. He found it extraordinarily comforting. Just the simplicity, the completeness of it. He stood for a while leaning on the bridge, looking, listening. It made him smile.

At the entrance to the garden he had to take off his shoes, slide into slippers. The place must be crowded, going by the number of shoes stacked in racks. He gave a nod to the attendant, an old man in a thick plaid shirt and baseball cap, and he shuffled in over polished wooden floorboards.

He shouldn't have expected silence in the place, not with so many people. But it was the level of the noise that surprised him, louder as he got near. Babble of voices, the high excited prattle of schoolchildren, and some tape-recorded tourist guide blaring out.

The garden itself looked incredible. The raked gravel intensely white. The rocks placed just so. But there was nowhere just to sit quiet and take it in. As one group of schoolchildren was marched out, another in identical black and white uniforms was marched in. A few of them caught his eye, called out *He-rro!* and gave him the two-finger peace sign.

'*Konnichi wa!*' he called back, and they laughed, amazed and delighted. The *gaijin* speaks. What was that Doctor Johnson thing about women preaching? A dog on its hind legs. Not that it's done well, but that it's done at all.

'So this is it!' said a young American to his friend. 'Rio-angie.' He pronounced the second part like the girl's name.

A cold bedsit in Edinburgh, so long ago. A girl he'd known called Angie. A guitar-track by Bert Jansch. Angie had given him a book called *Zen Flesh Zen Bones*.

'Seriously awesome,' said the American, looking around.

Another bunch of Japanese tourists came in, all wearing

153

wigs – a plastic samurai headpiece, a silver frightwig, a dayglo green Mohican tuft. They clowned around, posed for pictures in front of the garden.

Behind him he heard a loud English voice, a man asking, unironic, 'Tell me. What exactly does *Ah so* mean?'

Time to go.

Turning, he glanced in to one of the inner rooms, caught the eye of a young monk looking out. The look was a kind of amused detachment. The monk bowed and he did the same. A glimpse in.

He collected his shoes, made his way back down the path towards the gate. The water-sculpture made him smile again.

Thunk.

Further on he sang mindlessly to himself, a single phrase over and over, the fingerpicking riff to Bert Jansch's *Angie*.

Persistence of memory. *Di diddly dang.* So long ago. Zen flesh Zen bones.

★

He had showered and changed, sat watching the TV in his hotel room, channel-popping, not able to follow the commentary. More than one channel carried the same report on the Empress. Old newsreel footage of her early life, her wedding, great state occasions. Then the same sequence, over and over, long shot of her car driving out through the palace gates, fuzzy close-up through the car window, the Empress giving the slightest bow, a graceful inclination of the head.

At first he thought it was an obituary, that the Empress had died. Then he realised it couldn't be. There were other news items, and that wouldn't be happening. Some politician had killed himself. A jogger had been shot with a crossbow. The Japanese football team were getting geared up for tonight's big game with Iraq. But the broadcast ended with that same image. The Empress inclining her head.

At 7.30 the phone rang. A lady was downstairs waiting for him.

He saw her when he stepped out of the lift. Standing by the desk looking poised and contained. Neat in a dark suit, a green silk scarf tied loose at the throat. That black black hair in a kind of pageboy cut, short at the back, hanging longer at the sides. She turned her head and smiled at him.

That was all. Just turned her head and smiled. And it turned him inside out, an implosion in his chest. Awkward and tongue-tied as some dumbstruck schoolboy he stepped forward and shook her hand.

★

Her name was Yumiko. She spoke English with the slightest trace of a French accent. Her father's business had taken the family to Paris where she had grown up, gone to school. This he learned in the taxi on the way to meet Yamamoto.

'How is your French?' she asked him.

'About as good as my Japanese.'

'Fine.' She smiled. 'We'll stick to English!'

Her husband – mentioned very early in the proceedings – was French, a business associate of Yamamoto's.

'Will I meet him? Will he be there tonight?'

'He's at a conference in Osaka. But maybe later in the week. How long will you be staying?'

'Don't know yet. It depends.'

'On what?'

'How it goes.'

'Of course.'

She did occasional translation work for Yamamoto, into English and French, when he needed it in a hurry.

'He invited me along tonight', she said, 'to make things easier for you. In case you should need an interpreter.'

'Well,' he said, suddenly awkward again, 'I'm glad he did.'

A moment's silence, the taxi gliding through traffic, then

she asked, 'Have you had a chance to see any of Kyoto?'

'This afternoon,' he said. 'I went to Ryoan-ji.'

'Oh yes?'

'It was murder,' he said.

'Murder?' She looked alarmed.

'The crowds. It was like being at the Vatican.'

She laughed, and he noticed she didn't cover her mouth with her hand like other Japanese women.

'You should go back early in the morning,' she said. 'When it's quiet.'

'I might just do that,' he said. Then he told her about the water-sculpture, how much he'd been taken with it.

She nodded. 'It's called *shishi-odoshi*. I also like this very much'.

'*Shishi-odoshi*,' he said. And she laughed again, at his earnestness, or his pronunciation, or whatever.

★

Yamamoto had arranged a surprise. After they had eaten, they went through to the lounge bar. On one wall was a giant TV screen, and they settled to watch transmission of the game, the final World Cup qualifier, Iraq v Japan, live from Qatar.

'I thought you would like this,' said Yamamoto.

'It's incredible!' he said. 'Thank you!'

Their table was near the screen, and he sat between Yamamoto and Yumiko. Turning to her, he asked, 'How about you? Do you like football?'

'It's all right,' she said. 'My husband is a fanatic. He still thinks Michel Platini is God.'

On the screen, the pre-match build-up was interrupted by the same news items as before.

'What's the story with the Empress?' he asked Yumiko.

'She had some kind of collapse. They took her to hospital. It's very strange. She's a little paralysed and she can't speak.'

The car moving out through the gates. The close-up,

bow of the head. Tiredness and sadness in the eyes.

Next up was the suicide story. Nomura Shusuke. Age fifty-eight.

'I knew this fellow,' said Yamamoto. 'Well, I met him once or twice. He was leader of right-wing party, Kazenoto. And this newspaper, *Asahi*, published cartoon making fun of him. So he had meeting with directors of the paper, to make protest. And right in middle of meeting he pulled out two guns and shot himself.'

The footage on the screen showed the room where it had happened, homed in on a spatter of bloodstains on the pale carpet.

'Crazy,' said Yumiko.

Now on the screen was an advert, he couldn't work out what for. A manic housewife hitched up her skirt, slapped both her thighs and ran screaming and laughing from the kitchen. Then it was back to the football. Japan's Dutch manager said the team would lose over his dead body.

'Not another one,' said Yumiko.

'Yes,' said Yamamoto. 'He has become Japanese!'

Yumiko laughed, covered her mouth with her hand. Yamamoto ordered a round of drinks as the sides lined up for the kick-off.

★

It was into the last five minutes and Japan were going to win. They were 2–1 ahead, held possession in midfield. Ramos the Japanese Brazilian flicked the ball up languidly, stroked it with the outside of his foot into space on the right wing. Kazu the striker chased after it but couldn't keep it in play. It didn't matter. It was more time wasted, seconds ticked away towards victory.

The drink and the atmosphere were getting to him. He heard himself shout out *Ganbate!* Go for it.

Yamamoto laughed, slapped him on the back. The room was jampacked now. Word had spread, and more and more kept crowding in to share the great triumph. His eyes nipped from the smoke. He rubbed them, blinked, looked across at Yumiko. She was side-on to him, chin resting on her left hand. Meant he could gaze at her profile, take it in. The hair, curve of the neck, shape of the eyes. The small nose, full mouth. Sum of the parts, but so much more. Perhaps she sensed him watching, turned and looked straight at him, half-smiled. It felt like he had known her a long time.

The drink, the atmosphere.

Something was happening in the game. The ninety minutes up. Into injury time. Iraq throwing everything into one last attack and winning a corner. Cut to a section of Japanese supporters in the crowd. Mostly young, all dressed in royal blue replica strips, chanting *Nippon!* Movements choreographed like aerobics, punch with the left hand. *Nippon!* Take two steps and punch with the right. *Nippon!* The people about him in the room started chanting along. *Nippon!*

The corner was swung over. Somebody connected and the ball was in the net. The Japanese players looked in shock. The ball was centred. They kicked off. The whistle blew. Finished. Word was already through from the other games. Saudi and South Korea had both won, would go through. Japan were out.

The aerobic supporters on the terracing were in tears, hugging each other, sobbing. Players hung their heads, threw themselves to the grass, beat the ground.

The reaction in the room was anguish, disbelief. One man beat the table with his head. Another howled like a dog. More drink was ordered.

'I can't believe it,' he said to Yamamoto. 'I thought these things only happened to us. I mean it is *so* Scottish! Going out on goal difference. Glorious defeat.'

Yamamoto managed a smile. 'Unfortunately, is also very Japanese.'

★

Back at the hotel, his head fuzzy, he decided to soak in the hot tub before bed. The communal bath was down in the basement. There were directions in his room, the clothes he should wear laid out at the foot of the wardrobe – starched black and white patterned *yukata*, plain navy blue robe to wear over it, rectangular flip-flop straw sandals. He bowed to his image in the mirror, laughed. Then the strange thing happened. The image seemed to shift, go slightly out of focus, like somebody else looking back at him, somebody Japanese. Yet somehow this other was himself, was someone he had once been.

The moment passed, though it left him shaken, staring once more at his own everyday face. He took himself out and along the corridor, down in the lift.

The attendant gave him a towel, a blue plastic basket for his clothes. He folded them up neatly, slid open the glass door into the steaming room. At intervals along the walls were taps, and in front of each a small plastic bucket. He crouched down and ran the hot water, soaped himself all over. He filled the bucket and emptied it over himself, repeated it three, four times till all the soap was rinsed off. Then he stepped into the bath.

It was only when he had eased down into it, immersed himself, untensed in the deep heat, that he looked across at the other men in the tub. There were four of them talking in those low guttural voices, quickfire aggressive bursts. They were all covered in elaborate tattoos that marked them as *yakuza*, gangsters. One had a dragon curving over his shoulder, another what looked like Mount Fuji on his chest. The third was turned to the side, and all he could see was the tip of a stylised branch of cherry blossom. The fourth man said something and laughed, climbed out of the bath. Across his back was an image from an *ukiyo-e* print, an elegant lady of the floating world.

He thought of Yumiko. The curve of her neck. Light shimmered on the surface of the water. Steam hung in the air. The deep gruff voices rumbled, boomed. He felt lightheaded, unreal.

★

Yamamoto had to be out of town, wouldn't be able to see him till the next afternoon. Another free day in Kyoto. He could get used to this.

Late morning he found himself downtown, wandering through a shopping arcade, an indoor marketplace, row after row of stalls. One whole section was a fishmarket, brisk sea-smells, the stink of something pungent and raw, catching the back of the throat. Raised voices haggled, hustled as he passed. The same highpitched mantra was called out to him again and again. *Irrashaimase!* Welcome!

Further over were fruit and vegetable stalls, stacked, then places selling other kinds of food. Beanpaste cakes and loose green tea, noodles, pickles, blocks of tofu, takeaway savouries – sushi and deepfried tempura. Maybe later he would buy a lunchbox, find a park bench. He crossed another aisle and was in a different section again, souvenir city, T-shirts and baseball caps, kamikaze headbands and samurai paper-knives. He bought a postcard of the stone garden at Ryoan-ji.

Making his way out, he found himself back in the food section, among the fruit and vegetables. He stopped in front of a basket of orange-red persimmons, ripe and perfect. He picked out two that were just right. The old woman selling them smiled and nodded encouragement, as if he had made the best possible choice. She talked away at him as she wrapped them, put them in a paper bag, her voice a high nasal singsong. All he could do was smile and nod and bow. As he walked on, the weight of the fruit in his hand, he felt ridiculously elated. Then up ahead, twenty, thirty yards away, he thought he saw Yumiko.

But it couldn't be. In a city with a population of over a million, to bump into the one person. And even then, to think he would recognise her at that distance, someone he hardly knew, seen from the back, in a throng of other people, half of them small thin blackhaired Japanese women! It wasn't possible. But again he caught a glimpse of the woman, through a gap, and there was definitely something, a familiarity in that turn of the head. Then she was gone again, lost in the crowd.

He started moving towards her, and each time she reappeared he was more sure, and less sure. The clothes were wrong, blue jeans and a denim jacket, the collar turned up. But still there was that something, in her bearing, the way she moved. He was close now, close enough to call out. But he didn't, felt foolish. Then she turned round and looked at him.

Just turned round and looked. Again. That way. And Godalmighty yes it really was her!

She smiled, surprised.

'I thought it was you,' he said.

'Well,' she said. 'It was. It is!'

'Wonder what the odds are. City of a million.'

'Million and a half.'

'Even more incredible!'

Another of those little silences hung there between them, nothing said. Then he broke it, came out with 'Would you like a persimmon?' Heard the words out there, his own voice strange to him.

She laughed. 'Sounds like an offer I can't refuse!'

'I bought two,' he said, as if that explained anything. She reached in and took one, wrapped in tissue, from the bag he held out.

'*Merci*,' she said. 'Thank you. *Arigato gozaimasu*.' She sniffed at the fruit. '*Kaki*. That's what they're called in Japanese. Don't you think it sounds like autumn?'

'*Kaki*,' he said, trying out the word.

'When I was very small,' she said, 'we used to visit my grandparents in the country, in Kyushu, near Fukuoka. And it must have been this time of year. And I always associate the two things, the smell and taste of the fruit, and all these red red fields with crows flying over going *Ka! Ka!*'

161

'*Kaki*,' he said. 'That's beautiful.'

'Our famous Japanese poetic sensibility!' she said, suddenly ironic, European. 'Listen, have you got time for a coffee?'

'Took the words right out my mouth!'

★

The coffee shop was crowded, mostly young or middle-aged women, in twos and threes. The tables and chairs were white wrought-iron. Pale hessian-covered walls hung with framed colour photos of Fuji, the Grand Canyon, the Matterhorn, Niagara Falls. Laidback easy-listening on the sound system. The old Cyndi Lauper hit, *Time after time*.

'It's nothing special,' said Yumiko as they sat down. 'But the coffee's all right.'

'It's fine,' he said. 'It's great.'

The waitress brought them two glasses of water. Yumiko ordered two *cafés au lait*. He picked up his glass, read out the little inscription printed on the side, a kind of poem.

A glassful of drops.
Each drop is tomorrow's dream.
Sip your dreams by drops.

'A haiku!' he said.

'More like high kitsch,' she said.

'*Haikitsch!*' he said. 'That's good!' He took a drink from the glass. Sipped his dreams by drops. 'You get some wonderful stuff on T-shirts.'

'It's one of the first things visitors notice.'

'Saw a couple of nice ones this morning. *Body Fitness Believing*. And what was the other one? *Blue Persons Racing Team*.'

'I almost don't notice them any more,' she said. 'The last one that caught my eye was *Humble Mojo Wetback*.'

'It does have a ring to it!'

162

The waitress brought their coffee, discreetly placed the bill face-down beside his cup. Yumiko had put the persimmon in front of her on the table. She picked it up, sniffed its fragrance again.

Kaki. Taste and smell of autumn.

'I watched the news on TV this morning,' he said. 'Mucked about and got this channel with English subtitles.'

'Mucked about,' she said. 'Sounds a very Scottish thing to do.'

He laughed. 'But what got me was the weather forecast. Right at the end it showed a map of Japan, with areas marked in red. And this was where the maple leaves were turning. And they gave a report on the best areas for viewing! I mean what a culture! What a beautiful thing to do!'

'I can see you're in love with the place.'

'How could you not be? Maple-viewing!'

She smiled. 'The French also love these things. The whole aesthetic.'

'They like Zen?'

'They like *Japonisme*. It's not always the same thing.'

She shrugged in a way that was very French, gave a little nod of the head that was wholly Japanese.

'So you spend half your time here, the other half in Paris?'

'That's the way it works out, yes.'

'Which do you prefer?'

'It's hard. When I'm here I feel European. When I'm there I feel Japanese.'

'Sounds tough!'

'You may not have noticed. But it's not easy here for women. Especially westernised women who've picked up unacceptable habits. Like speaking their minds!'

'I thought all that was changing,' he said. 'I was reading about women being appointed to government posts.'

'Only one or two. A drop in the ocean.' She sipped her coffee. 'You know you were asking about the Empress? This sudden illness and not being able to speak? Well, there's been speculation that the whole thing is psychosomatic. It seems a lot of the old hard-line traditionalists at the palace have really disapproved of her speaking out. And they've made her life a misery.'

'Caused this breakdown?'

'Silenced her.'

'Incredible.'

'And that's how it is here. Even the Empress gets hammered down.' She smiled again. 'I get a lot of it because of my Western ways. If I forget to speak with just the right amount of female deference to some businessman, I'm put in my place with real ferocity. No, I mean it. I can feel it right here, in the pit of my stomach. Like being punched.'

'I know the feeling. If somebody's having a go at you.'

'Even our friend Yamamoto, who's really quite liberal. He's caught me by surprise a few times.'

He remembered the gangsters in the hot tub, told her about them.

'They probably own the hotel,' she said. 'Or at least have a share in it.' He must have looked surprised. She shrugged. 'It's the way it is.'

On the tape, Joni Mitchell was singing *Chinese Café*.

'This is a great song,' he said.

Nothing lasts for long.

'I know it,' she said. 'I love the way she takes these old songs and weaves them into it, like they're playing on the jukebox.'

Here in this Japanese café the waitress came over and asked if they wanted more coffee. He didn't. But then he didn't want Yumiko to leave. Didn't want this to end.

Nothing lasts for long.

Yumiko picked up the persimmon, said 'Let's go and eat these. I know a good place.'

★

The little square was quiet, though it wasn't too far back off the main road. In the centre was an old wooden shrine, grey and weathered, doors shut and barred. A bike rested against the steps. Houses backed onto the square, modern two-storey blocks. From an open window came the sound of a samisen, not a tape but the real thing, somebody practising scales and patterns. In the far corner stood a red vending machine selling cold drinks. Coke. Pocari Sweat. Ice Tea. They sat on a bench under a willow tree, eating persimmons on a perfect autumn day.

The fruit's rich sticky sweetness filled his mouth, left a subtle, rounded aftertaste, far back. He looked across at Yumiko who was delicately licking her fingers.

'*Oishi desu ne?*' he said. Delicious, isn't it?

'*Hai!*' she said. '*So desu!*' And they laughed, and he couldn't remember when he'd last felt this happy.

'It's really strange,' he said. 'I feel so at home here. I know a lot of folk don't.'

A sudden memory came to him, from his childhood, playing in a Glasgow back-court, and he told her about it.

'We used to play this game called Best Fall. Somebody would crouch down with a bit of wood for a machinegun. And the rest of us would take turns at running up to him and being cut down, dying a horrible death. The more spectacular the better! Now, the thing is, in the films we saw and the comics we read, the Japanese were always the baddies. I mean, it wasn't *that* long after the war. But for some reason, when we played these games, I always wanted to be a Jap soldier. I could see myself in the leggings and the wee cap, and I'd run up and launch myself into the air, yelling out *Banzai!* at the top of my voice.'

'I can just picture it!' she said.

'And then there was a time – you know, I'd just about forgotten this! I was nineteen and I'd hitched through to Edinburgh to see some stuff at the Festival. And I wandered into this photographic exhibition in some church hall. It must have been free! And I stopped in front of this picture. Big black and white print. A Buddhist monk with his head bowed. Mount Fuji in the background. And I just stood there staring at it and couldn't move. Absolutely rooted to the spot. Transfixed. And the next thing I knew I had tears in my eyes, rolling down my face.'

'It must have touched something deep,' she said. 'A memory.'

'You mean, like from another time? Another life?'

'Who knows?'

He remembered that *other*, looking back at him from the mirror in his hotel room.

'Do you believe in all that?' he asked. 'Reincarnation?'

'Part of me does.'

'The Japanese part?'

'Maybe. I don't really understand it. But sometimes you just catch a glimpse, and it seems to make sense. Or you can find yourself thinking, I know this place.'

'Or this person?'

'Yes.'

Again a small silence between them. This quiet square. Sound of a samisen. The two of them sitting there, brought together by time and circumstance.

Yumiko opened up a brown paper bag she'd placed beside her on the bench. On their way here, in one of the winding sidestreets, she had stopped at a stall, bought two lunchboxes. Now she unpacked them, handed him one. Assortment of sushi – rice wrapped in toasted *nori*, stuffed tofu pouches, little blocks of omelette. Thin slices of pickled ginger. A tiny plastic bottle of soya sauce, shaped like a fish. Neatly folded napkin. Wooden chopsticks in their own paper envelope. Everything just so. The effect was exquisite, gave a sense of formality even to this, eating a packed lunch on a park bench.

He took out the chopsticks, snapped them apart.

'*Itadakimas!*'

'*Bon appetit!*'

When they'd finished eating, they sat for a while, not talking. A young couple, maybe eighteen or nineteen, were passing through the square. They came over and bowed, and the boy handed Yumiko a disposable camera, a small green cardboard box. They wanted their picture taken. Yumiko smiled, squinted through the viewfinder, asked them to step back a bit, got them in frame and clicked. The boy thanked her and took the camera back, raised it to his own eye to take a picture of him and Yumiko sitting on the bench. The boy motioned to them to move closer together, and they did, elbows touching. He could smell her perfume, something French and subtly floral, a hint of jasmine. The camera clicked. The moment was caught.

Now Yumiko was saying something to the boy. She rummaged in her handbag, brought out a business card, wrote on the back of it and handed it over. There was more bowing and thanking, and the couple went, waving back as they left the square.

'What was that about?' he asked.

'I asked him to send me the picture he took of us. A souvenir.'

She was already placing the moment in time, framing it, consigning it to the past. Something to look back at.

'I could send you a copy,' she said. 'Make one of these colour photocopies.'

'I'd like that.' He didn't have a card with him, searched through his pockets, found the stub from his JAL boarding pass. He wrote his name and address on the back, handed it to her. She took out another business card, wrote on it. It was her husband's card. Rene. Kyoto and Paris addresses. The same in Japanese on the reverse. She had put a little stroke through *Rene*, written *Yumiko* underneath. On the back she had written what he took to be the *kanji* for her name.

'*Yumiko?*' he asked, pointing to it. She nodded. He put the card carefully in his pocket. It was all going too fast. Exchange of addresses. Been nice. Keep in touch. Goodbye. She must have sensed it too, turned to him again.

'So tomorrow you see Yamamoto?'

'That's right.'

'Then you go home.'

'The day after. Back to Tokyo and out from there.'

KyotokyotokyoTokyo

'What about you?' he said. 'When does Rene get back?'

'The same day you go. He said he'd call tonight from Osaka.'

He realised the samisen had stopped, became aware of its absence.

'You are also married?' she said, more a statement than a question.

'Yes.'

'Any kids?'

He shook his head. 'Decided against it.'

'Like us,' she said. 'Not what we wanted.'

An old woman came into the square, was walking round the shrine. She picked up leaves, twigs, berries from the ground, dropped them into a plastic bag.

'What's your wife's name?' asked Yumiko.

'Anne.'

'And what does she do?'

'Teaches English. In a high school.'

'Tough job.'

He nodded. He found it difficult to focus on his life back home. It seemed far away, in time as well as space. The old woman with her plastic bag had found a single glove on the ground, in against the steps of the shrine. She picked it up and put it on her right hand, flexed the fingers. The glove was soft, off-white. The woman laughed, delighted. She caught Yumiko's eye, came over and started talking. She was dressed in an old grey smock, black baggy trousers. Her craziness seemed harmless, childlike, for all the world like some mad Zen character in a Hokusai sketchbook. He couldn't follow any of what she was saying, but Yumiko seemed happy enough talking to her. The old woman laughed again, waved her gloved hand in benediction, went on her way.

'What was she saying?'

'Nothing much,' said Yumiko. 'Just wishing us well. She thought we were a couple.'

'Nice.'

She smiled. 'Feel like walking a bit?'

★

They walked, down narrow streets to the Kamu River and back again, through a park, along the main drag and into a huge *dipato* store, just for a look. Late afternoon they sat in a little tearoom she knew – dark panelled wood, traditional low tables, *shoji* paper screens opening onto a miniature rock garden, water trickling over stones. They sipped green tea, ate soft *mochi* ricepaste cakes. A tape played the sweet piercing music of a *shakuhachi* bamboo flute.

'It was either this or McDonald's,' she said.

He laughed, sang a jingle he'd heard on TV. *'Macudonarido!'*

'The place is getting to you!' she said.

'I know!' he said. 'I know.'

He drank more tea, the taste of it flat and pleasantly bitter. 'Maybe I'll get to come back. If it works out tomorrow. I mean, if the meeting with Yamamoto goes well.'

'I'm sure it will,' she said. 'I think he liked you. That football business was good.'

'I suppose that's what it was,' he said. 'Football business!'

'When you went to his office, did he tell you about his paperweight?'

'That globe thing, with the beads in it?'

'That's the one.'

'Not really. I noticed it right enough. Only thing on his desk! All he said was, there's a story to it.'

'Well, if he tells you the story, you're in!'

'Good,' he said. 'Thanks.'

He looked out at the little rock garden, outside but somehow included in the room.

'I guess you didn't make it back to Ryoan-ji,' she said.

'Not yet.'

'Another time.'

Again that sense of things going too fast, slipping away. He felt it in his stomach, in his chest. An emptiness.

'I have to go,' she said.

From his jacket pocket he brought out the postcard he'd bought of Ryoan-ji, handed it to her. 'A souvenir.'

'Could you write something on the back?'

He thought about it, wrote.

Haikitsch

Japanese café.
Sip your dreams by drops.
Nothing lasts for long.

Out in the street, it was just beginning to get dark. Purples and reds in the sky. Warm yellow lights in the shops and cafés and bars. Neon *kanji*. They walked to the corner and she waved down a passing taxi.

'It's been a really nice day,' he heard himself say.

'Yes.'

'You realise this might be it. I mean, it's quite possible I won't see you again. Ever.'

'If it's meant, it'll happen,' she said. 'And you do have my phone number!'

The taxi door swung open automatically.

'Right then,' he said. 'Goodbye. *Sayonara. Au revoir.*'

She took his hand, held it a moment lightly. 'See you.'

Even climbing into the cab she did with effortless grace, and the door was closed and the cab moving off, and he knew if she turned and looked back at him they would meet again, and he concentrated hard, tried to will it, just turn your head look back at me and wave, and she did.

★

He had food sent up to his room, tempura and rice, pickles and miso soup. He tried to read the business page of the

Japan Times, but he couldn't concentrate. *US targets financial marts./Leading index up but gloom still prevails.* He watched a samurai drama on TV.

He had meant to call Anne, but he kept misjudging the time. He was out of synch. Nine hours ahead, so right now for her it was mid-morning and she'd be at work. The chalk face. Trying to teach a bunch of adolescents in a housing scheme. Scheme of things. A whole other reality.

He flicked through the paper again. An article caught his eye, under the headline *Deus Ex Machina*, the story of a mechanical priest installed in a Yokohama cemetery.

This ecumenical 'ghost in the machine' can conduct ceremonies for deceased from Shinto, Shingon, Rinzai, Soto and Christian faiths. After the ceremony the robopriest ascends into the ceiling.

He was tired.

He took out the card Yumiko had given him, read her name, turned it over and looked at the Japanese script. The card smelled of her perfume. He thought of phoning her, changed his mind, put the card on the bedside table, propped against the base of the reading lamp.

★

He woke early and couldn't get back to sleep. He put on his old T-shirt and shorts, his tracksters and training shoes, and headed out on the road. His intention was to run to Ryoan-ji. He had worked out the way. But somewhere he took a wrong turn, found himself heading out of the city, up into the hills. He decided just to go with it, one foot after the other, see where it led.

The road was narrow, winding. The traffic was just beginning to pick up, and he ran on the right, face-on to what was coming. A couple of times it was too close, a heavy truck, a bus off a tight bend. As soon as he could, he turned onto a side-road, kept climbing. He passed the massive wooden gateway to a temple, stopped and turned back, looked in. A bell was struck, clang of wood on iron. A row of black-robed monks crossed the compound, shaven heads bowed. Again that sense of something remembered. He shivered, his T-shirt, the back of his neck, damp with sweat. He ran on.

Further up he branched off again, along a dirt track that led through woods, past a grove of bamboo. It was hard going now, real slog. The track came to an end in a thicket of pine trees, and up through it was a rough narrow path. He kept on, every step an effort. He pulled up at the sudden shock of something clinging, sticking to his face, like thick tacky thread. He clawed and tore at it, strands of spiderweb catching at him. He looked up, saw the huge span of it, strung between the trees, giant orange-bodied spiders hung there, predatory. He ran on again, trying to be careful, look where he was going, but it happened three more times, he ran smack into the tangle of it. The last time it caught his mouth and he spat and spat, wiped at it with the back of his hand. After that he walked, one hand out in front of him. Made it into a clearing. Sat on a rock. Breathed hard.

From here, the way the hills curved, he couldn't see the city at all, just the tops of the trees, the odd small building in the distance. Gradations of autumn colouring, from gold through rust. One patch of intense red must be maple trees turning. Maybe they would be on tonight's weather map, with a guide to the best vantage-point.

A slight breeze chilled the small of his back where he'd sweated most. He had to keep moving or he would stiffen up. From somewhere he could smell woodsmoke and he tried to head in that direction, follow his nose. The trees thinned out and even the semblance of a path disappeared. He was picking his way over bare rock. Then he came round an outcrop and there it was, sheltered in the lea. A rickety wooden shack, huddled as if thrown there by the wind, and next to it a single old gnarled dwarf pine that looked as if it had grown right out of the rock. The smoke he had smelled was curling out through an aperture in the roof of the shack.

He called out good morning. *Ohio gozaimasu!* A screen

door slid open and an old man grinned out at him.

'*Ohio gozaimasu!*'

They bowed to each other and the old man laughed. He wore monk's robes, an old woollen cardigan on top. When he laughed his whole face crinkled up. Most of his front teeth were missing. His skin was brown, mottled with the darker brown of liver spots on the backs of his hands, on the top of his bald head.

'*Amerikajin?*' the old man asked.

'*Ie,*' he said. No. '*Sukoturandojin.*'

'Ah!' The old man looked pleased, laughed again, motioned him to come in. '*Dozo.*'

He bent and unpicked his laces, prised off his muddy shoes and left them at the door.

Inside, the hut was warm from the old stove against the far wall. On top of it sat a shiny aluminium kettle, a chipped ceramic teapot. Straw matting on the floor. The window a shoji screen, its paper panels yellowed, patched here and there with assorted bits and scraps, some that looked like Christmas giftwrap, red and green. A few books lay on a low table in the middle of the floor. The old man's futon and quilt were rolled up in the corner. The place smelled of the straw mats, old and dusty, the woodsmoke from the fire, tang of dried fish, a hint of incense, maybe pine.

He managed to make it clear that his Japanese was minimal. And the old man had no English at all. So their communication would have to be through mime and good will.

He indicated he was thirsty, swigged from an invisible glass. The old man nodded, brought him water in a cup.

'*Arigato.*'

The old man laughed again. '*Sukoturandojin!*' And he mimed pumping with his elbows, whined out a nasal and just about recognisable bagpipe version of *Auld Lang Syne*.

Should auld acquaintance be forgot.

They both laughed at that. Then the old man made a pot of strong green tea, brought it to the table with two bowls.

173

He looked around, took in more of the room. Behind him was a small shrine. Dried flowers in a vase. Iron incense-holder. A kind of urn. A brass bowl-shaped bell. On the wall behind hung a piece of calligraphy drawn with thick bold strokes, and beside that, curiously, an old tinted photo of a World War II battleship. Above that was the same map of the world he'd seen in Yamamoto's office, Japan at the centre of things. And above that again, spread out, was the old Imperial rising sun flag.

Nippon.

The old man had brought out a glazed clay flask, was pouring sake into two little cups.

He sipped, said 'Cheers. *Kanpai!*'

'*Kanpai!*' said the old man, and knocked back his drink, filled both cups again.

Maybe it was tiredness from the run. And not being used to drinking this early. Either way, by the third cup he could feel it. A certain mellowness, a letting-go. He looked about him. 'This is too weird!' he said. 'What am I doing here?' He knew the old man didn't understand, but he kept talking anyway. 'How did I get here?' He grinned across. 'I mean *here?*' The old man made to pour another drink, but he covered the cup with his hand, said 'No. Thanks but, enough.' He pretended to be holding the top of his head in place, let out an exaggerated *phew* of breath. 'Got to keep my head clear. Got a business meeting this afternoon.' He stopped and laughed, the words somehow funny, the idea absurd. 'I'm here on business!'

He stood up, the need to piss suddenly intense. He wondered how to mime it without being seriously mis-understood. He could probably just excuse himself, go outside and water the ground. But he couldn't be sure, didn't want to breach any etiquette, cause offence. Merci-fully, he remembered how to ask.

'*Toire?*'

The old man nodded, led him outside, waited while he put on his shoes. Past the pine tree, he pointed out a ramshackle hut, down at the edge of the woods. Inside was a hole dug in the ground, some kind of chemical solvent mulching away. He held his breath against the stink, got out quick, breathed the fresh air.

The old man was waiting for him. He pointed further into the trees at another building, headed towards it, beckoned him to follow. It seemed to be some kind of shrine, raised on stilts above the uneven ground. The roof was tiled, pagoda-shaped. Steps led up to the doors held shut with a wooden bar. At the foot of the steps was a low trough full of water that was surprisingly clear. Resting above it was a bamboo ladle. The old man used it to scoop up some water, the way they did in the temples, pour it over his hands, rinse out his mouth. He took the ladle and did the same. Then he helped the old man lift off the bar, open the doors. The smell from inside was musty, old dark wood and the residue of that same pine incense. The old man took off his sandals, kneeled on the straw tatami mats. He tugged off his trainers, left them beside the sandals on the top step, sat cross-legged inside.

In the alcove in front of them hung a single scroll, covered with more calligraphy. A low wooden cabinet, various caskets and boxes on top of it. On a lacquer tray, what he took to be offerings, a carton of soya milk, packet of rice crackers, opaque bottle of some energy drink. Above, hanging from a beam, was a heavy bronze bell.

The old man leaned forward, lit an incense stick and placed it in a holder. He wafted the smoke over himself, clapped his hands three times. The keeper of the shrine. Then he bowed, sat back on his heels, his back straight, and started chanting, intoning some prayer or *sutra*, his voice rough and gravelly.

At first as he listened, and dealt with the discomfort of trying to sit still, the front part of his mind was ticking away, functioning, running ahead to his meeting with Yamamoto, thinking he should get moving, head back. Then the chanting cut across, held his attention.

175

Yumiko's face, the way she smiled. The utter strangeness of this whole trip. How could growing up in Glasgow have led him here, to this? And yet. That recurring sense of something familiar.

The old man chanting.

Best fall. Yelling *Banzai!* and dying a spectacular death. Sudden awareness of himself in this body, this time. Black and white photo of a Zen monk, Mount Fuji in the background.

The old man chanting.

For a moment he lost all sense of who he was and where. Smell of incense. The wooden walls creaking. Wind in the pines. The old man stood up and struck the bronze bell and the sound was inside his head, reverberating, driving out all thought. When it passed, when the sound had faded, he had tears in his eyes. The old man nodded, grinned.

Back round at the old man's shack, he said goodbye. He really did have to go. The old man motioned him to wait, went inside and came out with something for him, a gift, dark soft cotton folded up neat. He opened it out. A black T-shirt with one of those messages on it, the best he'd read yet.

how would you like keep 3 cats! look you?

'I'll meditate on it!' he said. The old man grinned.

He pulled the T-shirt on, over the one he was wearing. A little on the small side, tight under the arms. But that didn't matter. It was the thought. The old man walked with him part of the way, then waved him off. He ran slow at first, his legs stiff. When he looked back the old man was gone. Downhill through the woods he picked up pace, let his momentum carry him. A couple of times he crashed through the spiderwebs, but he kept going, brushed them off as he ran.

★

Given that this meeting was the crucial, the important

thing, was what he had come here for, halfway round the world, it lasted no time at all. Yamamoto had already decided. They could do business. It was quick, brisk, efficient. They shook hands on the deal.

Yamamoto seemed relaxed, spoke briefly about the football the other night.

'It was disappointing, to come so close. And getting to America would have been great achievement. But this kind of disappointment can bring strength. We are good at rebuilding. You say, bouncing back?'

'That's right.'

'You know our Daruma dolls?'

'I do, yes.' Fierce Zen patriarch reduced to a child's toy.

'They are round at the bottom, so each time you knock him over, he bounces up again. There is a rhyme that says it. Seven times down, eight times up.'

Bouncing back.

'I told you there was a story to this paperweight.'

'You did.'

'All right. Did you know I was born in Hiroshima?'

'I didn't, no.'

'It was where my father had his business. I was youngest in family. Had one older brother, one older sister. In 1945 I was six years old. On sixth August, just by chance, I was here in Kyoto with my mother, visiting my grandparents. Just by chance. Rest of family were back home. When bomb fell were all destroyed. Father brother sister. Whole house disappear. Nothing left. No trace. Never found bodies, anything. One week later, maybe two, I don't know about time, we went back. Went to where house had been. Nothing. Only rubble. Everything dark and muddy. This black rain you maybe read about. Mother was very sad. You say, desolate? Because no bodies, nothing to bury, to have funeral. Usually in that case, if body lost, we bury something belong to person. But nothing left. Everything gone. So mother search around in rubble for something, anything.'

177

He could see it, the darkness, the mud, the utter desolation, this woman scrabbling around in the ruins.

'Heat of blast had melted all glass in house. Windows, everything. Made into glass beads. Mother gather up handful, to take away. Some she bury, rest she give to me, to remember. I keep them. Few years ago I have them made into this.' He picked up the paperweight, cradled it in his hand. Clear perspex globe with the four grey beads set in it. 'We move here to Kyoto to stay with my grandparents. Of course we knew nothing about radiation. Mother got sick with cancer and died. For some reason I didn't catch sickness. Some kind of miracle. I am survivor.' He put the globe back in its base. 'So. That is the story.'

There was nothing to say. Nothing.

★

Again he'd got the time wrong for phoning home. He had left it too late. Would have to wait till early in the morning. Instead he dialled Yumiko's number. To tell her the meeting had gone well. To say goodbye, it's been real, keep in touch. Any excuse.

It rang three times then clicked to an answering machine. Yumiko's soft voice. *Moshi Moshi* . . . A message in Japanese. Then a man's voice, her husband, with what he supposed was the same message in French. A pause. A bleep. He hung up.

The day had taken it out of him. He felt adrift, cut off from his moorings, didn't recognise himself. He looked at the backs of his hands, flexed his fingers. This body, something he inhabited. He pulled open the top drawer in the table. Hotel notepaper, envelopes, a pen. In the second drawer a Gideon Bible, but also a book with a bright orange sunrise on the cover. *The Teachings of the Buddha.* He took it out, leafed through it, read.

Do not pursue the past. Do not lose yourself in the future. Look deeply at life as it is.

Your true nature is never lost to you.

178

He closed the book, put it back in the drawer.

This almost oppressive sense of significance. Like being on acid, or in love. Japan was doing a number on him. He called Yumiko again, listened to her voice on the machine, hung up.

★

He slept deep, woke alert and clear. Still dark outside, just the slightest trace of first light in the sky. He put on his shorts and trackpants, laced up his trainers. On a whim, he wore the T-shirt the old man had given him, with its wonderful crazy koan across the front.

how would you like keep 3 cats! look you?

Maybe if he really did meditate on it, he would batter through to some kind of enlightenment!

This time he was clear about where he was going, had checked and rechecked the map, wouldn't lose his way.

The desk clerk bowed to him as he passed. Out through the automatic doors into the early morning cool.

He ran easy, a steady even pace. No hurry. He took his bearings at every street corner, made it to Ryoan-ji in half an hour. This early there was no one at the gate, no one to take his money, sell him a ticket. He slipped in, had the whole place to himself. He remembered the path to the garden, followed it, breathed in the pure air, the smells of wet vegetation. Heard only his own footsteps, rustle of leaves, chirp of some tiny bird. Then the sound of the stream, and above it, gradually louder, that steady beat. *Thunk*. Bamboo on rock. *Shishi-odoshi*.

Even the old attendant at the garden wasn't there. He took off his trainers, eased into a pair of the slippers, glided in.

Ryoan-ji. Rio-angie. *Di diddly dang.*

Angie had been the first one ever to talk to him about these things, lend him books. She had told him a story, about life being an illusion, a dream. She'd said it was Zen, but he had an idea it was Hindu. It didn't matter. It was a

179

good story. Hesse had used a version of it in *The Glass Bead Game*.

This master is meditating with his disciple, a young man, and he sends him to fetch some water from a stream. On the way, the young man meets a beautiful girl. He is captivated by her, and follows her home. He courts her, marries her, they have children. In time he comes to rule the village. He accumulates wealth, becomes the ruler of the state, then the whole country. He has great armies at his command, owns everything he could ever desire. Then a neighbouring ruler attacks him. There is war. He is beaten, his capital city destroyed, his wife and children killed. He is driven out, a fugitive wandering the country. He finds himself by a stream and he stops to take a drink. He recognises the place. He remembers. His master sent him to fetch water. He finds a broken gourd, scoops up some water in it, stumbles to his master's hut. His master is waiting for him, smiles and asks, *What kept you?*

A good story.

He had almost married Angie. Hadn't. She'd gone to Canada. Died at twenty-five. Some kind of drug overdose. Di diddly dang. How to make sense of any of it. Zen flesh. Zen bones. He had met Anne. They'd had something good. Still had.

A life.

The sky was lightening now. The raked gravel seemed to hold the light, hold the silence. The placing of the stones was perfect, created space. Islands in a still sea. Mountaintops in mist. But that was image, comparison, metaphor. The place was just what it was. Stone garden. He breathed it, filled his head with nothing. Shining emptiness. And nothing in his whole life, nothing that had ever happened to him, had any meaning. Only this now. He just sat here as if he just sat here.

Then it wasn't that he heard anything, saw any movement. But he sensed it, somebody standing there behind him. And even before he turned, he knew it was Yumiko.

He stood up and faced her. Dark coat and the same green scarf. That scent, hint of jasmine. In this light her face was pale, almost white. Shimmer of lacquer-black hair. That turn of the head.

'I came out early,' she said. 'Took a cab. I thought, no, I knew you would be here.'

He moved towards her, and it felt like stepping back into something he had once known.

Someone he had once been.

Auld acquaintance.

'Love the T-shirt,' she said.

'There's a story to it.'

The stone garden dreamed itself, beyond it all. Her hair felt cold against his face.

Nessun Dorma

It's the first thing I hear when I step out into the street. Pavarotti at full volume, belting out *Nessun Dorma*. Half past six in the morning, the streetlights on, the sky above the tenements just starting to get light. Three closes along, on the other side, the ground floor window is wide open, pushed up as far as it can go. That's where the music is coming from. It builds to its crescendo. *Vincero*. It stops. There's a brief silence. Then it starts all over again.

I peer across as I pass by, but I can't really see in. The lights are off in the house. All I can make out is a faint glow that might be from a TV in the corner. The curtains are flapping, whipped about by that freezing Edinburgh breeze, straight off the North Sea.

In the papershop at the corner, Kenny from upstairs is buying his *Daily Record*, his cigarettes.

'Early shift this week?' I ask him.

'That's right. It's a bugger,' he says. 'Wife still away?'

'She'll be back at the weekend. Hey, did you hear that racket in the street?'

'The music?' he says. 'That World Cup thing?'

'Pavarotti.'

'I think it's been on all night. I got in the back of ten and it was going full blast then.'

'Weird.'

'The thing is.' He has pulled open the door, set the bell

above it jangling. He stands half-in, half-out of the shop. 'I couldn't help wondering if she was OK. The wifie in the house, like. I mean, I looked in the window when I was passing and she was just sitting there in the dark wi the TV on and that music blaring out. Over and over.'

'Could be a video and she's rewinding it.'

'Aye.' He looks uncomfortable. 'Anyway. Maybe somebody should make sure she's all right. I'd do it myself but I've got my work to go to.'

'Sure.'

'So.'

'Right.'

He lets the door go and it closes behind him.

Thanks, Kenny.

Christ.

Back along the street with my milk and rolls, the paper, I have to look in and see for myself. The music is still playing, louder the nearer I get. Right outside the window it's deafening. The curtains are still being tugged about by the wind, white net gone grubby. They flap out and I catch their dusty smell.

Inside, the TV flickers bright and harsh. Pavarotti is in close-up, the colours lurid and wrong, his face orange. Silhouetted in the blue light from the screen, I can make out the woman, sitting in an armchair, her back to the window. I lean right in and call out hello, above the music. My eyes adjust to the light and a few things take shape. A stack of newspapers on the table, an empty whisky bottle, ashtray full to overflowing, a carton of longlife milk. And the smell hits me, reek of drink and stale tobacco and somewhere in at the back of it a pervading sourness like old matted clothes in a jumble sale. The room stinks of misery. It's a smell I remember.

I call out hello again, hello there, and this time her head turns, she makes some kind of noise.

'Are you all right?'

She heaves herself up in the chair. She's a big woman,

heavy. I recognise her, I've seen her in the street. Not old, maybe late forties, fifty. She steadies herself, peers at me blankly, takes a careful step or two towards the window. She looks terrible, her face blotched and puffy. Her hair is flattened, sticks up at the back, the way she's been leaning on it. She wears a thick wool cardigan, buttoned up, on top of what looks like a nightdress.

'What's that?' she says, bleary, looking out.

'Just making sure you're all right.'

'All right?' She has no idea who I am, what's going on. 'Yes,' she says. 'It's all right. Each one that has wronged me will come undone. Nice of you to take an interest. I would offer you a drink but it's not on. They sent for the police you know. But I told them. No uncertain terms. So now they're looking into it. Full investigation. I'll show them. Would you like a drink? No, of course. It's not on.'

She suddenly stops and looks confused, stranded in midstream. The voice of Pavarotti swells, fills the room. She lets herself be caught up in it again, lost in it. Her face crumples, folds in a grimace, a tortured smile as she stands there swaying in her stinking kitchen. The aria builds to its climax, again.

Vincero.

She finds the remote control and winds back the tape.

★

The Chinese dragon I painted on the wall of my room, in Glasgow, all those years ago. Eight feet long in bright primary colours, straight onto the blank white wall.

No reason why it should come to me now, but it does. I see it floating in its swirl of cloud, fire flaring from its nostrils, its long tail curled and looped round on itself like a Celtic serpent.

The room was the first one I'd ever had completely to myself. The twenty-third floor of a highrise block. My father and I had been moved from the room and kitchen where I'd grown up, where I was born. The room and kitchen that had come to have that stink of misery I recognised just now. The smell of hopelessness, my father not coping, myself useless in the face of it.

But all that was past. The tenements were rubble and dust. We had been transported to this bright empty space, high in the sky. I remember us laughing as we walked through it, shouted to each other from room to room, intoxicated by the cleanness and newness. It still smelled of fresh putty and paint. And the view from the windows had us stand there just staring. Instead of blackened tenements, the back of a factory, we could see for miles, clear down the Clyde.

I kept my room simple and uncluttered, a mattress in the corner, straw matting on the floor. And I started right away on painting that dragon. I copied it from a magazine, divided it up with a grid of squares, pencilled a bigger grid on the wall and scaled the whole thing up. That way the proportions would be right, exact. And when I'd drawn in all the lines, traced every delicate curve, I set to colouring it in, with poster paint and a fine-tip brush.

I worked on it meticulously, a little every day, with total concentration and absolute care. After a week it was finished, except for one small section, the last few inches, the very tip of the tail. I decided to take a break over the weekend, finish it the following week. But I never did. I lived in that house for four years and never completed it. That section of tail stayed blank. When anyone asked me why, I had no idea. I just couldn't make myself pick up the brush. The dragon remained unfinished.

★

When I head out later along the street, Pavarotti's *bel canto* is still ringing out. *Tu pure, o Principessa nella tua fredda stanza.* Princess, you too are waking in your cold room. Again that smell wafts out as I pass by.

My father had a record of *Nessun Dorma* – an old scratched 78 – sung by Jussi Bjorling. So I know the song from way back. He used to play it loud when the drink had made him maudlin, sometimes alternating it with records of mine he liked in the same way, records that moved him to tears, Edith Piaf's *Je ne regrette rien*, Joan Baez singing *Plaisir d'amour*. In the years after my mother died, I grew to dread hearing those songs. I would stop and listen on the stair, halfway up the dank close, knowing the state I would find him in, guttered into oblivion.

It must have been those songs that made him want to learn French.

'Got to do something about myself,' he said. 'Haul myself up by my bootstraps.'

So he'd signed up for an evening class at the University, gone along once a week.

'Gives me something to look forward to,' he said.

He made lists of vocabulary in a little lined notebook.

'That tutor's some boy,' he said. 'Really knows his stuff.'

He had told the tutor he was hoping to go to France on holiday, someday.

The night I came home late and that smell hit me as soon as I opened the door. No music playing, but in the quietness the hiss and steady click of the recordplayer, the disc played out, the needle arm bobbing up and down in place. And behind that, my father breathing heavy in a deep drunk stupor. He slept in the set-in bed in the recess. I didn't want to disturb him, but I wanted to turn off the recordplayer. I switched on the light, turned and saw him.

Sprawled across the bed, still dressed, shoes on, his clothes and the bedding covered in blood, a blood-soaked hanky wrapped round his hand.

I managed to wake him but couldn't get him up on his feet. He had drunk himself senseless, beyond all comprehension and pain, anaesthetised and numb.

I sat up all night, dozed in the chair. A couple of times he shouted out, nothing that made any sense. At first light I shook him awake, took him down to casualty at the hospital. He had lost the tip of a finger, had no recollection where or how. The doctors stitched him up, gave him injections.

'I was on my way to the French class,' he said. 'Met a guy I used to work with, in the yards. Drinking his redundancy money. Just the one, I said. Got somewhere to go. That was it. The rest's a blur.'

'What about your hand?'

'No idea,' he said. 'Except maybe.' He stopped. 'Just a vague memory. Getting it jammed in a taxi door.'

'Where in God's name were you going in a taxi?'

'I haven't a clue, son. Haven't a clue.'

For a while after that he was ill. A low ebb. He never went back to his evening class, never finished the course. He was giving up on everything, until this move to the new place, the highrise. A fresh start.

★

I like to get settled in the library early, get a good stint of work done in the morning. But today I just can't seem to focus. So I'm glad of the distraction when Neil comes in, sits down at the table next to me.

'How's the mature student?' he asks. 'Working on something?'

'Dissertation,' I tell him. 'Zen in Scottish literature.'

'Wild!'

'Of all the people on the planet, you're the one most likely to appreciate it.'

'Hey, thanks!'

His beard and long hair are grizzled these days. The archetypal Old Hippy.

'Passed these young guys in the street the other day,' he says. 'And they're looking me up and down. And one of them says Hey, man, tell it like it was! He shrugs, spreads his hands. 'Thing is, I'd have been glad to!'

I hand over one of my sheets of paper to him, point to the passage at the top. It's a story from the legend of Fionn.

Fionn asks his followers, What is the finest music in the

187

world? And they give their various answers. The call of a cuckoo. The laughter of a girl. Then they ask Fionn what he thinks. And he answers, The music of what happens. 'Beautiful!' says Neil, handing me back the page.

'I'm writing about MacCaig at the minute,' I tell him. 'He once described himself as a Zen Calvinist!'

'Ha! He won't thank you for that!'

'Listen. Do you fancy a cup of tea?'

'Hey!' he says. 'Is the Pope a Catholic?'

In the tearoom he says, 'Stevenson's your man.'

'Stevenson?'

'Have a look at his *Child's Garden*. Then check out a wee book called *Fables*. It's the two sides, you see. Innocence and Experience. Here, I'll tell you my favourite one of the fables. This man meets a young lad weeping. And he asks him, What are you weeping for? And the lad says, I'm weeping for my sins. And the man says, You must have little to do. The next day they meet again. And the lad's weeping. And the man asks him, Why are you weeping now? And the lad says, Because I have nothing to eat. And the man says, I thought it would come to that.'

Neil throws back his head and laughs. 'There's Zen Calvinism for you!'

'The Ken Noo school!'

'Lord. Lord, we didna ken!'

'Aye, weel, ye ken noo!'

He thumps the table, laughs again.

Over more tea, I find myself telling him about the woman this morning, listening endlessly to *Nessun Dorma*.

'Sad,' he says.

Then I tell him about that dragon I once painted on the wall. And he stares at me.

'Now, that is something.'

'How do you mean?'

'There's this Chinese story', he says, 'about an artist that paints a dragon. And his master tells him he mustn't complete it. He has to leave a wee bit unfinished. The artist

188

says fine, no problem. But sooner or later his curiosity gets the better of him. And he finishes it off. And the dragon comes to life and devours him!'

I stare back at him.

'I've never heard that story in my life. How could I have known?'

'We know more than we think,' says Neil. 'I mean everything's telling us, all the time. Only we don't listen.'

'Sure.' For some reason, his story's disturbed me. 'Better get back to my work.'

'The dissertation!' He looks amused.

Outside in the High Street he asks, by the way, how's Mary? And I tell him she's fine, she's away in the States, she'll be back at the end of the week.

'Good,' he says.

We stop at the corner.

'Right.'

'One last thing,' he says. 'Do you know the story of *Turandot*, where your *Nessun Dorma* comes from?'

'Just that it's set in China.'

'Aye.' He nods, grins. 'Check it out sometime. I think you'll find it interesting.'

Back at the library, I look in the music section, find the libretto.

An unknown prince arrives at the great Violet City, its gates carved with dragons. In the course of the story, he finds his long lost father. He solves three riddles, which grant him the hand of the princess Turandot. The answer to one riddle is the name of the princess. The answers to the others are hope and blood.

The word Tao catches my eye as I flick through the pages. The prince is told, *Non esiste che il niente nel quale ti annulli*. There exists only the nothingness in which you annihilate yourself. *Non esiste che il Tao*. There exists only the Tao.

One last passage jumps out at me, a paragraph in the introduction, explaining that Puccini never completed the

opera, it was left unfinished when he died.
I see Neil's grin. Everything is telling us. All the time.
I close the book, put it back on the shelf.

★

When I'd lived four years in that white room with a view, the painted dragon unfinished on the wall, I met Mary and moved out. We travelled a bit, in France then Italy. We got work teaching English, enough to get by. I sent my father postcards from every new place. When we came back home I went to see him. The flat had come to have the old familiar smell, staleness of booze and fags and no hope. He was listening again to his sad songs. He had lost his job, been laid off. He was months behind with his rent, and we were too broke to bail him out.

In the end he had to give up the flat. I helped him find a bedsit near the University. He liked it well enough, liked the neighbourhood. The bedsit was his home for five years, till he died.

★

Ten o'clock at night and *Nessun Dorma* still going strong. She's been playing it for twenty-four hours at least.

At the World Cup, Italia 90, in one of the games Scotland lost, the song was played at half-time, the video shown on a giant screen in the stadium. Someone shouted, 'Easy the big man!' And the whole Scottish crowd started chanting,
One Pavarotti,
There's only one Pavarotti.
Scotland in Europe.
Wha's like us?

My old neighbour Archie next door has started up on his accordion. He plays it most nights, runs through his repertoire. *Moonlight and Roses. Bridges of Paris. Spanish Eyes.* A taste for the exotic. He plays with gusto, undaunted by the odd bum note. I find it unutterably melancholy.

The long dark night. This wee cold country.
Ach.

★

I know the noise has something to do with me as it batters
into my awareness, harasses me awake. The phone ringing
at 3 a.m. So it must be Mary calling from the States. Still
groggy, I pick it up, hear that transatlantic click and hiss,
then her voice, warm.
Hello?
'Hi.'
'*I know it's late, sorry.*
It's one of those lines. The person speaking drowns out
the other. When you talk you hear a faint, delayed echo of
your own voice. Not great for communication. Those little
phatic responses keep getting lost. So I just listen as she tells
me the story. New York's been hit by a hurricane. Roads
are flooded, bridges closed, subways off. The airports are
shut down, all flights cancelled, no way she can get out.
Sorry.
'So it'll be, what, a few more days?'
Whenever.
I listen to the wash of noise down the line, feel the
distance. Then she's telling me about a call she made to the
airline, and the woman she spoke to knew nothing about
the situation.
*So I says, Haven't you been watching the news on TV? And
she says, You think I'm sitting here watching TV? I'm working!*
I laugh at that, miss the next bit.
and I ask her what I should do, and she says Stay tuned!
'Nice!'
What?
'I said, Nice.'
Yeah, right.
'So.'
So this is costing.
'Who cares?'
What?

'Never mind.'
I'll call when I know what's happening.
'See you soon.'
Take care.

I put down the phone, stare at it. I shiver and realise I'm chilled from sitting. I know I won't get back to sleep, so I pad through to the kitchen, put on the kettle, light the gas fire. Then I hear the commotion out in the street, voices raised, an argument, crackle of an intercom. I pull back the curtain and peer out, see the flashing light on top of the police car. Two young policemen are at the ground floor window, trying to reason with the woman, and she's screaming out at them, 'I know the score here! I know what's going on!'

Finally she bangs the window shut. Then the music stops, cuts off.

A man's voice shouts out from an upstairs window, 'Nessun bloody dorma right enough! How's anybody supposed to sleep through this lot?' And he too slams his window.

The car drives off, and everything is quiet again, so quiet. For no reason I get dressed and go out, walk to the end of the street. I stand there a while, looking up at the night sky. The winds are high. The way it looks, the clouds stand still, the stars go scudding past.

Somewhere a dog barks. A taxi prowls by.

The music of what happens.

Stay tuned.

That ground floor window is open again, just a fraction. Smell of my father's house. Things left unfinished. The music is playing one more time, but quietly now, so I have to strain to hear it. I stand there and listen, right to the end.

Vincero.

THROUGH THE WALL

It isn't the way I remember it. At least not on the surface. Glasgow's been upgraded, refurbished. Old grey tenements buffed up new. Sunday morning and ten thousand of us converging on Glasgow Green. So many. I had not thought. I'm carrying a change of clothes in my knapsack. Wearing an old tracksuit I don't mind throwing away. I'll wear it till the last minute. Take it off just before the start of the race. Ditch it. Like that verse in the *Gita* talks about dying. As a man casts off an old worn-out garment. Chucks it when the soul's had enough. Moves on.

Down Candleriggs and along to Saltmarket. Past the High Court, the park up ahead on the left. Clock the mortuary on the other side of the road, and realise I've been trying not to remember the last time I was here. Then it hits me like a punch in the stomach. A sickener.

Push it away.

Into the park. Find the tent where I can leave my stuff. Smell of trampled grass and mildewed canvas, sweat and embrocation. Folk milling about, scared and nervous, under sentence. Some talking and laughing in that too loud way, others quiet, turned in on themselves. I'm yawning, sure sign of nerves. Feel it in my stomach, in my teeth. Slap vaseline on the inside of my thighs, at the groin where the shorts might chafe. A good dollop on each nipple or they'll end up raw.

Ten minutes and counting.

Over to the start and find where I should line up. Around the three hour mark. A bit of last minute stretching. Right leg over left and touch the toes, then left over right. Stretch out the calf muscles, the hamstrings. Legs apart, bend and touch the ground, palms flat. Stand on each leg, pull up the opposite foot out behind. Hope the knees hold out. No space to do any more, the pavement suddenly crowded. Jostle of spectators, runners shoving past. A minute to go.

Off with the tracksuit, top first. A bit of trouble with the pants, the legs catching on my shoes, but manage to tug them off. Look around for somewhere to dump them. An old woman catches my eye.

'Want rid of them son?'

'Aye.'

'I'll take them for you. Find a bin.'

I'd forgotten this. The sheer gratuitous friendliness, simple warmth. I hand the bundle over to her. 'Thanks a lot.'

'My grandson's running,' she says. 'He wants to break three hours.'

'Same as me.'

'He's wearing a Partick Thistle jersey.'

'I'll look out for him!'

'Good luck to you.'

'Thanks.'

Then I'm under the tape and into the crowd of runners, finding myself a space. Smooth down my number pinned to the front of my vest. Nod to the guy next to me wearing a plastic bin bag, a hole poked for his head.

'Aye aye.'

'This is it, eh?'

'This is it.'

He peels off the bin bag, throws it to the side. Half a minute. A tape playing *Chariots of Fire*. Somebody up ahead shouts *Oggie! Oggie! Oggie!* The crowd shout back *Oi! Oi! Oi!* Who starts these things? Picked up from the London

Marathon on TV.

Then it's a countdown, last ten seconds. Zero my stopwatch. 3 . . . 2 . . . 1 . . . the gun and off. Hit the start button. A great roar like a football crowd and in spite of myself I'm moved by it, caught up and swept along. This is it.

At first we have to move as a pack, the same pace. Keep getting blocked, having to check my stride. Up past the Tron and the Tolbooth, old heart of the Merchant City. Somewhere near here was the Sloan's warehouse my father once worked for as a tick man, collecting money round the doors. Earned a tenner a week. The fifties.

Up the High Street past the dosser's hostel. The Great Eastern. Poor bastards out in the street. Glasgow's miles better.

A bit easier to move now, not tripping over the people in front, but still carried along at a pace. So far it feels comfortable, good to be moving, a release, rush of adrenalin. Carries me to the one mile point quicker than I'd planned. 6:41. Allowing for the slow start means I'm running about 6:30. A bit too fast, try to ease back, put on the brakes. Along George Square I used to cut across on my way home, every schoolday for six years. Shriek of starlings on dark winter afternoons. Past Queen Street station. Relax my shoulders, sit on my stride. Hold to an image of Abebe Bikila running barefoot through the streets of Rome, gliding. Old black and white footage, the 1960 Olympics. Year after my mother died. First year at secondary school. Interminable greyness and desolation. My father falling apart. I watched the marathon on TV, head stuck in Latin homework. Amo Amas Amat. Conjugating love. Pad pad of Bikila's feet on the hard Roman roads. The thought of it.

My own feet now in lightweight adidas racers, TRX Comp, white with the three blue stripes. Can't get them any more. Every time I find a shoe I like. Planned obsolescence. These have just enough cushioning but not too much bulk. Light enough I can feel the ground. Hi-tech German design churned out in the sweatshops of Taiwan and Korea. Keep my eyes on the road ahead. Beat beat beat of my feet. Abebe Bikila. Along Sauchiehall Street, still a good crowd on the pavements. Gives you a lift and you wave back, take the acclaim.

Gawn yersel!

Looking good!

Only twenty-five mile to go!

And there's always some smartarse shouts *Get those knees up!* There he is. Bawface. Mister Happy. *Hup-two-three-four!* Only makes me laugh. I'm immune, I'm gliding, Abebe Bikila. On past what once was Charing Cross, ripped apart by the motorway. Bridge to nowhere on concrete piles. Garnethill where we lived when we first got married. Bedsit in Hill Street, six quid a week. A big sunny top flat room with a great view across the city. We shared the flat with an Irish navvy, a Chinese student who cooked crab that stank the whole place out, a suave Iranian who lolled about the manky kitchen in a silk dressing-gown. We stayed there a year. Read in the paper a month after we moved out somebody was murdered in what had been our bright room. Never know the minute.

2 miles. 13:41. Have to work it out. Seven minus twenty. 6:40. Still a little fast. Aiming for even 6:50. Still. Allowing for the start. And anticipating the slowdown at the end. Good to save a few seconds now. Money in the bank. Pass a drink station, grab a paper cup and try to drink on the run. Gulp in air with the water, slop some down my vest. Drop the empty cup. Push on.

Oggie! Oggie! Oggie!

Oi! Oi! Oi!

There's an old guy up ahead, looks in his fifties, club vest and old washed-out cotton shorts. A tough old customer. Wiry and lean, not a pick on him. The kind who'll die with his trainers on, out on a long run, or when he's about eighty, going for an age-group record in the 10 k. Way to go. He's running easy, within himself, getting it just right. Fall in behind him, watch his feet. Lock on to his pace. Focus on the rhythm. Beat. Beat. Beat.

Up Kelvin Way to University Avenue. See myself coming out of a Law exam in 1966. Losing it. Not a clue who I was. Mod suit and Small Faces haircut. Out of it in the Union beer bar. Pie and beans and a pint of heavy. Slop of beer on the tables. Redneck medics, engineers, bawling out rugby songs. Roll me over lay me out and do it again. Living for Saturday night and the Union dance. Bands thumping out Tamla, Atlantic, Stax. Sweet soul music. Who I was. In and out of love. Sunburst of '67, turned on tuned in dropped out. Acid high, the first time up there on that hillside in Kelvingrove spreadeagled on the green grassy slope blasted wide open all of it pulsing through me the Ding Dong of the Uni clock in its mock Gothic tower every fifteen minutes one note high one low bringing me back reminding me time was a joke. Some joke.

3 miles. 20:12. Can't work it out but it's under seven. Fine. Walked up here with Mary a summer evening so long ago dressed in velvet castoffs from Paddy's market carrying flowers we'd picked. Jesus it was sweet. Ding Dong. One note high one low. Bonnie lassie O.

Let us haste.

Up the Avenue to Byres Road. All those years. The bedsit I found for my father. Poky wee hole but he liked it here, liked it fine. Take another slug of water, kick discarded paper cups, keep the old clubrunner in my sights.

Past the Botanics, Kibble Palace. A story I wrote and turned into a play. About my father when he lived in that bedsit. Sat in the Kibble for a bit of brightness and warmth. Always summer. There is a flower that bloometh. Just finished writing it, typed the last line and the phone rang. Bit of bad news.

Was that 4 miles? Not paying attention. Away in my head. The time would be right enough. 26:53. Catch up to the old guy, run alongside him.

'Eh, was that the four mile point?'
'I hope so! Otherwise my split times are jiggered!'
'Right. I missed it. Just wanted to make sure.'
'Wandered already? That's bad!'
'I know!'
I know. Run side by side for a bit, feel a strength from him. Economy of effort. Knows what he's about. Got to ask.
'Going for under three?'
He's not quite irritated by the question, weighs it up.
'Good chance. If it happens it happens. Not going to kill myself.'
Pad. Pad. Even pace. His vest has little rips front and back, threads snagged and torn by years of safety pins, race numbers. Roadrunning punk. He spits, accurate, hits the gutter.
Spat!
'Yourself?'
'Under three'll do me fine.'
Done it before?'
'Once. 2:55.'
'No reason you can't do it again. If you're trained.'
'Right.'
'If you hit the wall remember you can run through it. Just got to hang in, keep going.'
'I will.'
'Do it!'
And maybe he cranks the pace up just enough, I fall back a yard or two, let him move ahead. Up into Maryhill, gapsites between tenements. Wee Indian kid at a third floor window, waving. I wave back and laugh. It's great this, the freedom of it, running down the middle of the road, a different perspective, looking up. A feeling like being on holiday. Through an open window hear *Keep on running* come to an end and start again. Spencer Davis. Stevie Winwood at fifteen with that great raw voice. *One fine day*

I'm gonna be the one to make you understand. Beat Beat Beat.
Keep on.
Driving on up Maryhill Road. Merryhell. Fleet once
ruled OK. Tiny Mental Fleet Kill. Had to be careful which
pub. Once got it wrong had to run like fuck down this same
road. Fleet of foot. Keep on running.
Past Garioch Road, the dole where I used to sign on.
Available for work. Trying to write. Marking time. 33:43.
Five miles. Still on course but the first time now a stitch in
the left side, catches my breath.
Read somewhere the thing is to breathe out hard from the
diaphragm, push it out, grunt. Dig my fingernails into the
palms of my hands. Kind of acupressure. Dig. Grunt. Push
on and after a while it's eased, almost gone. Get back the
rhythm. Beat. The veteran still up ahead, keeps his steady
pace. Not going to kill himself.
Story about a guy that took up running to end it all. Sick
of living. But insurance wouldn't pay up for a suicide. Wife
and kids to think about. So he figured he'd run himself into
the ground. Unfit and out of shape, shouldn't take much to
bring on a heart attack. Wrote his last will and testament,
everything. Went out. Couple of times round the block.
Knackered and aching but not dead. Next night a bit
further. And the next. After a month of it still not dead,
running a mile. Then another month two miles and starting
to feel good. Tore up the will. Kept on running. Kept on
living.
Running to keep fit. Fit for what? Fit to run. *Correo ergo
sum.*
Temple, past Dawsholm Park and down Bearsden Road
towards Anniesland.
Six miles. 40:34.
Why Temple? Something masonic. And who was Annie
if this was her land? And did bears ever really have a den
round here? Things you never think about. Names. *Nama
Rupa.* Name and form. Christ, another stitch. This time the
left shoulder, seized. Breathe Grunt Dig. Need a mantra to

keep focused. Try the old Buddhist job. *Gate Gate*. The right rhythm. Good pace.

Gate Gate Paragate Parasamgate Bodhi Svaha.

Gone. Gone beyond. Gone beyond the beyond.

Heard Ginsberg chant it years ago at a reading in Blythswood Square. Played harmonium. Sang *First thought is best thought*. Remember that. But it doesn't help the stitch, it won't go away. Just have to run through it.

Gate Gate.

On.

To 7 miles. 47:25. OK. Great Western Road.

That time walking Mary home all the way out here, 3 a.m., all the way to Drumchapel down the middle of the Boulevard, central reservation. Walking on grass. Walking on glass, tentative. She'd been away, travelling, and there was that distance. Take heed take heed of the Western wind. On the brink of splitting up. We walked, right out this road. Past the Goodyear factory, gone now. Lapwings circling. Peewit. Middle of the night. We talked things out, found something to hold on to, thank God. Out this road.

Turn off now down towards Scotstounhill, up there the high flats, middle block of five, my father and I moved to when the tenements were pulled down. The last ones to go, the whole close empty, boarded up. I'm lying in bed one morning, sick, and I hear a racket up on the roof, hammering and ripping, and stuff starts flying past the window. Bricks and slates and guttering, TV aerials, chucked down into the back-court. And *Hey!* I'm shouting. *What the fuck?* Somebody hears and they stop. Jesus Christ! They'd thought the building was empty, had started demolition. Another half-hour and the chimney stack would have been down, through the ceiling on top of me. Never knew the minute right enough. Could have been flattened. After that got moved out right away, the same week. Up there to the twenty-third floor.

8 miles. 54:15.

A white room to myself, a view down the river as far as

Dumbarton. Rush mats and incense. Stringband on my old Dansette. Everything's fine right now.

Right now. All there is. Keep on. Up and along the Expressway. A stretch of it closed to traffic for the day. Brilliant. Freedom of the city. Next drink station I take a sponge. A young girl hands it to me, dripping from a bucket. Thanks. Squeeze it on top of my head. Shock of the cold water streaming over my face, down the back of my neck, soaking my vest. Cools me down rapidly, a quick boost. Keep the sponge with me, dab at my arms, the fronts of my thighs. Realise the legs are stiff, tightening up, beginnings of fatigue. It happens. A last wipe at my face and neck and drop the sponge. Armies of helpers will clear up the mess. Incredible the scale of it, the organisation. All so we can run ourselves into the ground. Crazy. 9 miles. 1:01:06.

A Partick Thistle jersey up ahead. Red and yellow, black trim. The Jags. Firhill for thrills. The word they used was *unpredictable*. Wonder if that young guy's the grandson of the old woman at the start. Catch up to him, run alongside.

'Some race, eh?'

'It is that.'

'Going for the three hours?'

'Hope so, aye.'

'Well, we're bang on course.'

'Aye, so far!'

'Thistle supporter?'

'Aye, God help me! Don't know why I bother.'

'Ach well. We've all got a cross to bear!'

'Right enough.'

We pad along in step for a bit. At this pace casual conversation is not easy. But I make the effort.

'Listen. Was your grannie at the start of the race?'

'Eh?'

I suppose it does sound strange.

'Auld woman. Grey hair. It's just, she was looking for her grandson. Said he was wearing a Thistle jersey.'

201

'Aye. That's me! She said she'd be there but I never saw her.'

'Well there you are then.'

'Small world, eh?'

'Isn't it.'

That's all we can manage of philosophy, on time and chance, concidence. Small world right enough. So it is but. So it is.

That wee surge to catch him up felt good. Try it again and I'm easing ahead, striding out. Past Minerva Street. Goddess of Wisdom and Social Security. By Finnieston Quay and the massive great structure of the crane, tracery of iron. Glasgow made the Clyde, the Clyde made Glasgow. Another time, gone. My father a young man worked in the yards, sailmaker to trade. Laid off after the War, the old heavy industries running down, in decline. Entropy.

Need more water. Grab another sponge. 10 miles.

1:07:55.

Past another crowd of spectators, a big cheer. Some of them offering drinks, slices of orange, squares of chocolate. Don't need any but thanks all the same. Kids holding hands out for a high five. Slap as I run past. American-style.

Running New York, remember the high school band blasting out the theme from *Rocky*. Bam! . . . Bam! Bam! Bam! Eye of the tiger. And the Jewish neighbourhood, Williamsburg, orthodox Hassidics in black coats and hats, beards and the long sidelocks. Stood in total silence watching us pass. And the twenty mile point, dead on my feet, dragging myself through the Bronx. And this big black guy calling out *Hey man! If I was you I'd keep going. I mean do you really want to stop in the Bronx?*

No way.

Oggie! Oggie! Oggie!

Oi! Oi! Oi!

Broomielaw where the steamers left for doon the watter. The river Clyde the wonderful Clyde. Used to play that at Ibrox when I stood on the terracing. Before the game and at

202

half-time. That and Shirley Bassey. Let the great big world keep turning. Smells of cigarette smoke and brylcreem in the open air. My father started taking me when I was three. He lifted me over the turnstile. I cried when Rangers lost. Hit some cobblestones, hard underfoot. A twinge in the left knee. Hope I'm not going to suffer for speeding up. Good protestant attitude that. I'll pay for it. I'll pay for it. 11 miles. 1:14:43. Harder to work out now. Seventy-four and a bit. Still good, under seven. Try to glide more, Abebe Bikila, ease forward, not pound down. Take the weight on my heel. Feels OK. Heel and roll to the ball of the foot, push off. Easy. No problem. The pain stops but a worry all the same, a niggle. Off the cobblestones onto tarmac again. Better.

Miles better. Milesmilesmiles. A concrete poem. Smile-smilesmile. Story in the Ramayana. A thief and murderer tries to say the name of God. *Rama. Rama.* All that comes out is *Mara. Mara.* Darkness. But he perseveres, keeps repeating *Mara Mara.* And eventually it becomes *Rama Rama.*

Amazing the stuff that floats around in your head. *MaraMaraMaRamaRamaRama.* Darkness to light. *Miles-MilesMileSmileSmile.*

Smiles Better. Nice bit of PR hype. Development here like Docklands, executive flats on the waterfront.

Brando in black and white. Coulda been somebody. Coulda been a contender.

My father's hands. Bigger than mine, stronger. A worker's hands. Was an amateur boxer. Useful. Knew Benny Lynch. Tried to punch his way out but never made it. Never quite good enough. Or bad enough. Lost it.

But that time a couple of years back, a van driver giving him grief. The old reflexes still there, my father laid him out with an uppercut. Bam! Like that.

Could have been a contender. Slugged it out. A life.

My father's hands.

I've caught up with the old club runner again, just up

ahead. Ticking off the miles. 12 now. 1:21 and a bit. One more to halfway. Getting there. Heel and toe. Bit of a breeze off the river, resistance, running against it, but nicely cooling. Shiver for the first time, strange because I'm hot. Electric feeling down the spine, the backs of the legs. Remember it from before. A forewarning. For the moment it passes. A hard right and we're crossing the bridge at Central Station. Oswald Street. George the Fifth. Up and over the river, exhilaration. Yes!

Onto the Southside, right again off the bridge, easier with the wind at my back, gives an extra push, a boost. Weave in and out, pass a few people beginning to slow. Before I know it I'm easing past the clubrunner.

'Aye aye,' he says. 'Feeling frisky?'

'No bad, considering.'

'Can only go by how you feel.'

'This is it.'

'Might as well go for it.'

'Aye.'

'But mind there's quite a bit to go.'

'I will.'

'Right then.'

'See you.'

Go for it. I take strength again from talking to him, drive on over more cobblestones, past old dock buildings, sheds, on to the 13 mile point, halfway give or take a couple of hundred yards, whatever is half of 385. Halfway in 1:28. Perfect. The time I ran my best it was even halves. 1:27 out, 1:28 back. In Edinburgh, out the coast, field of sixty runners. Ran half the race on my own. No pack to carry me along.

So this is good, it's good. Same time and all this support. Halfway. *Mezzo nel cammin.* Just a momentary sinking at the thought I've to run the same again, only halfway, and the fatigue. But can't think that. I'm past halfway. Heading home.

Under the flyover, concrete supports, approach to the

Kingston Bridge. Traffic roaring overhead. Cuts through what was once Tradeston. Street where my father grew up, Houston Street. Gone.

Never knew my grandfather, industrial blacksmith, worked in Howden's all his days. Died when I was a baby, and his wife before I was born. Only seen old photos, cracked box-Brownie portraits, sepia, kept in a biscuit tin. My grandfather walked from Campbeltown to Glasgow to get a start. Hard as iron. The other grandfather on my mother's side worked in Dixon's Blazes. Only one of my grandparents that lived into old age. Longevity doesn't run in the family, my mother died at 38. Christ. Why think about it?

Consciously try to relax the shoulders, breathe deep, run easy. Up past Lorne School where the Orange Walk used to line up. Uncle Billy in his regalia. Big Orange headbanger. A good man too, decent. But all that madness and hate. Insane division, to keep folk fighting each other instead of what's wrong. On and on.

Past Cessnock subway and turn onto Paisley Road West. Brownstone tenements. Another twinge in the knee there. Limp a little, favour it till it settles. Fine.

Fourteen miles. 1:34. Along past Ibrox. Runner in a Rangers strip punches the air. Hullo! And down there I can see the high rise blocks, on the site. The tenement where I was born was right there. Now it's just a gap between tower blocks. The third floor room and kitchen was somewhere in that space, a capsule in midair. The building gone. The street gone. Mother long dead and now my father. Our life there only in my head, will die with me.

The Albion. Now Rangers' training ground. Was the Dogs, where my father worked at the turnstiles, a couple of nights a week. Had the odd wee bet on the side, sometimes lucky mostly not. A punter. He brought home photo-finish pictures to show me. Almost abstract, streaks of light, the greyhounds elongated rippling towards the line. He

brought them home to show me, that was all. My Da.
Christ.

That shivering again even though I must be overheated.
Wet vest, my sweat and spilling the water and the sponges
down my neck. That electric feeling like some kind of short
circuit in the arms and legs. Breathing a bit harder, this is
starting to hurt. I'd forgotten.

Turn in to Bellahouston Park. Who was Bella Houston?
The same as in Houston Street? More water, gulp and spill.
A woman handing out glucose sweets, a packet of dextro-
sol. Take one and crunch it, chalky, let it dissolve and
swallow it down. Leaves a strange sensation of coldness in
the mouth, an aftertaste. But the quick hit of it gives a lift,
almost instant. Pick up the pace again, on through the park.

Think that was a mile marker. Should have been 15.
Check the time, 1:41 something. Would be about right. I
think. Past the Palace of Art. I once took part in some
Lifeboy show. Singing. Marching. God knows. *O the
wanderlust is on me, and tonight I strike the trail.* That was it.
Swing along to a hiking song on the highway winding west.

The Palace was left over from Empire Exhibition. My
father helped make awnings and tarpaulins, tents and
marquees. He pointed out the site to me. Summer evenings
we would walk here, my father and mother, me hoisted up
on the old man's shoulders. We'd sit up there on the hillside
above the bandstand and he'd smoke his Senior Service and
we'd listen to the brass bands play popular favourites.
Younger than springtime. Sometimes we'd bring my ball and
we'd kick it back and forth while my mother sat. Back and
forth. The ball was rubber, had a brown smell. Made a
rubber noise when you kicked it. Even more when you
headed it. *Boing.* And the noise was in your head and flashes
of colour behind your eyes. Red. Tiredness and back up on
my father's shoulders, down the road home.

Flashes of light in my head, the smell of cut grass, this is
now. Out the park. Mosspark Boulevard and Corkerhill
Road. Pass sixteen in just under 1:49. Only know that's still

under seven, and that'll do, that'll do fine.

Houses with gardens here, semi-detached postwar dream, kind of thing my parents always imagined, never had. A few kids at a corner, giving the high five again. One of them holds out a bottle of Lucozade. I stop and take a swig, warm fizz hitting my throat, and I'm belching bubbles the next half-mile right back up my nose. Still, the caffeine rush to the brain is good. Good. Surge again. *Gate Gate Paragate.* Beat Beat. Hard tarmac. Eyes on the road ahead. Occasional glitter and sparkle, glint of particles catching the light. Beautiful and hypnotic. Lose myself in it. Stars in a tarmac firmament. And those flashes of light in my head again. Pulse. Deep space. But the feet on the ground, what running does, keeps your feet on the ground. Again and again, in between the flight. When you're running just run. This is Pollok. Housing scheme. Pebble-dash blocks.

Once ran Barnsley. In December. Exotic or what. Out and back, past coal tips, slag heaps. The first four miles sharp downhill. Meant the last four a grinding climb. Killed me completely. One old guy shuffled past me up the last slope, still had the breath to speak. 'Bloody fell race this.'

Bloody right. So this one could be worse. Should be grateful. The ball of my left foot is beginning to cramp. Try to ease it, untense, flex the toes. Down on the heel again. There. Must be 17 coming up. Yes. 1:55.

Straight sevens would be what? 7 times 10 is 70. Plus 7 times 7 is 49. Add them together is 120 minus one, is 119. Is a minute under 2 hours. 1:59. So I'm 4 minutes under. Divide 4 minutes by 17. Subtract that from 7 to get my pace. Christ. 17 into 240 seconds. Long division in your head is hard enough at the best of times. But when you're wasted 17 miles into a race. And trying not to think that 9 miles is a hell of a long way still to go.

17 into 24 is 1 and 7 over. 17 into 70 is what? 4 times 17 is 68. Near enough. So what does that make? Must be 14. 14 seconds off 7 minutes is 6:46. Not bad. Not bad at all.

Up Barrhead Road, long straight slow drag, a golf course on either side. And the wind's whipped up from somewhere, turned against me. A headwind. Keep pushing into it. Up the gradient. Against the wind. Slog. Milesmilesmiles. Maramaramara. *Gate Gate.*

In amongst the smells of sweat and Ralgex and Deep Heat I catch a whiff of perfume. Look across and see a girl gliding past. Blonde hair back in a ponytail. Towelling headband. Thin and light on her feet. At this pace shouldn't be too many women ahead of me. But bound to be a few. And this one looks good. Trailing four or five men in her wake, determined not to let her beat them. Keeps them going I suppose, something to work at. Seems to matter. On she goes, the pack of them in tow. I tuck in behind them for a bit, hitch a lift, get through this patch. 18 miles and over the 2 hours. 2:02. Give up on the arithmetic. Can't be bothered. It feels fine.

Pollokshaws Road. Another crowd of folk. Big cheer for the girl, still setting the pace there, dragging us along. Mary would be running this if she hadn't got sick. Couple of days ago, a bad flu. Wiped her out, too late to get back. Stuck at home in bed feeling wretched. Damn shame. I'll run a good one for her. God but she helped me through the bad time. Sounds like country and western. Sometimes the way of it, truths are simple and obvious, even banal. Everyday life is the way.

Into Pollok Park, the smell of cut grass again. Coming here as a kid was a long trek, miles, across three main roads. Tadpoles in a jamjar. Baggieminnies. They never survived.

The game of soldiers. Came here with my wee pal Brian to play in the big open space across from the Estate. Called it the Cunyon. Canyon I suppose. Fell in with a bunch of kids from the big houses round about. Played at soldiers, best fall. Brian went over on his ankle, twisted it. Couple of them helped him back to their house. Huge great place with a garden, a driveway. House from a storybook. The father sounded English. Gave us all glasses of orange juice, cold out of the fridge. Checked the ankle, Brian squirmed. The father offered to drive us home. First time we'd ever been in a car, took no time, minutes. And the street looked so different, gliding into it, seeing it out the window of a car. Like a film. The rundown tenements, the pub at the corner. Like seeing it for the first time. This is where we live. Stopped at Brian's close, a swarm of kids round the car as we climbed out. Said thanks and waved goodbye, and as soon as the car was out of sight Brian skipped through the close, no problem with the ankle at all. 'Was sore at first,' he said. 'Then I saw the house and I thought fuck this!'

Fuck this for a game of soldiers.

Aye.

19 miles and I'm toiling. 2:09. Keeping up with that pack and the girl. Grab a cup of water and try to drink on the run, drop the lot, got to stop and take another, let the pack go. Good luck to them. I need to drink. Knock it back. And another. Get moving again, and even as short a stop as that, few seconds, makes the legs start to seize again, stiffen. Hobble the first few strides, get back into it, pick it up. Get those knees up. Not possible. Locked in. Path winding, up and down, through the park. Pollok Estate. Pollok House and the Burrell.

Chinese figure of a monk in meditation, a lohan. Almost life-size, ceramic, in green robes. Sat poised and still, background of trees through the glass wall. Need that stillness, that poise, in the heart of action, in the middle of pushing to the limit, like this. Was meditation got me into it in the first place. My teacher the Indian yogi. Came to Glasgow, caught me with his simplicity, his luminosity. Most of all, his directness. This is it. Live it. Got me up and running instead of just sitting on my arse. No, as well as just sitting. Run and become. Him to thank for this. Hammering myself. Push. Push. Push. Be right here in the moment. Nothing else for it. Feet on the ground.

This. This. This. This. This.

The road ahead. Long way home. Don't think about it. Don't think. Try to keep the breathing right. Smell of the grass. That shiver again. Walking on my grave. Won't have a grave. Be cremated, like my father.

Be still my soul.

That electricity down the back, the legs. Short circuit. Calf muscles hard knots, thighs and hamstrings taut like cord coiled tight.

But 20 miles is something. A landmark. 2:16 and 42 seconds. Should be able to work that out, simple division by 20. Divide by 2 then 10. But that part of the brain won't work. Can't get it to kick in. Come at it from the other end, 6 miles left. If I can just hold a 7 minute pace, that's 42 minutes. Add that onto 2:16 is 2:58. I'd settle for that. God yes. But it means not slowing and that's hard. No flexibility, every step an effort. 20 miles the longest training run, now I'm out beyond. *Gate Gate.*

Once watched a friend set out to try and swim the English Channel. In October. Crazy, too cold. Left at night. Just remember the light of the boat going with him, disappearing into the dark, into the unknown. Sense of vast emptiness. The Void. In the end he didn't make it, had to pull out halfway. Got the boat back.

Here the only way back is going on. Back to the start. One foot after the other. On. Hold that 7 minute pace. Like training, the long run. In the long run. 7 minutes. No problem. A skoosh. Keep on keeping on.

Oggie! Oggie! Oggie!

Where did he appear from? Haven't heard him in a while. Did he start too fast and I'm catching him up? Or the other way about, is it him gaining, me going backwards? The *Oi! Oi! Oi!* is more muted now, less enthusiastic. At this stage everybody's struggling. 7 minute pace. In Barnsley by the end I was down to 9 minute miles, maybe slower. But that was a bloody fell race. No hills here. I can do it.

Out the park and hit the street again. Dumbreck Road.

Dumb break. Dumb wreck. I'm wandering. Uncomfortable with the camber of the road, climb up onto the pavement, sidewalk, feels a huge step up, straining. One giant step. Moonwalk. Could do with being weightless, floating. Instead the drag of gravity. Legs are lead. Dumb. 21 miles.

2:23.

Now the pavement feels harder than the road. Negotiate the step down. Shit. Another stab in the left knee, this one sharper, has me limping again, hurting when I take the full weight. Get myself to a lamppost, something to lean on, anything. Grab the left foot with the right hand, pull it up behind. Something crunches, clicks. No stretch in the muscles. Switch and do the other leg, start to move again gingerly, the sharp pain dulled to an ache. *Chondromalacia pattelica.* Runner's knee. A bugger.

Work my way to the centre of the road where it's flatter, less of a curve. On the level. Even keel. Maintain forward motion. Minimal knee lift. No option. Couldn't sprint if I tried. Reduced to a shuffle. Ali shuffle, float like a butterfly. I wish. Harlem shuffle. Sam and Dave. *You slide into the limbo, how low can you go?* Good question.

And where is this? Where am I now? Unremarkable suburbia. Looking for a sign. I seek wonders, I would see. This one reads Fleurs Avenue. Nice name. *Avenue des Fleurs.* Somebody's dream. The flower way. The primrose path. Head down eyes on the ground.

This. This. This.

Grind. Into the limbo. I'd forgotten this, I really had forgotten. Like they say about childbirth. If you remembered, if you really remembered you would never go through this again. And I'm beginning to remember, God yes it is always like this. I am seriously losing it.

Another sign. 22 miles.

Hard to focus on the watch. Screw up my eyes. 2:30. Don't know what that means. But there's 4 to go. In half an hour. That's right. Just have to hold on, not die. Tell

211

myself it's only glycogen depletion. Lack of blood sugar, that's all. I have been here before. I have run through it. But Jesus fuck it hurts, it hurts.

A woman, young mother with a baby in a pram. She's holding something out and I veer, lurch across, see it's half an orange, peeled, and the goodness, the simple loving kindness is overwhelming, it gets to me. I can hardly say thanks, just grunt and grab the fruit, stuff it in my gub eat/ drink the lot swallow it down. God bless you. Plowter on, and it helps it definitely helps. At least for a couple of hundred yards. Then it all starts to go again, slipsliding away. I'm treading water. Running on empty. Why the fuck am I doing this? No sense.

If that bastard shouts Oggie Oggie Oggie one more time.

Did I miss a water station? Too long since the last drink. All these cartoons, the guy on his hands and knees crawling across the desert. Oasis that turns out a mirage.

Somebody at my right shoulder, heavy step pounding.

'Hellish, eh?'

The Thistle jersey. He looks as bad as I feel but he's moving better, stronger. Easy the Jags. All I can do is grunt out 'Aye.' And he gives me a wave, moves ahead of me, going so slow but every step further away.

Water.

Stop.

Take a cup in my shaking hand. Drink it down, drop the cup. Here they're ankle-deep. Take another and force myself to drink it, even though it feels like drowning. Drop the second cup, kick it, scuff through the debris.

Now. The thing. Is. To get moving. Again. Don't know if I can. All I want is to sit down in the middle of the road. *Mezzo nel cammin.* Folk that get lost in the snow, in blizzards, the middle of nowhere. Just want to curl up and die. Can understand it, totally. Oblivion.

Fuck it.

I can't go on, I'll go on. Yer man Sam Beckett knew the score there. Knew this place. Last words in the trilogy.

Read the whole thing straight through when I was 19 and laid out with the flu. Good state of mind to appreciate it.

I am in the process of hitting the wall. Have to push through it. One step. Another. Interesting territory. I remember it now. I can't go on. I'll go on.

The Unnamable.

What was it they used to call pakora in Indian restaurants? In Glasgow and nowhere else. Hey pal, gie's a plate ae yer unnamables. Yer unpredictables.

Indescribables!

That was it. Only in Glasgow.

A plate of indestructibles. Ineffables.

Immortal invisible.

And where in God's name am I now? Or for that matter, who?

That Gauguin painting. *Who are we? Where do we come from? Where are we going?*

Pollokshaws!

I know these streets from sometime.

Had an auntie who lived here. My mother's sister. We used to come and visit. A while after my mother died my father fell out with her whole side of the family. Some stupid feud. To do with money borrowed and never paid back. Story of his life, he said.

Saint Andrew's Cross. Cross to bear. Andrew got himself crucified upside down on the diagonal. Our patron saint. Right enough.

Mortification. What I'm doing now? No, this is for it's own sake, for the doing of it. Transcendence. Going beyond. Beyond the beyond. *Parasamgate.*

Down Eglinton Street past the Bedford and the Coliseum, past the mess they made of the Gorbals. The sixties God help us. A few years more and they'll rip it all down again. On to Jamaica Bridge. And I did miss a mile marker, this is 24. But my vision is blurred now, I can't read the watch. My eyes are dim I cannot see, I have not

213

brought my specs with me.

The auld man again, used to sing that on bus trips. Away for the day. Largs or Troon. Gave it laldy conducting the sing-song. Or doing a solo on Danny Boy. *O come again when summer's in the meadow.*

Och Da. Ya stupid auld bugger. I loved you.

The phone call. A bit of bad news. Your father, I'm afraid. Out on his lunchbreak from the shop. Worked as a storeman round the back. Out for a breath of air, a walk. Fell down dead in the street. Like that. Outside what used to be Tom Allan's church. Buchanan Street, pedestrian precinct, the lunchtime crowds. As good a place as any, to go.

That wind off the river is chilling me again. I'm shivering. Hands and arms numb. Take heed take heed.

I used to come through from Edinburgh to see him every couple of weeks. Or I'd phone, keep in touch. But I'd been away, been travelling for two months. Sent him a card, was all. The plan was to come through and surprise him the next day. His birthday for Christsake. Would have been 64. *Will you still need me.* Not phone, just turn up at his work, end of the day. *Drop me a postcard, send me a line.* If I'd written, or called.

Fuck.

Yours sincerely wasting away.

Those flashing lights in my head again, pulsing star.

'You OK pal?'

The old clubrunner passing me. Paced it just right. I make some incoherent noise.

'You look bad,' he says. 'Maybe try and eat. Bit of fruit or something.'

I manage to nod, wave him on. He waves back and he's gone.

Next clump of people handing out food I take what I can get. Crisps and chocolate, bit of a doughnut, half a banana. Eat it like an animal, wolf it down. More water and on. Again.

The mortuary, when I saw it this morning, that punch in the guts. Had to go there to identify the body. Mary came with me, helped me through it. The chemical smells, formaldehyde. Bracing myself to see him one last time. Touch him. But the briskness of it. Into this room and a video screen high up in the corner. Black and white image, an old man's face contorted, the mouth turned down in a grimace of pain.

'Your father?'

The shock of it. 'Yes.'

Yes, but.

Just as briskly out, back into the waiting room.

Yes, but no. Him but not him. The body but not the man. Not the Da.

And so quick, a matter of minutes, the coroner out telling us the post mortem was over. A heart attack. Coronary artery atheroma. And he's keeping up this bantering cheerfulness, getting me to sign for my father's belongings. Wallet with a few quid in it – a fiver, some loose change. His specs. A betting-slip. A pen.

'The clothes were burned of course. They were marked.'

Of course.

'And he was carrying a plastic bag. A loaf and a pint of milk in it. But the likes of that doesn't keep.'

Of course.

'So if you'll just sign here, that's everything. Hunky-dory.'

Porter at hell's gate.

A loaf and a pint of milk. And the specs. My eyes are dim I cannot see. Christ.

Be still my soul. What we sang at the funeral, as the coffin slid through. To be consumed, reduced to its elements. As a man casts off an old worn-out garment. Gone. Gone beyond.

Now my breath comes in gulps, in sobs. This harsh world draw breath in pain. All sense of time gone, don't care any more. Everything screaming out to stop. I can't go on I'll go on, whole existence focused down to this. All that's left just the will the sheer will to continue to keep going. Something against dying. Something against nothing.

Pulse of light in my brain. Noise washing over me, fading out, an ebb. And suddenly, like that, I'm not running any more, body down and out, it lies there on the ground and I float disembodied somewhere above, looking back down at it. Sad and comic the wee body lying there in its vest and shorts, the white trainers with the blue stripes. That's me. But so is this floating free above it all. Rising into light. Sweet release after all the effort. It's as easy as this, letting go.

Then I'm back down in it, re-entry, feel the weight of me. There are voices by my head.

'Easy now.'

'Got him.'

And hands, arms are underneath me lifting me up and carrying me. *Pietá*. I'm laid down on the pavement and a blanket's over me, a woolly hat pulled onto my head, my arms being rubbed to get me warm. I love these people. Two men and a woman, angels in St John's uniforms.

'Had us worried there. You blacked out.'

It's a struggle but I get the words out. 'How long?'

'Eh?'

'How long was I out?'

'Must have been five, ten minutes.'

Now the next question. 'How far to the end?'

'Couple of hundred yards.'

There is no way I am not going to finish. Not now. Get to my feet, still shaky. They help me up, hold on just in case. But I know I can do this, know I have to.

'Thanks,' I tell them. 'I'm fine.'

Glasgow Green again. Full circle. Just one last push on through. Every step jarring. Body in shock. Drag it, last hundred yards, is nothing. So close. Can see it, the finish line, the gantry. Digital clock, the flick, flick of seconds ticking off. Reads 3:07:28. Tick. 29. Tick. 30. Crowds along the final straight cheering us in. Last. Few. Steps. Mind over matter. No mind? No matter! Push. Over. And done. 3:07:48. Do me fine. Arms raised. Some sharp photographer taking everyone. Catches it. The moment. Immortal. Yes. Is all.